MOCKINGBIRD IN THE MOONLIGHT

MOCKINGBIRD IN THE MOONLIGHT

By
Jaclyn Weldon White

Indigo Custom Publishing, LLC

Publisher	Henry S. Beers
Associate Publisher	Richard J. Hutto
Executive Vice President	Robert G. Aldrich
Operations Manager	Gary G. Pulliam
Editor-in-Chief	Joni Woolf
Art Director/Designer	Julianne Gleaton
Designer	Daniel Emerson
Director of Marketing and Public Relations	Mary D. Robinson

© 2007 by Indigo Custom Publishing, LLC

Disclaimer: Indigo Custom Publishing LLC, does not assume any legal liability or responsibility for the accuracy of any information or content in this publication. The statements, views, and opinions presented in this book are those of the author, based on his own research, open public records, and do not reflect the opinions or views of Indigo Custom Publishing LLC, its staff or associates.

Printed in U.S.A.

Library of Congress Control Nmber: 2006938442

ISBN: (10 Digit) 0-9776711-7-8   ISBN: (13 Digit) 978-0-9776711-7-5

Indigo Custom Publishing, LLC books are available at quantity discounts with bulk purchase for educational, business, or sales promotional use.

For information, please write to:
Indigo Custom Publishing, LLC · SunTrust Bank Building · 435 Second St. · Suite 320 · Macon, GA 31201, or call toll free 866-311-9578.

Cover Design: Julianne Gleaton

DEDICATION

To Carl Dean White, Jr.,
the son of my heart

ACKNOWLEDGMENTS

Thanks to the lunch bunch – Jackie K. Cooper, Louise Staman, Van Henderson, Carol King Pope, Skippy Davis, and Sterling Everett. They kept my feet on the ground and my eyes on the prize.

Thanks to Henry Beers. He took a chance on this one.

As always, thanks to Carl. Without his love and support, none of it would mean a thing.

DISCLAIMER

This book is a work of fiction. Names, characters, places, and incidents are either products of the author's imagination or used fictitiously. Any resemblance to actual events or persons, living or dead, is entirely coincidental.

The Friends of the Library is a fine organization. In Macon, Georgia, this group of dedicated volunteers works tirelessly collecting used books and conducting the annual Old Book Sale that raises thousands of dollars for the library. The members of that organization portrayed in this book are entirely fictitious and are not intended to resemble anyone in Friends of the Library.

PROLOGUE

She was comfortable in the Research Room. It was dim and quiet there and no one paid any attention to her. The only sounds were the buzz and whir of the microfilm machines and the occasional rustle of papers. Hunched forward in her chair, her eyes never left the screen. She slowed the advancing film and paged through the images until she found the item she sought. The newspaper page was fuzzy and she manipulated the wheel until the focus was sharp. Minutes later, she almost laughed out loud. It was even better than she'd hoped. So that's what he'd been hiding. She'd been sure there would be something; there always was. Everyone had a secret and she never gave up until she found it. Her greatest virtue was patience.

She knew she was not popular. She wasn't pretty. She wasn't rich and she wasn't famous. But after years of disappointment and rejection, she didn't care anymore if people liked her. And once she stopped working so hard for acceptance, getting the things she wanted had turned out to be surprisingly easy. It was almost comical how quickly people changed their attitudes once they were aware of the knowledge she possessed. Instead of ignoring her, now they couldn't do enough for her. They were eager to please and so frightened of upsetting her that it made her laugh. She reread the article on the glowing screen and wondered what he could do for her?

CHAPTER ONE

My name is Dixie Anne Sheridan McClatchey. We might as well get that out of the way up front. I've already heard all the jokes about the land of cotton, looking away, and Louisiana beer. And, yes, a few folks have made sure that I know the word "Dixie" has unpleasant connotations for the more politically sensitive. But it's been my name for thirty-four years and I'm not about to change, modify, or start apologizing for it now.

That morning I wasn't thinking about names or even appreciating the splendor of the early spring day. I was driving as fast as was reasonable along Poplar Street. I braked for a jaywalking pedestrian and glanced at my watch. There was still a chance I'd make it by noon. Every Tuesday morning I met with several other Friends of the Library volunteers to sort and price donated books for our annual sale. It was a worthwhile cause and I enjoyed participating, but if our session ran long as it had today, it could make me late opening the shop.

I parked the Blazer in the alley and grabbed a sweater from the back seat before getting out. My loose cotton dress was comfortable this warm March morning, but I knew the day could change with a single gust of wind. A visitor to middle Georgia might easily believe spring was here to stay. Daytime temperatures had been flirting with the low seventies for two weeks. Daffodils and flowering quince splashed color all around. The Japanese magnolias were in full, deep purple bloom and even some of the cherry trees showed faint color. But we who live here know that these beautiful days are precariously balanced above a late freeze. A few clouds and a northwest wind could knock us right off the edge of spring and smack back into winter.

After two years, I still get a little thrill of ownership every time I turn the key in the lock of Chapter and Verse, my new and used bookstore in downtown Macon. It was the first place I'd ever owned completely by myself. I flipped on lights as I made my way through the office to the front where I unlocked the door and turned the cardboard sign around to show OPEN.

I was sweeping the office floor a few minutes later when Edward Swanson came in the front door, loaded down with paint jars and brushes.

"Is your air conditioning working, sweet thing? I've got my thermostat turned down to sixty, but it's eighty-five in my place if it's a degree. If it gets any hotter over there I'm breaking out the cutoffs and tank tops and ordering a daiquiri machine!"

His appearance brought a smile to my face. I believe Edward could brighten up a cave.

"No. It's quite comfortable in here," I said, propping the broom against the back wall and joining him in the middle of the shop.

"Oh, dear, I suppose I'm going to have to call the ogre again," he said, referring to his seldom seen landlord, the ancient Mr. Carson. "Not that it will do any good. He simply doesn't respond. But I want you to remember this conversation, Dixie. Make note of it in your girlish diary, so when I die of heat stroke, my heirs will be able to prove that I did register numerous complaints. It should be of great help in the wrongful death suit."

Edward set the jars and brushes on the counter, tossed a lock of blond hair off his forehead, and helped himself to coffee.

"I'm here to paint your window, as promised."

Every year in the middle of March, we downtown merchants turn our attention to the approaching Cherry Blossom Festival. Due to an extraordinary planting program begun in the late fifties, Macon is home to nearly 300,000 Yoshino cherry trees. The annual festival, which coincides more or less with the blooming of the trees, brings over half a million people to our town and "Think Pink" becomes the watchword of the day. Women dress in pretty pastels and men, including city officials, don bright pink blazers. Mailboxes and front doors sprout floral wreaths and big pink bows, and store windows are painted with pink flowers intended to resemble cherry blossoms. Edward was one of the volunteers who not only painted a masterpiece on the window of his own business, but also kindly recreated that magic on his neighbors' windows.

I followed him outside and held the jars as he dipped brushes in pink, white, and green paint. Two teenaged boys stopped behind us to watch.

"I really appreciate this," I told him. "If I had to do it myself, the place would look like it was being overrun by giant pink spiders."

"You're very welcome," he said, stepping back a few feet to give his work a critical look. "But my services are not free. You know that the Children's Hospital is having its annual auction in May."

"Sure. I'll be there with bells on."

He grinned. "I'm certain that'll be worth seeing, although bells might be a little over the top. But that's not what I had in mind. We need things to auction off, and," he peered through the window at the interior of my shop, "if there's one thing you've got, sweetie, it's things. Could you manage a donation?" He added a few darker lines around the center of the last flower. "There. I think that will do. What do you think?"

"It's gorgeous." And it was. Edward was such an accomplished artist that his talent was obvious even on so insignificant a canvas as my window. "What kind of donation do you want?"

"Well, money to start with, the more the better. It costs the earth to put on that auction. Last year we spent nearly eight hundred dollars on the floral arrangements alone, even with the discounts. I'm donating a painting. So is Shirley Stafford." He grinned again. "Of course, you don't paint, so I guess you might give me some books. Six or eight of them in a nice basket with lots of tissue paper and a big bow, I think." He raised an eyebrow at me. "Two or three baskets would be even better than one."

I smiled and surrendered. "You got it. When do you need them?"

"I'll take the money any time you want to give it to me and the books by the first of May. And you can depend on me to remind you when we're a bit closer to the event."

We went back inside and the boys moved on. While I wrote out a check to the Children's Hospital, our talk turned to the fast-approaching festival. As he had been for ten years now, Edward was in charge of the parade that kicked off the celebration.

"Oh, my God, the details," he moaned. "It's less than a week away and I know half the floats won't be ready. And the Junior Cherry Blossom Princess is driving me mad!"

"A little six-year-old girl? Now what could she possibly do to you?"

"Well, it's not her," he admitted grudgingly. "But her mother! That woman is the stage mother from hell! First it was the banner, then the flowers. Now she wants us to change the color of her little darling's car. It seems that red overpowers her baby's delicate beauty and couldn't we just get a powder blue convertible instead? If I get through this without committing some terrible act of mayhem, it will be a miracle."

I couldn't help laughing. "Oh, Edward, you're always frantic before the parade, but we both know it will be just as big a success as it always is. Why only this morning Marian Saxby was saying what a great job you do every year. She was very complimentary."

He looked moderately pleased at the praise, then his eyes narrowed. "Was this at your Friends of the Library soiree? I suppose Glynnis McCullough was there, spewing her usual poison?"

"Yes," I said reluctantly, "she's always there." There was no question about it—Glynnis was an unpleasant person. She thrived on gossip, oozed malice, and was never happier than when she was destroying a reputation. She'd had several victims that morning and some of her nastiest comments had been about Edward. But I wasn't about to tell him she'd declared that, since he was gay, he must also be a child molester. She'd gone on and on about pedophiles and their crimes until I thought I'd scream. In fact, as it turned out, I needn't have worried about Edward's feelings. He was well aware of the tales she was spreading.

"You know she called the hospital about me?"

"What? Why would she do that?"

"Who knows? She told them that I was a danger to the children." His voice was hoarse with disgust and an angry flush crept up his cheeks. "How anyone could think . . . those poor, precious children . . . " He shook his head as if to clear it of such offensive thoughts.

"Surely the people at the hospital didn't pay her any attention. Why, you're one of their greatest assets."

"No, of course, they didn't. But it's still a horrible thing for her to have done."

"You won't get any argument from me," I told him. "I don't understand people like Glynnis. She gets such pleasure from bringing people pain. You should have heard her this morning, needling poor Cassie Waycaster about her children. And for some reason she really had it in for Reg, acted like he was immoral for wanting to take a vacation." I sighed with self-pity. "And I've got more of her company to look forward to this afternoon."

"How did you ever let yourself be talked into that?" he asked.

"I didn't have a choice. She said she was coming by – wants some information about a book, I think. The only way to avoid her would be to close the shop."

Edward finished the last of his coffee. "Might be worth it."

He looked like he might have more to say on the subject, but took a deep breath instead and moved on to other things. He got a determinedly negative answer when he inquired about my love life.

"But, sweet thing, it's time for you to do something good for yourself." He reached out to refill his cup. "It doesn't have to be the love of your life or even a moderately grand passion. Just go out and find yourself some gorgeous young thing to dally with . . . "

"Edward!" My outcry was unintentional, but when he reached for the coffeepot, his shirtsleeve edged up to reveal red and purple bruising around his slender wrist and forearm. "What happened? Are you all right?"

He hastily pulled down the sleeve. "I'm fine."

"The hell you are! What happened?"

He tried unsuccessfully for a smile. "When I went up to Atlanta last weekend George and I had a tiny disagreement."

"George? Oh, no. You're not seeing him again, are you? That man is poison and you know it. We've talked and talked about this."

He nodded. "I know, but there's just something about him . . . And things only get out of hand when he's drinking. He's such a complicated man."

"Complicated? He's simple. He's an abusive jerk. Look how he treated you at Christmas. And what about the money he borrowed from you last year? I thought you said it was over between you. If he could do that," I nodded to his arm, "he might really hurt you next time. Why do you waste your time on him? Get out and meet some new people."

I knew I sounded disturbingly like my mother, but Edward was a good friend and I hated seeing him mistreated by trash like George Bennett.

He smiled sheepishly. "I know you're right, Dixie. As usual. But logic just flies out the window where emotion is concerned."

I crossed the few feet between us and gave him a quick hug. "I know, but I worry about you."

"Thanks, sweetie." His grin came back. "But the only really dangerous person I'm facing right now is the Junior Cherry Blossom Princess's mother. George and all other men pale in comparison."

"Speaking of Cherry Blossom threats, isn't the dinner tonight?"

He rolled his eyes. "Oh, why did you have to bring that up? I'd almost succeeded in forgetting it." He sighed. "Yes, tonight is the banquet and I'd rather be beaten with a big stick than have to go."

The Parade Banquet was one of the crosses Edward bore. Every year, the Festival organizers invited all of the parade participants to a dinner. It was a huge affair with over two hundred guests. Edward, by virtue of his position, was expected to not only function as host, but also as the main speaker. And therein lay the problem.

Edward was a talented painter and an astute businessman. He was unfailingly generous when it came to supporting deserving causes, and a good and loyal friend. However, he was a most reluctant public speaker. The experience terrified him.

"Oh, my God, I hate getting up in front of all those people. I can hardly breathe when I start that speech."

"You'll be great. You always are. It's just getting started that's so hard."

He shook his head. "I don't know about that. But I'll get through it, I suppose. Then I plan to hurry home and drink heavily."

He left a moment later, carrying his paint jars with him. "Two more windows to do this afternoon."

I wasn't surprised that there hadn't been a rush of waiting customers when I'd opened up. My walk-in business had never been very brisk, although it was slowly improving. I perched on the stool and reflected just how fortunate I was that my husband had had a knack for investment. When he died three years before, he left me with a more than adequate income, which was why I could afford to run a marginally profitable business.

The thought of Donald and the knowledge of how much I'd lost still had the ability to stop me cold. I was almost paralyzed by how much I missed him. We were married only six years. He was a partner in a fast-growing technology firm and I was working my way up through the ranks of the Atlanta Police Department. We were an unlikely combination, but a good one. I'd just made sergeant when Donald was killed, the victim of a street robbery. My drive and desire for police work – and everything else – died with him. I couldn't stand living in the new Peachtree Street loft we'd bought and decorated together. With Donald gone, it was just an echoing shell where I never seemed to get warm.

Several months after Donald's death, my widowed grandmother, Evelyn Sheridan, decided to give up her rambling old house in Macon and move into a condo near my parents' Atlanta home. It was on a weekend trip to help Grandma Evelyn sort through seventy-five years of accumulated possessions that I first entertained the thought of living here. Although it was a bit rundown, the big house on High Street was as familiar and comfortable to me as it had been when I spent summers there as a child.

Thanks to Grandma Evelyn's endless stories, my young mind had perceived Macon, Georgia, as a fascinating place packed with history, romance, and intrigue. The passing years had given me a more realistic perspective, but it was still a pleasant, pretty town. When the bookstore on Cherry Street came on the market a month later, I took it as an omen.

I sold the loft and bought the shop and its inventory with the proceeds. I'd been more than willing to purchase the house as well, but Grandma Evelyn wouldn't hear of it. Instead, she signed it over to me, declaring she was just relieved that she wouldn't have to imagine strangers living there.

I turned away from the door and surveyed my shop for a long, quiet minute. It looked as I'd always thought a bookstore should. Tall wooden shelves lined the walls and stood in ranks in the center of the store. Only three areas of the big room were bare of books. At the front a scarred, wooden counter was equipped with a cash register, telephone, computer, and a tall stool where I could sit and watch the world go by on Cherry Street. Farther back on the left were a couple of mismatched easy chairs, a reading lamp, and a beat-up sideboard that held a coffee maker. My customers were encouraged to get comfortable with the books. On the right stood an old refectory table that was used for everything from craft displays to book signings.

Of course, it hadn't always looked like this. When I bought it, this building was in desperate need of work. The two-story structure dated back to the 1920s and had spent most of its life as a dry goods store. But even in the shabby condition it was in when I first saw it, it was love at first sight. I adored its ornate front, complete with plaster curlicues and gargoyles, but the interior was a disaster. There were structural and cosmetic repairs that couldn't be put off.

A leaky roof, neglected for years, had created water-stained walls and ceilings. Faded linoleum covered the floors and a damp, musty smell permeated the whole place. The first things to go were the stained plaster walls. Once those were torn out and the original red brick revealed, nothing could have convinced me to cover it again. That and refinishing the wide-planked pine floors had given the whole store a nice mellow glow. I'd painted the exterior brick a Victorian blue and the trim around the windows a deep burgundy.

While the ground floor was now just what I'd hoped it would be, my money and enthusiasm ran out before I got to the upstairs rooms. Someday I hoped to add a second-story sales floor, but that ambitious project was going to have to wait a while.

All things considered, I was content to be here. Over the past two years, I'd gradually become involved in the life of my new hometown. I joined the Chamber of Commerce and the Friends of the Library. And, much to my mother's surprised delight, I even occasionally attended St. Paul's Episcopal Church. Mother saw this as a prodigal's return to the fold after a misspent youth, but I didn't give it that much significance. God and I still had some things to work out in the wake of Donald's death.

I'd met a lot of nice people and even made a few good friends, but Macon didn't feel like home yet. I wasn't sure anywhere ever would without Donald.

The press of a button brought the computer screen before me to life. I selected an Allman Brothers CD and slipped it in the player. It was almost too much of a cliché for Macon, but I'd recently sorted through some boxes at home and come across Donald's beloved four-CD *Dreams* set and wanted to hear it again. The opening chords of "Statesboro Blues" filled the shop and brought a smile to my face. I remembered Donald dancing me around our living room to that song. It seemed a long time ago now. I adjusted the volume to a level that wouldn't distract customers.

It was a little on the solitary side, but the existence I'd fashioned here suited me. There were no romantic interests on the horizon, but I had friends when I chose to be sociable. I had a comfortable routine and, although business was still slow, my customer base was growing. When I decided to sell used books as well as new ones, I took a course in web design at Macon Tech and got myself a web site. Now more than half of my sales were made via the Internet.

There were just enough customers Tuesday afternoon to keep me awake. My clients' tastes in reading material often surprised me. Arthur Penney, branch manager of a local bank, came in to check out the latest action adventure books. Arthur was a mouse of a man – small, hesitant, and easily startled – yet he devoured violent suspense novels at a rate of four or five a month. Hannah Mackey always wore a demure dress, high heels and a hat when she visited me. She was the picture of a soft-spoken Southern lady and was eighty if she was a day. She regularly purchased the latest bodice-ripping romances. That afternoon she left the shop with three paperbacks, their lurid covers hidden in a plastic bag.

Harriett Black, forty years old and never married, was truer to type. She stopped by after lunch, as she often did, on her way back to the furniture store. Her interests were local history and genealogy. But she was on a strict budget and, more often than not, left without making a purchase. I could see a copy of *Immigrants of Pennsylvania* tempted her, but she was discouraged by the $35 price tag.

I was printing out computer orders at the front counter when a young woman on the sidewalk caught my eye. Dressed like a refugee from the Sixties in embroidered bell-bottom jeans and a fringed gypsy shawl, she stared at the window display for several minutes before coming in. After we exchanged hellos, she spent some time roaming around the shop, looking at several books as if she might make a purchase. But after a while, she came empty-handed to stand beside the counter.

"Would you want me to do a tarot spread for you?" she asked in a voice that was sharpened by a slight Appalachian accent. "Or a palm reading?"

I smiled. "No, I don't think so. Not unless you can see something in my future to improve business."

She brushed long, beige hair back from her face and looked around the store. Her gaze finally settled on the front shelf that contained local writers' work. "You could start with that rack there. You ought to move it."

"Move it?"

"Yeah, if you moved it about two feet out from the wall, it would be directly under this light here, see?" She talked fast, as if afraid I'd interrupt her. "And if you turned it so that it faced the door, people would stop to look at it when they came in, especially if you changed this around. See, you can turn a few of these books out so the fronts show." She demonstrated with Jackie Cooper's *Halfway Home* and Louise Staman's *With the Stroke of a Pen*. "You've already done that on some of the other shelves. Why not this one? Right now, all anyone sees when they come in is the side of the shelf. It just seems, I don't know, kind of awkward." She smiled apologetically. "I'm not criticizing. It's just an observation."

The last thing I needed today was a wandering palmist dispensing marketing advice. I forced a smile. "I'll think about it."

She stood awkwardly, moving from one foot to the other, as if she wasn't ready to leave yet. Finally, she took a deep breath.

"Look, I . . . uh . . . my name is Pandora Bryant. I'm a sophomore at Mercer – an English major." Her sentences all ended with rising inflections, as if each one was a question. "I thought you might need someone to work here part time."

Who on earth, I wondered, would christen a child Pandora? I smiled as kindly as I could to soften my refusal. "I barely make enough here to pay myself. There's no way I could hire somebody else."

"Not even for a few hours a week?"

"Sorry."

"Well, thanks anyway."

She left the store and wandered across the street to the corner bakery, and I turned my attention to the local writers' bookshelf. It looked all right to me, but I did pull out Milam Propst's *Ociee On Her Own* and arrange it so that the front cover showed. I couldn't see that it really improved the display.

Several people came in during the next half-hour, but only one middle-aged woman bought anything. She was excited to find a 1950 hardcover edition of *I Capture the Castle*. The book had always been a favorite of mine and I was glad to see this one would get a good home.

"I can't wait to read it again," she declared. "I remember discovering it in the school library as a child. It was the most magical thing I'd ever read. After work, I'm going home and make a pot of hot chocolate and turn off the telephone. Then I'm going to read it from cover to cover in one sitting!"

It sounded like a fine evening to me and I was sorry that it was the quarterly tax report and not a beloved book that awaited me. At six, I locked the front door, turned on some soft Brazilian jazz and retreated back to the office where I jumped into the taxes with both feet. It's not a difficult task, but it is one I truly hate. Because of that I usually put it off until the last minute, but this time I was determined to get a head start. I worked uninterrupted for over an hour and, at the end of that time, was close to being done. In two weeks I'd plug in the end of March figures and the report would be ready to go. I stretched in my chair and let my head fall forward, trying to relieve the tension in my neck and shoulders.

After a last quick circuit of the shop to make sure the front was secured, I switched off the computer and CD player, pulled on my sweater, and let myself out the back door.

My mind was focused squarely on food and what I might find in the refrigerator at home, so at first the faint noise didn't register. However, by the time I'd reached my car, I recognized it as the cry of a small animal. It seemed to come from a pile of boxes a few feet down the alley.

I approached cautiously, not wanting to be bitten by an injured dog or a rabid raccoon, but I couldn't ignore what was obviously a cry for help. The scrawny tabby kitten huddled against the brick wall didn't look as if it could do anyone any damage. I picked it up. It was so small that its weight barely registered when I held it in my hand. The little creature didn't even move, but my touch did evoke a low purr.

"What are you doing here?" I asked in a soft voice.

It cried again, as if in response. I wondered when the poor thing had last eaten. There was a carton of half-and-half in the shop's refrigerator that might not have gone bad yet, so I took my small charge back inside. I put it down on the floor, found a clean cup and, after sniffing to make sure it wasn't sour, poured in the half and half. When I put the cup on the floor in front of the cat, it fell on the milk with noisy laps, the small head nearly disappearing into the cup.

How could someone abandon such a helpless little animal? But was it really abandoned? Maybe something had happened to the mother. Could the rest of the litter be in the alley? Back outside, I stood very still, listening, but there were no more cat cries. I started slowly down the alley. I shifted the pile of boxes where the kitten had been, but there was nothing there.

The hulking profile of the trash Dumpster loomed a few feet farther on. I'd never realized before just how poorly lit our alley was and decided to talk with some of the other storekeepers about changing that. Inadequate lighting was just an invitation to burglars. There were no more strays behind the trash container. I decided I'd walk a little farther on, but I drew the line at looking inside that big, smelly garbage bin.

The body of the woman lay just beyond the Dumpster, right behind Clarice Evans's shoe store. Her legs, encased in blue polyester slacks, sprawled at awkward angles. She was missing a shoe and her torso half-covered her purse. For one heart-stopping moment I was transported back to another death scene, to another body lying on another street. Then I got control of myself and did what had to be done.

I knelt beside her. Even before my fingers touched her wrist, I knew it was too late. Every sign of life was absent. There was no rise of breathing and her skin had that empty feel peculiar to the dead. The nauseating odor of evacuated bowels reached my nose. Knowing it was futile even as I did it, I leaned closer to check for a pulse in her neck and got a shock. The light was dim and the woman's face was distorted, but I recognized her. It was Glynnis McCullough.

CHAPTER TWO

I hurried back into the shop, pulled the phone from my purse and dialed 911.

"Are you there now, ma'am?" the emergency operator wanted to know.

"Yes. I'll wait in the alley."

The cup sat empty on the floor. There was no sign of the kitten, but I didn't bother looking for it right then. It couldn't get hurt inside the shop. I dropped the phone in my dress pocket and went back outside, conscious of the fact that the alley was now a crime scene.

In less than five minutes a marked patrol car rolled up the alley to where I waited. His flashing blue lights cast weird, circling shapes on the building walls, but at least he hadn't used a siren. I approved of his restraint. The responding officer was slender, with dark skin and eyes, and looked like he was about fifteen years old. Police officers, doctors, and other figures of authority were looking younger to me every year. I pointed down the alley and walked with him past the Dumpster.

When we came to where Glynnis lay, he knelt and checked for a pulse, just as I had.

"I found her about ten minutes ago," I said, angling the face of my watch to catch the feeble light. "Say 7:30."

He made some quick marks in a small notebook, keyed the mike at his shoulder and asked that investigators and a crime scene unit be en route. Then he turned his attention back to me, although his eyes were never still, constantly moving around the alley.

"What happened? Did you see anything? And what are you doing here this time of night?"

I made my reply as concise as possible. "I own the book store," I indicated its location with a nod, "right there. I was working late and when I came out, I heard a cat crying. I found a kitten right over there and took it inside to give it some milk. Then I wondered if the rest of the litter was out here. I came out to look. There weren't any more cats, but I did find Glynnis."

He looked up sharply at that. "You know her?"

I nodded. "Yes. Glynnis McCullough." I spelled it for him.

15

"She's a . . . an acquaintance of mine."

He wrote that down. "Does she work around here?"

"No." When he didn't speak, I continued. "Anyway, I checked her pulse – wrist and throat. It was clear she was dead, looks like she was strangled. I didn't touch anything else and nothing's been disturbed since I called you."

He got my name, address, and date of birth. "I'll need you to stay right here for now, ma'am. The detectives will want to talk to you. So stay right here."

He looked so serious that I thought he just might tackle me if I tried to go back inside. There was undisguised suspicion on his face and I knew he'd already found his prime suspect. We stood in silence until a second car – unmarked this time – arrived.

The two men who got out were a study in contrast. The passenger – short, trim and teeming with energy – reached us first. He practically bounced over to where we stood. His pinstriped suit was stylish, immaculate and didn't conceal the muscular body beneath it. His light brown hair was razor cut with every strand in place. But his most notable feature was the size of his nostrils. His nose was of normal proportions, but his nostrils looked huge. I tried not to stare, but it was difficult. I'd never seen that feature before. He squatted beside the body for a quick look, then came back to us.

"What have you got?" he asked the young patrolman.

As the officer explained the situation, the second man ambled up. Taller and heavier than the first, I put his age near forty -- a good ten years older than his companion. He, too, wore a suit, but the tie was loosened and his trousers were a bit wrinkled. His face was lined from a lifetime of expressions – I guessed that laughter was chief among them. He, at least, acknowledged my presence.

"I'm Lieutenant Ballard. This is Detective Kaminsky," he introduced the short man, "he'll be the lead investigator on the case."

"I'm Dixie McClatchey. I called it in."

"She knows the victim," the patrolman interjected, "but says she doesn't know anything about what happened."

The three of them walked over and formed a semi-circle around Glynnis. I felt a flash of sympathy for her. Fiftyish and a good forty pounds overweight, with flat, mousy hair and blotchy skin, Glynnis had never seemed concerned about making herself attractive, but she'd have been horrified to be sprawled out in this way with strangers staring down at her. And I knew that there were worse indignities to come.

After a few minutes, Kaminsky and Ballard motioned for me and guided me away from the body for more talk. The detective asked the first question.

"You found her?"

"Yes, about 7:30."

He frowned. "You don't seem all that upset, finding a body like that."

I looked in his eyes to avoid gaping at his nose. "It's not really new for me. I was with the Atlanta police for nine years – the last three in Homicide. I've seen my share of bodies."

"Why'd you leave APD?" Kaminsky wanted to know.

I shrugged, not willing to go into the details right then. "I was ready to move on. You can check me out, if you want. My last supervisor was Dennis Brown. Dennis M. Brown. I heard he's made captain now and is working out of Zone Two."

He wrote that down. He'd be on the phone to Dennis at the first opportunity. He'd be disappointed, I thought, to learn that my leaving the force had been voluntary. I was an officer in more or less good standing when I quit.

I repeated what I'd told the uniform officer, elaborating this time on what I knew about Glynnis.

"I've known her for over a year – ever since I joined the Friends of the Library." I divided a glance between them. "Are you familiar with the organization? We're volunteers that work with the public library. Glynnis and I are both on the Acquisition Committee, along with some other folks. When people donate books, we're the ones that sort and price them. Then every year we have a book sale to raise money for the library. Our last one was only a couple of weeks ago."

"I've heard of it, sure," Ballard said. "Even went to a couple of the sales."

Kaminsky wasn't interested. "Where did the victim live?

All I could tell them was north Macon. "But I do know she lives with her mother. Her name is Delia."

"Same last name?"

I nodded.

"Do you know what kind of car the victim drove?"

I shook my head. "Sorry."

Ballard keyed the radio he carried and requested that uniform units check registrations on the cars parked in the vicinity of the shop. "See if you can find one that comes back to a McCullough."

A chilly breeze rushed down the alley and I pulled my sweater tighter. Kaminsky asked when I'd last seen Glynnis.

"This morning. We were both at the Friends work session. We meet every Tuesday morning to sort books from nine to eleven."

"Where is that?" His nostrils flared every time he asked a question.

"At the Washington Street library. In fact, Glynnis said she was going to come by and – " I was struck by the realization that she'd probably been killed while coming to see me. "I … I guess that's why she was here. She said she'd stop by the shop this afternoon. But it doesn't make sense. I mean, why was she in the alley? She would have used the front door."

"You were expecting her? Why was she coming to see you?"

I closed my eyes with the effort of trying to remember that last conversation with her, but it was useless. We'd all been walking out together and I simply hadn't paid much attention. I shrugged. "She said something about wanting information about books, I think; needing my expertise, I believe was the way she put it. I'm sorry, I just don't remember her exact words."

"What time was she supposed to be here?"

"There wasn't a set time. She just said she'd stop by, that's all."

"You must have had some idea of when to expect her," he insisted. "Weren't you concerned when she didn't show up?"

I was ashamed to admit that I'd just been relieved that she hadn't come to the shop. "No. There was no reason to be worried. It wasn't a definite appointment or anything. I just figured she'd gotten busy with something else and would come in another time."

"Too bad you didn't check on her," he said. "Might have been able to help."

My glare was wasted. He didn't even look in my direction. It was quiet downtown now. Then a city bus rumbled along Cherry Street.

"What time did you close tonight, Ms. McClatchey?"

"Six."

He looked at his watch. "What have you been doing since then?"

"Working on my sales tax report." I nodded at the rear door. "At the desk in there."

"And you didn't hear anything out here in the alley?"

"Nothing."

He stopped writing in his notebook and looked me in the eyes. "Can anyone vouch for you? Was anyone with you?"

"No … no one."

He expelled an impatient breath through those nostrils. "Nobody stopped by or called?"

"No, not a soul."

The crime scene technicians arrived then with a clatter of equipment and an assortment of boxes and satchels. Portable flood-lights were set up and illuminated the alley as bright as midday. The two techs – an Asian woman and a white man with a scraggly beard – began their slow, methodical work. Glynnis's body was their starting point. They measured, examined, and photographed it from every angle. Plastic bags were slipped over her hands and secured with tape. Next, on their knees, they searched the area immediately around her. From time to time, one or both would stop and confer in undertones with Ballard and Kaminsky.

The activity unfolding before me was both familiar and strange. I knew everything they were doing and why. I was accustomed to working as part of that team. In fact, I could have performed each task myself. But now I was separate from them, cast in the awkward role of a witness.

After a quick consultation with Kaminsky, the woman came over to me.

"Would you consent to have me examine your hands and forearms and take fingernail scrapings, ma'am?"

For a moment I was speechless, stunned by the knowledge that these people actually believed I might have killed Glynnis. The technician waited patiently for my answer. Kaminsky and Ballard had stopped talking and were watching me, judging my reaction. The decision was easy since I had nothing to hide. I took off my sweater, tied the sleeves around my neck and stuck out my hands.

"Sure. Go ahead."

Five minutes later we were done and the woman rejoined her partner in processing the scene. I put my sweater back on.

A patrolman I hadn't seen before trotted down the alley to report they'd located Glynnis's car. "It's a blue Toyota, parked around the corner on Second Street."

"Call a wrecker and have it pulled in," Kaminsky told him. I knew they'd process it for prints and other evidence. "And don't go putting your hands on it and messing up the fingerprints."

The patrolman rolled his eyes as he walked past me. I wasn't the only one who found Kaminsky hard to take.

The night had turned chilly and my sweater didn't provide much warmth. When Ballard joined me near the back door, I asked if I could go inside and make a cup of tea.

"Sure," he said agreeably, "as long as I come with you."

In the little office/storage room at the back of the store, he declined my offer of refreshment. He leaned against the doorframe and watched as I heated a cup of water in the microwave and plopped in a tea bag. He seemed to be one of those people who was comfortable in any circumstance.

Kaminsky came in as I was adding sugar to my cup.

"Where is that cat you say you found?"

I glanced around the office, but didn't see it. The front of the shop was dark. "Well, it's here somewhere." I retrieved the cup up from the floor. "It finished the milk."

"Yeah, but I don't see the cat."

Did he think I'd invented the story? I wondered if I'd have to produce the stray to avoid arrest. "I'm sure it's here. There's no way it could have gotten out."

He turned to Ballard. "We're going to need to search this place, Lieutenant."

"For the cat?" I asked before Ballard could reply.

"It's a crime scene," Kaminsky told me as if explaining something to a rather stupid child.

It wasn't, of course, not technically. The alley was a crime scene, yes, but not my bookstore. Glynnis hadn't set foot in here and I doubted that any judge would issue a search warrant for the shop. It would have been easy to make an issue of it, especially since I was developing a serious dislike for Kaminsky. It might do him good to be brought down a peg or two, but this wasn't the time to teach him a lesson. Getting in the way of a murder investigation just to spite one obnoxious man was foolish.

"Help yourself. Just try not to tear anything up."

He produced a "Consent to Search" form and handed it to me without a word. I signed the paper and gave it back. He folded it once and slipped it into his jacket pocket, then started toward the front of the shop.

I was right behind him, turning on the big overhead lights. He could search my shop all he wanted, but I was going to watch every move he made. Kaminsky clearly held no fond feelings for me and I knew from experience how things could get "broken" during a police search. Ballard followed several steps behind us as if he were a disinterested observer.

Kaminsky started at the front. He plundered under the counter and fumbled in the drawers. He even examined the CDs I had stacked up there. When he found nothing of interest, he moved on to the book-shelves. I stood to the side with the lieutenant.

"I always thought I'd like to own a book store," he said. His blue eyes were bright with good humor. "Must be great. I guess you can read any book you want without having to buy it, huh?"

I smiled. "Well, the used ones anyway. People kind of expect the new ones to be in perfect condition."

Kaminsky knocked a whole row of books off a shelf in the biography section. He looked to see if I'd noticed and, after locking eyes with me for a long moment, grudgingly began replacing them. I took a breath, but didn't say a word.

Ballard gave me a critical look. "You doing okay?"

"Sure. I don't think he did any damage and he's picking them up."

"No, I didn't mean that."

"Oh," I said, understanding dawning, "yeah, I'm fine. I'm really not upset. I mean, it was unpleasant, but, like I said, I worked homicide for years. So …" I shrugged.

"Still finding someone you know . . . must have been tough."

I didn't mind his questioning, even couched as it was in friendly, casual terms. He was doing what he was paid to do, what I'd have done in his place. And talking to Ballard beat dealing with Kaminsky all to hell.

"Look, Lieutenant, I knew Glynnis, but we weren't friends. I didn't even particularly like her. So I'm not going to pretend to be real upset about her death." He probably wouldn't tell me, but I had to ask. "Do you have any idea what happened?"

"Nothing definite." He shrugged. "Maybe a screwed-up robbery."

A plaintive, high-pitched cry came from somewhere on the far side of the shop.

"It's the kitten." I sent a triumphant look at Kaminsky, but he was on his knees behind the gardening books and didn't pay me any attention. I walked up and down the aisles, saying "Here, kitty" and finally zeroed in on the cries among the Civil War books. The cat had managed to crawl into the space between the bottom row of books and the shelf above, and was now feeling lost or hungry or something. I gently lifted it out and held it against my chest. After a second, the purring cranked up again.

I carried it back to the front of the store, passing Kaminsky who barely gave the animal a glance. He continued his search, pawing through every corner and seemingly putting his hands on every object in the shop. I could tell by the way he handled them that he had no love for books. When he'd searched through everything he could find on the ground level, he moved to the narrow stairs that led from the office to the second floor.

"What's up there?" he asked, craning his neck in an attempt to see the top of the stairs.

"Nothing. Just a lot of junk."

"Uhh huh." He started up the stairs. I stayed where I was.

"You're not going with him?" Ballard asked, unsuccessfully hiding a smile.

"No. It's a real mess up there. Everything's covered with dust. Most of it was here when I moved in. I don't think there's anything he can hurt." There was a crash above our heads, followed by the sound of something heavy being dragged across the floor. "I just hope he doesn't break his neck. He's just the kind who'd sue me if he injured himself."

Ballard shook his head, smiling. "Come on, cut the kid some slack. He's young and he wants to do the best he can. Just doesn't always know how he comes across. Give him some time and he's going to be a damned good detective."

I was willing to give Kaminsky the benefit of the doubt. I'd even chip in a pat on the back if he'd just wrap it up so I could go home.

It was near midnight before the search of the shop was finished. Kaminsky's forehead gleamed with sweat and his suit was now wrinkled and showed smears of dust. He didn't say anything about the search, no doubt sulking because he hadn't found evidence to incriminate me.

"What else do we have to do here tonight?" Ballard asked him.

"Should be just about done. I'll go make sure the Crime Scene techs have finished what they can for the night." Kaminsky inhaled deeply and turned to me. I quickly looked away from the depths of his nose. "You'll need to come to headquarters tomorrow and give a statement." He handed me his card. "Ask for me at the front desk."

"Okay."

Without another word, he turned and strode out the back door. I was too tired to react to his rudeness. All I wanted was to drive home and fall into bed. I said as much to Ballard. That's when I learned that the Macon Police Department had other plans.

"You're going to have to leave your vehicle here," he said, a note of apology in his voice. "It's a part of the crime scene and has to be processed. But they probably won't get to it till tomorrow."

I followed him out the back door into the glare of the work lights. Glynnis's body had been removed while we were in the shop and the alley was now roped off with bright yellow crime scene tape. A uniformed officer stood nearby, presumably to make sure nothing was disturbed before they could come back in daylight and go over the ground again. My Blazer sat within the bounds of the tape, a hostage to circumstance.

Ballard saved me from the six-block, mostly uphill, walk home by giving me and the cat a lift. Kaminsky would ride back to the office in the Crime Scene van.

"My house is on High Street, just off Orange." I fastened the seatbelt and the cat settled contentedly in my lap, gently kneading the fabric of my skirt with its paws.

"Yeah, I know where that is. Up on College Hill, right? Nice up there. The book business must be good."

I smiled. "I hate to disappoint you, but it's a family thing. It was my grandmother's house until she gave it to me two years ago."

Ballard drove out of the alley and turned right on Second Street.

"It's faster if you go the other way, up Poplar," I said.

"I know. I've got a stop to make first."

I waited in the car while he went into an all-night market at Spring and Riverside. When he came back, he had a box of cat food – or rather kitten food, according to the label – in his hand.

"Here you go. For your new friend. Consider it a gift from the Macon Police Department."

"Thanks." I smiled down at the tiny creature in my lap. "But I'm sure I could have found something to feed it at home."

He shook his head. "This is better. Babies need special food."

Two minutes later, he stopped the car in front of my house. "Don't worry about coming to headquarters. You were a cop – you know what to do. Just write up your statement and we'll pick it up some time tomorrow."

I guessed Kaminsky wouldn't approve, but Ballard outranked him and that was good enough for me. "I'll get it done first thing in the morning."

He offered me a ride to work the next day, but I declined. During the evening I'd caught him a couple of times looking at me in a less than professional way. There was no point in encouraging any unofficial contact. I thanked him and got out.

When I reached the house I turned and waved, and he drove away down the hill. It took some juggling, but I managed to unlock the side door without dropping my purse, the cat food, or the now madly wriggling kitten.

"Just a minute, just a minute," I told it.

As soon as the door closed behind me, I flipped on the light and released the cat. It shot off into the dining room as if it were pursued by devils while I rubbed the stinging scratches it left on my arm. I locked the door and surveyed the big old kitchen with a critical eye. Grandma Evelyn's house was over a hundred years old and, for the last twenty years or so that she'd lived here, she hadn't been able to do much around the place.

Although most of my attention and money had gone to the shop during the last two years, the house had had one problem that I couldn't ignore – the exterior was long overdue for painting. That expense set me further back financially than I'd expected and it had taken more than a year for my budget to recover enough that I could contemplate doing more. But now I was ready. Last week I'd given a contractor my wish list and he was coming by Friday morning to deliver his estimate on updating the kitchen.

I filled a small bowl with the cat food and the kitten materialized at my feet. No urging was necessary to make it eat. It fell on the food like a small, furry steam shovel, scooping up the dry morsels as fast as it could. I filled a second bowl with water and set it beside the first.

Some people cannot imagine lives without animals. Some people, but not all people. I'll be the first to admit I am not a pet person. Because of my sister's allergies, we never had any animals growing up, and I knew next to nothing about taking care of one. I knew the kitten should probably be put outside to relieve itself, but what would I do if it ran off? I decided we'd just have to take our chances inside for the night. I folded up an old quilt, and put it on the floor not far from the food. Then I finally went to bed. As I climbed the worn stairs, I couldn't remember the last time I had felt so tired.

The bedroom was cool, damp evening air drifting in through the open windows. As I climbed between the sheets, I was vaguely aware of the night sounds of crickets and far off traffic on the interstate. A train rumbled in the distance.

Sleep came quickly, but I couldn't keep it close to me the whole night. Once I was startled awake when the cat jumped on my chest, its tiny, needle-sharp claws splayed. My shout of outrage must have scared it sufficiently to keep it out of the room because it made no further appearances the rest of the night. But that didn't ensure peace. It wasn't Glynnis's death, but Donald's, that filled my dreams.

I woke around three, heart pounding and damp with sweat. The night seemed to press in on me. I could banish the darkness by turning on the light, but I resisted the impulse. Experience had taught me that once I did that, there'd be no more sleep that night. So I lay in the darkness playing "what if." Even though I knew that no imagined scenarios could change the past, I couldn't seem to stop myself from conjuring them up. Near dawn, exhaustion finally overcame grief and guilt and I managed a couple of hours of fitful sleep before the alarm sounded at seven.

I staggered into the bathroom to brush my teeth. As I worked the brush around my mouth, I regarded myself in the mirror. I was a medium sort of person – medium height, medium weight, and medium brown hair that I wore cut short to discourage its tendency to curl. Ordinarily I didn't mind the way I looked, but this morning my face had a pasty cast and there were dark stains under my eyes. I thought a run might make me feel better.

The exercise and the cool, fresh air worked like a tonic. After the first quarter mile or so, I began enjoying the run along the quiet city blocks. I did two miles almost before I realized it.

It wasn't until I slowed to a walk back at the top of High Street, my legs tight and my breath coming in hard gasps, that I let myself think about Glynnis McCullough's death. Ballard's suggestion of a robbery gone bad was the most logical explanation. I knew from painful experience that such things could happen and Macon was no more immune to violent crime than any other city. It was a rare day that at least one robbery didn't make the evening news.

Still, Glynnis's death didn't quite fit the pattern here. Most Macon robberies were committed in businesses. One-on-one street crime was still unusual, especially downtown. I tried to decide if Glynnis had been the type to resist a robbery. I didn't know her well enough to say for sure, but I had a hard time imagining her putting up a fight. She'd be more likely to hand over her purse and then sue the city for failing to protect her. What could have gone so wrong that the robber had killed her?

A few slow stretches smoothed the knots in my muscles. I started walking down the hill, my mind still on Glynnis. Try as I might, I couldn't imagine an alternative reason for her murder. Lord knows she had been a mean-spirited, irritating woman, but that fact alone couldn't account for her death. If being unpleasant were sufficient motive for murder, we'd experience a dramatic decrease in the population.

Lincoln Pryby wished me a cheerful good morning. In pajamas, tightly belted bathrobe and slippers, he was retrieving the morning paper from the end of his drive. Mr. and Mrs. Pryby had lived next door to Grandma Evelyn for as far back as I could remember. His wife, Anna, had died some years before, but Lincoln, now eighty-five, was still going strong.

I returned his greeting and picked up my own *Telegraph* from the lawn. I'd unfolded it and read the headline when a flash of gray and white caught my eye. A mockingbird flew low over the hedge and came to rest on the bare branch of a crape myrtle. Nearby several blue jays hopped over the grass in search of breakfast. I had Grandma Evelyn to thank for teaching me to identify the more common varieties of what she called her "yard birds." Since moving to Macon, watching them come and go with the seasons had brought me quiet contentment. I'd even set up a couple of feeders in the back yard.

The telephone was ringing when I opened the door. Calls before eight o'clock were unusual in my house. I was even more surprised when I recognized Marian Saxby's voice. It wasn't like her to behave in any way that could be considered less than courteous and an early call like this was a minor breach of etiquette for the most proper woman I knew.

"Is it true?" she asked, not even apologizing for the early hour. "They said on the news this morning that Glynnis was killed outside your store."

I told her what I knew.

"Oh, dear," she sighed. "Oh, dear. That's awful. What will her mother do without her? Delia's been in poor health for years."

I agreed it was a sad situation. No, I told her, I hadn't heard anything about funeral arrangements. "I expect it will be a day or two before there are any plans. The police have to . . . well, they'll need to keep the body for a while."

"We'll have to cancel the Thursday night meeting, of course." I wasn't surprised that Marian went straight to the practical problems created by Glynnis's death. Being responsible was what she did. She had served as president of the Friends of the Library for more than ten years and ran our Tuesday morning sorting sessions with the same iron hand she'd employed in her thirty-year teaching career. "It just wouldn't be respectful to go ahead with it."

"That's probably best," I agreed.

"And we'll have to nominate someone else for vice president."

To the surprise of many of our members, myself included, the nominating committee had put up Glynnis's name as one of the slate of new officers. Marian was an active member of that committee and I never thought she'd cared much for Glynnis, but after a bit of reflection I'd realized it wasn't such a bad choice. Unpleasant as she was, Glynnis was generous with her time and could be counted on to finish whatever task she was given.

"I don't suppose you would be interested in serving . . . ?"

"I'm sorry, Marian. I just don't have the time right now. What about Alexandra?"

We passed a few minutes discussing possible replacement candidates, and then said goodbye. I went off to find breakfast.

Tuesday's newspaper lay where I'd left it on the recycling stack at the back door. I saw the cat had been there ahead of me and shredded the top layers with its claws. Closer inspection revealed that it had been used as a makeshift litter box. I'd have to do something pretty quick or the house would be a disaster area.

After stuffing the soiled paper into a plastic bag and tying the top, I found a cardboard box in a back room that I thought would work. After cutting down the sides so the kitten could get in and out of it easily, I tore a couple of sections of old newspaper into strips and piled them in the box. I positioned it on the floor near the back door and hoped it would be acceptable to my guest. Finding the cat a home had just moved to number one on the list of things to do for the day.

Breakfast was simple – toast and fruit – and was interrupted several times. One friend and two casual acquaintances called to ask about the murder. Since Glynnis had been killed some distance down the alley, actually near the dry cleaning store, it seemed likely I had Kaminsky to thank for releasing the information that she was found behind Chapter and Verse.

Before I could finish my first cup of coffee, I had to go find the cat. It seemed to have a knack for getting lost. This time the panicky cries led me to the hallway where I found it halfway up the staircase, cowering behind a banister and howling for all it was worth.

"Idiot."

I took it back to the kitchen with me where the recently filled food bowl once again worked its magic. It was still gobbling when I left the house and caught a bus to Cherry Street.

CHAPTER THREE

The alley behind the store was still taped off and buzzing with activity when I arrived so I had to use the front entrance. After flipping the sign and turning on the lights, I went to peer out the back door. Patient people wielding small brushes were dusting shop doors, my car, the Dumpster, and any other surface that might retain fingerprints. Six uniformed officers were doing a grid search, walking slowly side by side, eyes on the pavement beneath their feet. Using this method, they'd cover every inch of the alley.

Wednesday turned out to be one of my busiest days since opening the store. It would have been nice to chalk it up to a renewed interest in reading on the part of Maconites, but I didn't believe my customers' motives were so lofty. They wandered around the shop, edging ever closer to the back door where they tried to get a peek at the alley. And, of course, they asked me what happened, what I saw, and what I knew. A murder had been committed only a few yards from where we stood and they were all hoping for a glimpse of the crime scene or some tidbit of confidential information. But they did more than snoop. Many felt obligated to make a purchase as they asked their questions. So, as it turned out, I actually profited from Glynnis's death. The idea made me a bit uneasy.

In between ringing up sales and saying "Don't know" to the morbid questions, I managed to write out a statement describing my relationship with Glynnis, her stated plan to come by the shop and what led up to my finding her body. Literary skill and imagination weren't necessary for this task. Since it was the truth, all it took was a little time to write it down. When Detective Kaminsky, immaculate in a gray suit and understated yellow tie, nostrils at full flare, came through the front door a little after eleven, I had the statement ready for him.

"All I have to do is sign it," I told him. "I was just waiting for someone to witness my signature."

If he was impressed with my efficiency, he didn't show it. He just scowled. Why didn't the PD invest a few bucks and send this guy to a communications skills class?

I scrawled my signature across the bottom of the last page, then handed him the pen. He signed beside my name, but still made no comment. I doubted he thought much of this method for taking state-ments and resented what he saw as my receiving special treatment from Ballard. Witnesses were expected to report to the police department and have their statements taken in the traditional way.

He leaned against the front counter and read what I'd written. I busied myself with the computer.

"So the victim told you she'd come by your store?"

I turned toward him. "That's right."

"And this was at a meeting at the library?"

"Yes, like I said last night, a work session for the Friends of the Library."

"Who else was there?" He gestured with the paper. "You didn't put that information in your statement."

I'd been hoping to keep the others out of the investigation, but he wasn't going to let me get away with omitting their names. "Let's see. Marian Saxby, Carlton Mabry, Cassie Waycaster, Reg Anderson, and Alexandra Michaels. And Glynnis and I, of course. I think that's all."

He looked at me, pen poised over his notebook. "You think you could give 'em to me one at a time?"

"Of course," I said, emphasizing politeness and speaking with exaggerated clarity.   "Marian Saxby. She's been with the Friends for years. She's a retired teacher."

"Address?"

I frowned. "I'll see what I have."

I pulled a Rolodex from under the counter and began flipping through the cards. I am fully aware that most everyone nowadays keeps information like that on their computers, but I don't. Somehow having it written on real paper is a source of comfort for me. The card with Marian's address was right behind the one for Satterfield's restaurant. I handed it to him.

As he copied the information into his notebook, he asked, "How did she get along with Glynnis?"

I thought he was maybe being a bit too thorough. If Glynnis was a robbery victim, her personal life should have been irrelevant. "Okay, I guess. Like anybody else."

He pointed those nostrils in my direction. "What were those other names?"

"Carlton Mabry. He and his wife used to run an office supply store, but their son handles the business now. And Alexandra Michaels. She's a doctor's wife. They live out in Barrington somewhere. Cassie Waycaster was there. She's a housewife with small children. And," I mentally ticked off all of the Friends who were at the library the day before, "oh, yes. Reginald Anderson. Retired Air Force, I believe."

I handed him the cards for all of them. Although I had only phone numbers for Reg and Cassie, finding the addresses shouldn't be too much of a stretch for a trained investigator.

"And, before you ask, as far as I know all of them got along okay with Glynnis McCullough."

He narrowed his eyes at me. "You don't sound too sure about that. What was the trouble between her and these people?"

I sighed. "There wasn't any trouble, not really. It's just that she wasn't a very likable person. She gossiped. She always thought the worst of people and she . . . I guess you could say she just wasn't very nice."

He had nothing to say to that, just finished copying the information and gave me back the cards.

When my statement was neatly folded and tucked away in his breast pocket, he gave me a hard look. "I called APD this morning. Talked with your old lieutenant. He said they didn't have any complaints about the job you did up there." He let two or three silent seconds pass and I knew what was coming. "Told me how your husband was shot. I'd have to say that resisting a robbery and endangering the life of a civilian was a stupid thing to do."

"I'd have to agree with you, Detective Kaminsky." There was no other answer because there was no excuse for what I'd done.

The telephone saved me from further conversation. It was Deannie Vandeusen, calling to confirm our dinner plans.

"I'll be there." Kaminsky left the store without a backward glance. "I wouldn't miss it."

"I'm looking forward to it, too." Her voice dropped in volume and took on a somber tone. "Are you okay, Dixie? You sound funny. I heard on the news about Glynnis. Did you really find the body?"

"Yeah, but I'm fine. Really."

"What happened?"

I sighed. I was still shaken by my conversation with Kaminsky and I couldn't face going over all of the events of the night before right then. "It's a long story. I'll tell you everything tonight. Oh, by the way, do you want a cat? A kitten, really. A cute little gray and white thing that I found …"

I stopped because I didn't think she could hear me while she was laughing so hard. "You and a cat! Of all the people in the world! You hate animals."

"I do not!" I protested. "I just don't like them all that much, I guess."

"Well, I sure don't need a cat. I've got two dogs. Remember? Why don't you keep it? It would do you good to have a pet." Laughter still bubbled just under the surface of her voice. "Having animals around is supposed to be good for people, isn't it? Lowers the blood pressure, I hear."

"No, thanks. That's the last thing I need. I'm just playing good Samaritan, finding it a home. That's all. And my blood pressure is just fine."

"How in the world did you end up with a cat anyway?"

I started to tell her, but a teenage boy entered the store and approached the front counter. "Tonight," I promised. "You'll get the full story."

"Okay, see you at seven. Come hungry."

The noon church bells had just stopped ringing when I glanced out the front door and noticed a man with a camera standing across the street, busily photographing the front of my shop. It was a small incident, I suppose, but it was the trigger that pushed me right over the edge of irritation into anger. I threw open the door and marched across the street, eliciting honking horns from the drivers I stepped in front of.

"Darren Bond, what the hell do you think you're doing?"

The young *Telegraph* photographer, and my sometimes customer, was only a year or so out of high school and probably hadn't encountered too many hostile people in his few months with the paper. He actually stepped back away from me a couple of feet and a slight blush showed under his freckles.

"Oh, hey, Dixie. I'm just getting a shot for the paper. Tomorrow's issue." He raised the camera and took two quick shots of me. "It's news, you know. Your store is a crime scene."

We were standing in the middle of the sidewalk, parting pedestrian traffic like boulders in a stream. I made a conscious effort to lower my voice.

"My store is not a crime scene, Darren. The alley is the crime scene. Go on back there and take pictures 'til you run out of film." I stepped closer, crowding him back against a store window. "And if you take one more picture of me, young man, I'll stomp that camera until there's nothing left but little pieces – and then I'll make you eat them!"

There was no sound of a camera whirring as I returned to my store. I might have lost a customer, I reflected, but it sure was nice to take my frustrations out on someone. I felt a hundred percent better.

As the parade of curious customers continued, I noticed that they rarely stopped at the display of local books. Of course, that shelf was located at the front of the store, far from the lure of the alley. Still I couldn't help wondering if the fortune-telling college student might have had a point about its arrangement.

In between sales, I made some calls trying to find the kitten a home, but struck out every time. Edward stopped by about two o'clock with a pizza to share. Actually he'd picked up a veggie pizza from Adriana's and already finished half of it. He'd brought me the leftovers. I felt sure I was an afterthought, but I didn't care. I was hungry and, even cold, it was delicious. I fetched a drink from the miniature refrigerator in the back and settled on the stool behind the counter. Edward wandered around the front of the store, looking at this and that as I ate.

"How did your speech go last night?" I asked.

He shrugged. "All right, I suppose. At least that's what people said. All I know is that I'm relieved it's over and that I didn't faint dead away when I walked up to that podium."

"I'm sure you were terrific."

And I was. Stage fright or not, Edward was an amusing, entertaining speaker.

"Whatever. At least it's over."

"Are the parade plans coming along okay?"

"Don't ask! I will not do this next year. You are my witness, Dixie. I will not do this again next year. It is simply not worth the abuse!"

I smiled sympathetically, but wasn't worried that the Festival parade would have to suffer without his help. "You say the same thing every year."

"Ah, but this time, I mean it! Now one of the horse groups wants to change its parade position. They say they can't come directly behind a marching band because the drums spook the horses."

"So change them."

"That would be the logical solution, sweet thing, but unfortunately the only place to put them is in front of the marching bands. As you might imagine, that creates a whole different problem."

"It's a problem all right," I said, biting into a second piece of pizza. "So what are you going to do?"

"Lord only knows." He shook his head. "Just the best we can, I suppose."

I chewed and swallowed. "You know it always works out by parade time. Are we still on for the Oldies Dance next week?"

He grinned. "Yes, we are. And thank you for mentioning it. It reminds me that life will, indeed, go on after the parade is over and done with." He brushed some invisible lint from his pant leg. "Would you mind terribly if someone else tagged along with us?"

"Of course not." Then came an unpleasant thought. "Not George?"

He looked embarrassed, but nodded.

"Oh, Edward." I sighed. "After the last time? How can you even think about seeing him again?"

"He's so distressed about that. I've never known him to be this upset. His job is just so stressful that sometimes it gets to be too much for him and he lashes out. He doesn't mean anything by it."

"Well, then he's the one who should be bruised, not you."

"I know, I know. But he's really sorry this time. It won't ever happen again."

"Right," I said with disgust.

He came to stand across the counter from me. "Come on, Dixie. Give him a chance."

"I can't stand the man. I don't want to give him a chance."

"Then do it for me. He'll only be in town for a few days and I know he'll think the dance is a hoot. He loves things like that, Americana and everything." He sighed. "I wish you'd just get to know him. He's really a fascinating person."

"He's an asshole." I shrugged. "But if you want him along, it's okay. Just don't expect me to go out of my way to be nice to him."

Two women who'd been hovering around the shelves at the rear of the store finally walked past us and out onto the sidewalk. When the door closed behind them, Edward looked around to make sure we were alone. "Is it true that the wicked witch of the west has melted away?"

"Edward," I scolded. "I know you didn't like her, but Glynnis is dead."

"Like her? I positively loathed her! She was a vile woman who did her level best to ruin me. Did I tell you she threatened to out me?"

"What? How could she do that?"

"Well, she couldn't, of course. I've always been out, sweet thing. Even as a toddler, I had a certain flair."

I giggled. "I don't doubt that for a minute. But what about Glynnis?"

He leaned towards me, resting his elbows next to the computer. "It was one day back around Christmas. She was in my shop wanting to buy one of Gloria Smith's paintings. You know, the one with the two roosters? Well, the silly woman tried to bargain with me, offering a ridiculously low amount for it." He rolled his eyes. "I told her I didn't bargain nor did I barter. A price is a price. I wouldn't lower it and I wasn't about to start trading paintings for livestock or produce."

"How did she take that?"

"She threatened me! She said if I weren't careful, she'd tell people about my strange sexual proclivities." He hooted with laughter. "Oh, my God. I told her to take her raggedy little butt out of my shop and not come back." He raised an eyebrow. "She never liked me much after that. And I couldn't stand her. So why on earth should I pretend to be sorry that the world is rid of her?"

"I didn't like her either, but I do feel sorry for her mother. I guess the poor woman will be all alone now."

"I can't see how Glynnis's absence could ever be considered a problem." Edward definitely wasn't feeling charitable. "Besides, it was probably her mother's dubious parenting skills that produced someone like Glynnis in the first place."

The telephone rang around five.

"Hello, dear." Even three years after Donald's death, my mother still managed to infuse those two words with sympathy. "How are you today?"

"I'm fine today," I answered, exaggerating my good humor for her benefit. I wasn't about to mention the body in the alley. "It's a beautiful day. Spring has definitely arrived in Macon."

"We're close, I think. We have jonquils in bloom up here and the Bradford pears are starting to show color. I believe we'll be able to start putting in some annuals in a few weeks. Now if we can only get a decent amount of rain this year, we should be fine."

Mother was, first and foremost, a gardener and had taken Georgia's recent drought as a personal affront. While she prattled on about her plans for the rock garden in the side yard, my father's business, and the latest achievements of my sister Anna's children, I listened with enough attention to make appropriate comments.

The rest of my mind was focused on the computer screen in front of me where the latest book orders were displayed. I printed out each one, still managing to respond to Mother's cheerful chatting. I was perfectly content to listen to a long story of Grandma Evelyn's blessedly minor health problems, but when the topic turned to Donald's death and what Mother perceived as my exaggerated period of mourning, I stopped the computer work.

"Mother, I'm doing just fine. I'm content here."

"Content? Content is for grandmothers and nuns. You should be out and about, seeing new people, having new experiences, finding romance. You can't mourn forever."

"I'm not interested in romance. I've got a business to run. I have friends. I don't need anything else in my life. I don't want anything else right now."

"You're not getting any younger, Dixie darling. If you're going to have children, you need to start thinking about that now."

"I don't want children," I told her definitely. "Anna is the one with the children. Enjoy them and let me be. Please, Mother, don't keep on about this."

There was a moment's silence and I knew I'd hurt her feelings.

"You know it's just that I'm concerned about you, don't you?" she asked in a subdued voice. "I love you, baby. And I want you to be happy."

My impatience drained away. "I know you do, and I love you, too. But I can't pretend to be interested in something I'm not. Maybe in another year …"

We broke the connection after I promised we'd talk later in the week. I returned to the computer. Mother, I knew, headed back outside to her beloved flowers. She wouldn't let a minute of nice weather get away from her.

A romantic interest just waiting to happen came in the shop a few minutes later. Rabb Kenny was a good-looking blond man in his late thirties, just beginning to go a bit soft around the middle. His interests were true adventure books and, as he had made abundantly clear, me. A local attorney, he'd let me know in more than a few ways that he would like to expand our acquaintance.

I really didn't understand his persistence. I'm certainly no beauty and I had done absolutely nothing to encourage him. But for some reason, Rabb was determined that we spend time together. I was friendly when he came into the shop, which was several times a week, but made sure I never crossed the line between congeniality and intimacy. He was a respectable man with a nice smile and a bright future, but I wasn't interested.

To begin with, I wasn't ready to venture out into romantic waters just yet. And even if I were, Rabb wouldn't have been my choice for the maiden voyage. I've never been attracted to the aging fraternity-boy type and Rabb had one characteristic I knew I couldn't tolerate. He thought he was funny. He wasn't. As far as I could tell, he didn't possess any spark of true wit. Instead he memorized clever things he heard other people say and spouted them out at what he thought were appropriate times.

"Lots of excitement today," he said, with a nod toward the alley. "Have they made an arrest yet?"

"No, I don't think so. How have you been, Rabb?"

"Terrific, just terrific. Went out to Las Vegas last weekend with some buddies. What a place! If you don't walk outside, you never know if it's day or night."

That sounded perfectly awful to me, but I gave him a smile. "Well, I'm glad you had a good time. Did you win?"

"Not hardly. They don't call it Lost Wages for nothing." He laughed and moved a bit closer to the counter. I had to force myself not to back away in response. Rabb was one of those people who gradually moved nearer and nearer as the conversation progressed. "I want to thank you for recommending that book on the Everest expedition. It's great, everything you said. I'm halfway through it and it's a real page-turner." His grin was almost a leer. "And that's good because I sure do need something to keep me entertained when I go to bed at night."

"Glad you like it." I ignored the implication.

He wandered to the shelf where his kind of books were displayed and examined a couple of new titles, but nothing captured his fancy enough this afternoon to prompt a sale. Before leaving, he made his habitual try at asking me out.

"There's a dinner dance at the country club Saturday night. Why don't you get all dressed up and let me take you? We'll eat, drink, and be merry, have a big time."

I knew what my mother would want me to do. My getting 'out and about' had become a near obsession with her. I smiled and declined as tactfully as I could.

"Sorry, I've already got plans. Maybe another time."

"You're the busiest girl I've ever known. Don't leave me waiting too long, Dixie, or I'll end up all broken up on the bottom of the ocean, twitching and shaking."

I'm sure I looked at him as if he were speaking Mandarin Chinese.

He grinned. "You know. I'll be a nervous wreck!"

He was still chuckling at his joke when he left the shop. I was pretty sure I couldn't stand a whole evening of that.

Late in the day, UPS delivered two boxes of books I'd purchased the previous weekend at an estate sale in Lizella. Because the alley was still closed off, the driver had to double-park on Cherry Street and lug them in the front door. I scooted the boxes across the floor to the middle of the front room, sat beside them and began sorting the books into categorical stacks. Among the Victorian novels and botanicals, I came across a biography of Sidney Lanier. I'm not really a poetry person, but this one caught my attention since I lived on the same street where the poet had been born in the early 1800s. I felt almost obligated to learn a little more about the man and his work. I set the book aside.

Locking up the front door for the day, I saw my strange visitor from the previous afternoon. The girl with the tarot cards and marketing ideas, still in full Retro style, stood on the other side of the street. She was leaning against one of the buildings, writing in a small notebook. Her face was a study in concentration. Once she raised her head and seemed to look straight at me, then quickly returned to her writing. If I'd had to guess, I'd have said it was poetry. I've never seen anyone who looked more like a poet.

Had she been hanging around the area late yesterday evening? If so, she might have seen Glynnis before the attack. I started toward the door, planning to ask her that question, but the telephone rang. By the time I'd convinced the caller I didn't carry magazines, vintage or otherwise, the girl was gone.

CHAPTER FOUR

It was only two blocks up Cherry Street to Chimera, one of the upscale restaurants that had blossomed with the downtown renovation. It was an eclectic establishment, blending Southern, Caribbean, and French cuisine – at least that's what the owner had told me. I wasn't qualified to pass judgment on the style of food served, I just knew I loved it. During the day, they served muffins, croissants, and some very creative salads and sandwiches. At night, the lights were lowered, candles were lit, and elegant dinner entrees replaced the daytime fare.

People were enjoying the spring evening at several of the sidewalk tables. When, a few years back, the first few downtown restaurants put tables outside their establishments, the move was met with doubt and laughter. The conventional wisdom was that no one in his right mind would ever venture beyond the air conditioning during Macon's blazing summers. And that was as true as ever. But in our mild climate, al fresco dining had proved really popular during the other three seasons.

I pushed open the heavy front door. Decorated in cool shades of blue and green, the restaurant boasted two dining rooms and a small lounge. Dinner at Chimera was never less than exceptional. The food was magnificent, the décor sumptuous, and the service impeccable. And when your meal was served at the chef's own table, the experience was even better.

The chef and owner of Chimera was Willadean Vandeusen, known to her friends as Deannie. She was bright, beautiful, surprisingly funny, and my best friend in the world. She was already seated, sipping a glass of red wine, when I arrived. At nearly six feet tall, she had the looks and stature of a high fashion model, but her world revolved around food. Tonight discs of hammered copper dangled from her ears and she wore an African-print caftan that emphasized her exotic looks. Her long black braids were interwoven with tiny red glass beads and few men in the restaurant could keep their eyes off her for very long.

Deannie's personal table, which seated a maximum of four people, was tucked in a tiny alcove at the back of the larger of the two dining rooms. There she and her guests could enjoy a certain amount of privacy while she was still able to observe what was happening in the room. On those rare nights when she chose to dine rather than cook, Deannie left her kitchen in the capable hands of her second-in-command Claude Mason.

He was an excellent chef and though there had been job offers from restaurants in Atlanta, Charleston, and Savannah, he always turned them down. Claude's mama, whom he adored, lived in east Macon and he wasn't about to move away from her. But even with such a paragon in the kitchen, I was sure Deannie wouldn't be able to get through the entire meal without slipping back a few times just to make sure everything was in order.

Moments after I slid into my chair, Kevin Lowry placed a glass and a frosty bottle of Samuel Adams lager on the tablecloth in front of me. He was my favorite waiter. He didn't pour the beer into the glass – knowing my preference for drinking from the bottle – and he was too polite to indicate that he didn't approve of such behavior. He did, however, always bring a glass – just in case I changed my mind. It's a fine thing to eat where they know your preferences.

"When would you like me to begin serving?" Kevin asked his boss.

"Give us about fifteen minutes."

I never ordered when I shared Deannie's table. She delighted in showing off her specialties and newest creations and I was a more than willing guinea pig.

"Well," she said, "you must have had a long day. Are the police still there?"

"No, they left a little while ago. I guess the shop's no longer a crime scene."

"Do they have any idea who did it?"

I shrugged. "If they do, they're not telling me."

She twirled her wineglass between tapered fingers. "They haven't mentioned me, have they?"

"You? Why would they mention you?"

"I don't know. Glynnis was in here a lot lately."

"Here?" I couldn't think of a less likely place for Glynnis to choose. First of all, I'd have expected her taste in food to be rather basic. The fare at Chimera was anything but basic and sure didn't come cheap. And that was the second reason. Glynnis had hated spending money. "What was she doing here?"

"Eating, just like everybody else," she said a bit defensively. "In the last few months she came in once or twice a week."

Could Glynnis have actually been seeing someone? "Who did she come with?"

Deannie elevated her elegant shoulders half an inch. "She was usually alone. I guess she just liked the food."

"Anyone would like the food," I told her with a grin. "But I don't think you'll be hearing from the police. They may not have much in the way of leads, but I doubt if they've reached the point where they're running down the owners of all the commercial establishments she frequented."

Kevin was back with our first course. He placed small, ice-filled bowls in front of us. Each mound of ice held three shot glasses containing a strange grayish substance. I looked questioningly at my hostess.

"Oyster shooters!" Her eyes twinkled with anticipation.

"These are not on the menu."

"They might be in the future. See what you think."

I wasn't quite ready. I picked up one of the glasses and gave it a critical look. "What exactly is in here?"

"A shot of vodka, winter savory, and marjoram. And an oyster, of course. Go ahead and try one."

I'm generally game for anything Deannie cooks up – or in this case, doesn't cook up – but I was a bit dubious about oyster shooters. It wasn't the uncooked state of the oysters that bothered me. I like raw oysters just fine, resting familiarly on shells where they belong, served with plenty of cocktail sauce and crackers. These, however, weren't especially attractive crammed into shot glasses with vodka and pieces of wet herbs.

I looked at my hostess. Her dark eyes were bright with merriment. She wasn't going to cut me any slack here. It was best to go ahead and get it over with. I emptied one of the glasses into my mouth and chewed. The familiar, salty flavor filled my mouth, along with something sharp and cold and peppery. I was pleasantly surprised – and more than a little relieved. Oyster shooters were good. I had no hesitation about finishing off the remaining two.

The rest of the meal was as flavorful and inventive as the first course had been. A tangy salad of diced vegetables led the way for grilled quail served with a mango and peanut salsa. Herb-roasted potatoes and carrots rounded out the entree. Dessert was a poached pear, coated with sourwood honey, rolled in toasted pecans, and drizzled with a port wine sauce.

Deannie did make a few quick trips to the kitchen during dinner, but even she couldn't find fault with the preparation and service of our meal. She didn't need my praise to know that dinner was a success. She only had to look at the empty plates Kevin cleared from my place.

"Did you have a big weekend?" I asked when we were a few bites into the dessert.

"Nothing special. Did a little work in the apartment. I was online almost all day Monday. I'm feeling real good about the last few months. The market's so much better now that the amateurs have been scared off."

I envied Deannie's skill with investments, but knew I'd never try it myself. I didn't possess her steely nerve and could never have endured some of the losses that she experienced on a regular basis. She often said it was all part of the game. I knew better than to play.

The conversation continued, pleasant and upbeat – but with the coffee came darker subjects. I told her what I knew about Glynnis's murder. She shuddered at my description of finding the body.

"But why was she coming to see you?"

"I don't know. I mean, it must have been something about books. What else could it be? We sure weren't friends. I don't think she'd ever once set foot in my shop."

"What do you think happened to her?"

"Probably one of those things you hear about – a really random act of violence. A robbery that went bad."

"Oh, she was robbed?"

"As far as I know, that's what the police think. And it's the only thing that makes any sense, isn't it? Why else would someone kill her?"

A frown creased her smooth forehead and there was an almost bitter note in her voice when she said, "Could be someone just wanted her dead."

"Why? She was a pill sometimes. Believe me, I know. I spent every Tuesday morning with her, but I can't think of a reason anyone would want to kill her." I lifted my cup and drank. "No, robbery is really the only logical explanation.

"And I'll tell you something else, this whole thing has started me thinking. It could just as easily have been you or me, couldn't it? You know, I've never felt uncomfortable in Macon before, but now … sometimes I'm late leaving the shop and I go out the back door right into that same alley. I believe I'm going to start keeping a gun with me when I'm downtown."

She wrinkled her nose in distaste. "A gun? I hate those things! They scare me to death." Then she smiled self-consciously. "But I guess you're used to them, huh?"

"Yeah, I guess I am."

She raised an eyebrow and Kevin hurried over to refill our cups. Deannie poured cream into her coffee and we both watched it swirl into the dark liquid.

"So, have you found a home for the kitten?"

"Not yet. I must have called fifteen people today, but nobody wants a cat."

She chuckled. "Face it, Dixie. It's fate. That's what it is. You and that cat are meant to be together."

"Not if I have anything to say about it."

A smile spread across her perfect features. "I don't think you do. As I understand it, fate doesn't ask for opinions or approval."

The yellow tape was finally gone from the alley behind the shop. My car, a four-year-old, gold Blazer, sat alone behind the wall of stores. The exterior and—unhappy discovery—the interior as well were covered with a fine layer of black dust. If they'd asked, I could have saved them some trouble. I knew the only fingerprints they found in my car were mine. I couldn't remember the last time I'd had a passenger.

I entered the house slowly, not sure what to expect after leaving the kitten unsupervised for almost twelve hours. Who knew what sort of destruction awaited me? Had the improvised litter box been a success? Did kittens chew things up or was that only puppies?

The little animal galloped into the kitchen when it heard me, winding itself around my legs and giving happy little mews. He – she? – seemed glad I was home. I picked it up and turned it over, trying to determine its sex, but after a minute or two of futile examination, I gave up. I hadn't had enough experience with cats to make even an uneducated guess. I released it and it stalked away, offended by the liberties I'd taken. What did its sex matter anyway? It wouldn't be with me long enough for that to make any difference.

Once the food and water bowls had been refilled, I took paper towels and spray cleaner out back. It took twenty minutes to get most of the fingerprint powder out of the interior of the Blazer. Back in the kitchen, I opened the refrigerator. I kept a variety of beer on the second shelf from the bottom. Other people might bring home seashells or matchbooks as vacation souvenirs. I brought home different brands of beer. Surveying my collection, I chose a bottle of Lone Star.

I took it and the Sidney Lanier book out onto the screened-in side porch. This was my favorite spot in the house. Furnished with a few old pieces of wicker furniture, a lamp and a ceiling fan, it was comfortable and welcoming – at least for three seasons of the year. During the hot, humid, summer months, it was as uninhabitable as the rest of outdoor Macon.

But it wasn't summer yet and I was determined to spend as much time as possible enjoying the pleasant weather. The temperate time wouldn't last long. Spring is fleeting here. Too often we have two or three weeks of it, then rush headlong into high summer. Temperatures in the nineties are not unheard of in April and by May any pretense of springtime is gone.

But tonight was perfect. There was no wind and the day's warmth lingered. Somewhere close by a bird warbled. I switched on the lamp and settled on the love seat. The cat had followed me. It jumped onto the sofa, curled up on the cushion beside me and was immediately asleep.

I had no expectation of riveting reading and I wasn't disappointed. I skimmed, rather than read, the first few chapters. But since Sidney and I were neighbors, albeit separated by a hundred and fifty years or so, I felt I should get to know a little about the man who'd been born up the street a century and a half ago. I'll be the first to admit I had some preconceived notions about poets in general and Sidney Lanier in particular. I expected to discover a pale, somewhat effeminate young man, who lived, perhaps, with his mother and never held a full time job. Just his name sounded wan and lethargic. I was way off the mark.

Sidney Lanier, son of a country lawyer, was born in his grandfather's house on High Street in 1842. The house, just a few doors away from my own, still stood and now belonged to a preservation group. I was surprised to learn that Sidney had been something of a ladies' man and had kept several young women on a string before meeting his future wife just around the corner at a house on Orange Street. At the start of the Civil War, Sidney and his brother enlisted in the Confederate army and became scouts, conducting clandestine operations and eluding bands of Federal soldiers behind enemy lines. I imagined the two of them in the dark of night, galloping along back roads, capes flying behind them. Pretty macho stuff for a poet.

After a while I switched off the light and stared out at the darkened street, trying to picture the neighborhood as it would have looked so long ago. There would have been fewer lights and less noise, of course, and horse-drawn carriages and men in uniform. Had the two parks been laid out then or were they later additions to the neighborhood? The kitten whimpered in its sleep and I put a calming hand on its back.

I fetched a second beer, then turned to the last half of the book. It was a collection of Lanier's poetry, with long-winded explanations of where and when each piece was written. As I've already said, poetry is not my thing. There was one that I liked about a mockingbird, but on the whole I could give it a pass.

At eleven I went inside for the local television news, hoping for word of an arrest for Glynnis's murder. Although WMGT ran a long piece on the killing, complete with a biography of the victim, a collection of downtown merchants expressing concern that such a thing could have happened, and a nice, clear picture of Chapter and Verse, no new information was forthcoming.

Whether it was the poetry or the hour, I could hardly keep my eyes open. And I didn't go to bed alone. The kitten claimed a spot near my left side and settled in.

"Don't get too comfortable," I warned. "Just as soon as I find some sucker to take you, you're out of here."

An elaborate yawn was its only answer.

Bright morning light woke me. I'd slept well and felt rested for the first time that week. I indulged in a long, luxurious stretch and sudden pain shot through my left foot. I instinctively yanked my leg to one side, unintentionally sending the kitten flying several feet across the room where it landed neatly on its feet beside the window.

It looked a bit surprised, but appeared unhurt as it left the room, tail high and indignant.

"That's what happens when you attack a defenseless foot," I called after it.

I dressed for my usual run, clomped down the stairs and let myself out the side door. It was seven-fifteen. The brisk morning and the newly risen sun filled me with a momentary certainty that anything was possible. The feeling rarely lasted more than a few minutes, but I enjoyed it while it did.

Some sidewalk stretches warmed me up and I set off at a medium pace up the brick-paved street. At Orange Street, I turned left and ran along the park. My only companions were the birds waking in the trees. I pressed up the hill to College Street; the wide boulevard was the spine of the College Hill area. I'd walked along it so many times with my grandmother, listening to her stories of the past, that I always felt her presence there. It was a reminder that I needed to give her a call soon.

The houses in this section of town had been built on the grandiose scale of the nineteenth century. It was here that Macon's early movers and shakers erected their trophy homes, high above the Ocmulgee where they could benefit from the river breezes. I passed the Mediterranean villa built for a long-dead hotel owner and several classic revival houses. The uneven sidewalk led me past the 1842 Inn and the huge house that had once belonged to Nathan Beall. Known locally as The Columns, it had served as a private home, a restaurant, and was now divided into offices. The Allman Brothers Band had used a photograph of themselves standing on its enormous verandah for the cover of their first album. Local legend said the place was haunted and Grandma Evelyn used to love amazing her impressionable granddaughter with the stories.

"There are spots in that house that are so cold they can make your teeth chatter on a hot summer day," she'd told me, delighting in my horrified reaction. "People have heard strange noises and seen lights in the upstairs rooms – even when no one lived there."

I doubted that she ever believed any of the ghost stories herself – Grandma Evelyn is an imminently sensible woman – but she'd sure enjoyed scaring the daylights out of me. Looking back, I kind of missed the delicious horror I used to experience just walking by the house. As an adult, I'd passed this way hundreds of times and even been inside The Columns on a few occasions, but I'd never seen anything unusual there. I sometimes wished I had. Tangible evidence of an afterlife would have been downright comforting.

Back home, I showered and dressed for the day. Then I replaced the soiled paper in the cardboard box with some freshly shredded pages of last month's Vanity Fair. I toasted an English muffin, sliced an apple and sat down at the kitchen table with the morning paper.

Glynnis's murder was front-page news in *The Telegraph* and, once again, "the alley behind local bookstore Chapter and Verse" was given as the location of the crime. According to the reporter, the police were following a number of leads and expected an arrest any day now. In other words, they still didn't have a clue.

Glynnis's obituary was on the back page of the local section. Visitation was that day from two to eight, with the funeral scheduled for early Friday afternoon. I hate funerals and I hate visitations – a sentiment I suppose I share with about 99 percent of the population. They've been especially miserable occasions for me since Donald's death. I considered several reasonable excuses I could use to avoid going, but I was only fooling myself. There was no real choice. I'd learned, with a strong helping hand from my mother, that the hardest things to do – the ones you really want to avoid – were usually the right things to do.

My last act before leaving the house that morning seemed totally foreign in my new life. I owned two guns. One was kept in the drawer of my nightstand. The second – a Taurus Ultralite .38 – I stored on the closet shelf. That was the one I tucked into an inside pocket of my purse. It was a less than ideal location for carrying a gun – a woman's purse was often the first thing dropped in an attack – but I was wearing a dress that had no pockets and I couldn't bear the thought of wearing a shoulder rig under a jacket all day. I wondered if I was just paying lip service to the idea of personal safety. In spite of the fact that Glynnis McCullough had met her violent end in the alley behind my shop, it was nearly impossible to equate danger with the Cherry Street I knew.

I left the house in time to see two mockingbirds battling it out in the driveway. They are territorial by nature and, in the spring, the males become obsessive turf guarders. The magnolia tree in the corner of the yard was evidently the point of contention for these two. They chased each other furiously, punctuating the fracas with angry squawks and darting beaks, until one finally fled for the safety of a camellia bush next door. The victor perched high in the magnolia and warbled a defiant song. A fragment of Lanier's mockingbird poem came back to me. 'He summ'd the woods in song.' Maybe my time with the poet hadn't been completely wasted. I was already feeling more cultured as I cranked the Blazer and backed out of the drive.

Edward stopped in to say hello shortly after I opened.

"It looks as if the cherry trees may have actually yielded to prayer," I told him. "I saw quite a few buds this morning."

His prediction was dire. "Something else will go wrong before Sunday."

I didn't react to that. There were more important matters at hand. Even though I knew it was a long shot, I was running out of prospects and had to ask. "Would you be interested in taking in a little kitten, a cute little tabby?"

He wrinkled his nose as if I'd suggested he move a flock of sheep into his Ingleside cottage. "I can imagine no reason to keep an animal, any animal, inside one's home. Think of the mess."

"A cat would be less trouble than some people I could name."

He laughed. "Isn't that the truth! There are all kinds of animals. But, no, sweetie, I am not interested in adopting a cat."

We both avoided any mention of George Bennett and, a few minutes later, he returned to his own shop, still muttering about the upcoming festival and the certain catastrophe that was to come. To tell the truth, I didn't mind seeing him go. Contact with Edward should be limited this close to parade time. The good news was that he'd be back to normal after Sunday.

The rush to see the crime scene had ended, but I still made a couple of sales during the morning and downloaded some orders from the website. I also racked up two more refusals on the kitten.

Cassie Waycaster came into the shop around lunchtime, asking if I was going to the funeral home that evening.

"I thought maybe we could go together?" she said tentatively. "I mean, since we all volunteer with the Friends, it just seems right to go together. Besides, it might be easier that way."

As she so often did, Cassie seemed to be coming apart here

and there. The tail of her shirt had worked loose from her skirt and a meandering run crept up one leg of her pantyhose. Wisps of hair had escaped from her ponytail and floated around her face. That might make some women appear waifish and adorable. Cassie just looked messy.

At our last book sorting session Tuesday morning, Glynnis had been especially mean to Cassie, insinuating that her six-year-old son Jason had severe behavioral problems. I thought she was being awfully charitable to even consider going to the visitation.

"Oh, I'm sorry," I told her, "but I'm planning to stop by late this afternoon. Want to come back around four-fifteen? We can go together then."

She sighed unhappily. "I wish I could, but Jason has soccer practice after school. I guess I'll have to go alone. I just hate that. I never know what to say."

She was getting dangerously close to whining and I was in no mood for that.

"Is Tiffany still taking ballet?" I asked to get her mind on something else.

"Oh, yes! From Leisha Carroll. And she's really doing so well. Their recital is coming up in May. Tiffany's class is doing a springtime theme and she's going to be a ladybug. She has the cutest costume you ever saw."

As she described yellow satin shorts and pipe cleaner antennae, I walked across the shop and pulled two books from a shelf. "I just got these in. They might interest Tiffany."

"Let me see."

She ended up buying a biography of Dame Margot Fonteyn. "Tiffany will love this. It has pictures of Fonteyn in *Firebird* and *Odette*! She'll be so excited."

I wasn't sure a fifth grader would be that impressed, but the purchase had taken Cassie's mind off less pleasant subjects and rescued me from a nasty dose of whining.

Before leaving, she returned to the subject of Glynnis's death. "It must have been just horrible finding her body like that."

"Well, it wasn't pleasant, no."

"I know I would have run screaming into the night. Who do you think killed her? And why would somebody do that?" We were alone, but she lowered her voice as if to prevent anyone overhearing our conversation. "You know Glynnis wasn't always nice, was she? I wouldn't be surprised to find out someone did it because she was so mean."

"Who knows?" I was in no mood to speculate. "I guess the police will sort it all out."

Just after two, I had a visit from a second Friends volunteer. Reg Anderson's green eyes twinkled in a face dominated by a mane of white hair and a thick mustache. I figured he must have been nearing seventy, but he was still a very attractive man. Anytime I encountered him away from our work sessions, he was dressed like an Esquire model and, more often than not, accompanied by a lovely woman. Today was no exception. He had no companion, but he was handsomely turned out in khaki slacks, a blue oxford cloth shirt and a navy blazer, complete with a bright silk handkerchief in the breast pocket.

"Terrible about Glynnis, wasn't it?" His expression softened with sympathy. "And it must have been awful for you, dear."

I agreed that it was.

He nodded sadly. "You just never know, do you? We can't take a single day for granted." Then he straightened his shoulders and smiled at me. The obligation to express sorrow was over and it was time to move on.

"Got anything I might be interested in today?"

"Nothing I can think of. But there's an estate sale next week and I'll keep my eyes open for you."

Reg's passion was modern first editions. Through his work with the Friends, he'd become something of an authority on the subject and had found quite a few nice specimens for us over the years. The sale of some of his finds had brought tidy amounts into our treasury and Reg, himself, was building a solid collection of Cornwell and Grisham first editions.

Of course, we volunteers couldn't just take any book we liked. All donated books were examined and priced when they were received. However, once the values were determined, the volunteers were usually given the first opportunity to buy them. It was one of the perks of the job. I'd occasionally taken advantage of the arrangement and so had most of the others. But it was a different story if a particularly valuable book came in. It was first appraised by an expert and then either included as a special item in our book sale or sold at auction.

"I ran across something recently that I thought you might like, Dixie." He pulled a paperback book with a bright cover from his jacket pocket and my heart sank a few inches. "It's a beginner's guide to wine. Looks like a pretty good one. I thought you might want to look through it."

"Oh, thanks," I managed, knowing I had no one to blame but myself.

Reg's interests weren't limited to first editions. He loved travel, fine dining, and fine wines, too. During a recent sorting session he'd been expounding on the delights of wine and, motivated more by politeness than honesty, I'd said I might want to learn more about the subject sometime. That had been a lie.

I've been a beer woman since my first taste of the lovely brew in college. From lager to stout, I've never met a beer I didn't like – at least a little bit. I don't like wine and, to paraphrase one of my grandfather's favorite expressions, don't know chablis from Shinola, and don't care to learn. But Reg had taken those few careless words to heart and now seemed determined to educate me. He'd already given me a guide to the California wine country as well as a cookbook of recipes using wine. At this rate, I was going to end up with a whole collection of books on a subject that bored me to death.

But I wouldn't have hurt his feelings for anything in the world. Even if I weren't interested, it was a thoughtful gesture. I obligingly thumbed through the book and gave him a genuine smile. "You're really sweet to do this, Reg. Thank you."

He waved that away. "It's nothing. Got it at a garage sale for a quarter."

He looked around the shop with that expectant attitude common to all real collectors. "I think I might just nose around a bit. You know, see if there's something you might have overlooked." He gave me a grin, then headed for the fiction section.

When he left forty-five minutes later, he'd found two books, both by Robert L. Parker, that he liked enough to buy.

I stood at the front door, gazing out at Cherry Street. In the warm sunshine, a few flowers were already blooming and a fuzz of green was beginning to show on some of the trees. I reflected that there weren't many people who regretted Glynnis's passing. In fact, I hadn't spoken to a single person who said she'd be missed. It was a sad thought on such a beautiful afternoon.

CHAPTER FIVE

Snow's Memorial Chapel had perched at the top of Cherry Street for as long as I could remember. I'd trailed Grandma Evelyn up the curving stairs between the white columns more times than I could count. It seemed like someone she knew was always dying. For a child, it was a mildly disturbing experience, but not a traumatic one. I never knew the person who had died and my memories of those events were chiefly of acute boredom, brought on by having to sit still and be quiet while dressed in uncomfortable clothes.

As soon as I walked through Snow's front door Thursday afternoon my senses were assailed by the quilted silence, the staid furnishings, and the smells of lilies and furniture polish. The familiarity of it made my heart beat faster. A gray-haired man in a dark suit glided across the thick carpet toward me.

It's astonishing to me how my attitude had changed over a few short years. I'd once been outspokenly disdainful of the whole business of mortuaries and funerals. So sure of myself and my enlightened modern viewpoint, I was quick to express the opinion that displaying the bodies of the dead was a barbaric custom. The long, mournful services, I insisted, just increased the pain of the bereaved. And the people who practiced the profession were little better than ghouls and scam artists, taking advantage of the bereaved at the time they were most vulnerable. Oh, I was a regular fount of cynicism and twenty-first century rationality.

Donald's death changed all that. I'll always remember with deep gratitude how the people at the funeral home in Atlanta guided me through the terrible process of final arrangements for my husband. They didn't push, they didn't pressure. Instead they very kindly and gently helped me through the formal part of the worst ordeal I'd ever faced.

I smiled at the man as he approached. When I pronounced Glynnis's name, he gestured down the wide hall to the right. Although it was just past four, the room was already full. Except for Delia McCullough, everyone there was a stranger to me. I could just make out Glynnis's profile in the casket at one end of the long room and knew I'd be expected to take that slow walk past the body before I left.

I milled around for a few minutes, looking at the flower arrangements that lined the walls. The one I'd sent, a basket of potted plants, sat on the floor near the guest book. After signing my name, I looked over to where Delia sat in a hard-back chair, surrounded by people who patted her shoulders and leaned close to speak to her.

We'd met a few times at Friends of the Library functions. She'd struck me as a pleasant, unassuming woman – a contrast to her often-contentious daughter. Today she sat rigid and silent, her expression frozen, her movements slow and heavy. A man with curly red hair and a florid face hovered near her. He resembled Glynnis enough to be recognized as her brother Teddy. Just behind him were a woman and two young boys.

I took my place in the line that moved past the coffin. Glynnis had that waxy, unworldly look common to those who've been on the receiving end of the funeral home employees' ministrations. Donald had had the same cold appearance in his casket. I tried to make my mind as blank as possible while I stood there an appropriate length of time. Then I moved on to the family.

"Mrs. McCullough," I said, extending my hand. Like Cassie, I had no idea what to say. "I don't know if you remember me. I'm Dixie McClatchey. Glynnis and I worked together at Friends of the Library. I'm so sorry for your loss."

She nodded automatically and I wondered if my words even registered in her grief-numbed mind. I spoke next to Glynnis's brother. He introduced himself to me, along with his wife and children.

"You own that bookstore, don't you?" he asked. The way he said bookstore made it synonymous with sleazy massage parlor.

I admitted that I did.

"They . . . the police said she was coming to see you. Why on earth would Glynnis be downtown that late in the day?"

I shook my head. "I'm sorry. I don't know."

"Well, why did she want to see you anyway?" He threw questions at me like a boxer throwing punches. "What did she say? She must have told you something about why she was coming."

"No, she really didn't, just said something about books."

He glared at me. I sympathized with his loss, but didn't like being considered a part of the problem just because his sister had been killed near my shop.

"I just don't understand this," he said angrily. "Crime is out of control in this town. When I grew up here, we left the doors unlocked, for Christ's sake. Now look at the place. Nobody feels safe anymore. And the police can't do a thing. Why hasn't an arrest been made? The predators own the streets and the so-called decent people won't do anything about it!"

I wasn't sure exactly who he was blaming. Maybe he wasn't either. From the perspective of someone who'd lived most of her life in a big city, I knew things weren't all that bad in Macon. But arguing with a grieving man would have been ruder than I was prepared to be. I repeated how sorry I was and gave my place to the person waiting behind me.

A quick walk down the carpeted hall and out the front door and I was free – back out on Cherry Street, breathing in the fresh air. I looked at my watch and was surprised. The whole ordeal had taken less than half an hour and the sun was still high in the sky. Then I was suddenly ashamed. Here I was fretting over an uncomfortable half hour out of my day when Delia McCullough's ordeal was just beginning. Not just hours, but years of empty days and nights lay ahead of her. Grief wasn't something you endured for a while and then left behind. It insinuated itself into your very being and became an indestructible part of you. It never went away. It only drew back into the shadows of your heart.

There was plenty of work to be done at the shop. There were orders to be filled and books to be priced and shelved. I started in on the waiting tasks with good intentions, but my attention kept straying to the display that Pandora had criticized on Tuesday afternoon. Was she right? I went and stood in front of it, trying to see it through the eyes of a customer. Then I changed position as if I'd just come in the door. Damn! I hated to admit it, but she had a point. It was almost invisible from that spot.

I closed promptly at six and set about moving the display. It took a while because I had to unload the bookshelf before moving it. Then, after I'd dragged the heavy wooden shelf across the floor, all the books had to be replaced. It was nearly seven before I was happy with the arrangement. I finished it off by putting my only copy of Skippy Lawson's *Dear Mom: Send More Money* on the top shelf, front cover out, right beside Cliff Chandler's latest police thriller. That, I decided, should bring more attention to the local books.

It was so quiet that the sharp knock on the front door made me jump nearly out of my skin. I turned and saw a grinning Lt. Ballard, backlit by the streetlights, on the other side of the glass.

"I was driving by and saw the light," he said as I let him in. "Wanted to make sure everything was okay."

"Yeah, everything's fine." He looked relaxed in slacks and a dark green golf shirt. I was suddenly very conscious of my sweaty, dusty self. "I'm just working a little late."

"You seem to do that a lot."

I shrugged. "Not too often. But when you own the business, something always needs doing. Have you found out who killed Glynnis yet?"

"No, not yet."

I remembered the palm reader. "By the way, there was a girl hanging around the neighborhood Tuesday afternoon. Early twenties, white, slender build, long light brown hair. She came in here and later I saw her going in one of the shops across the street – I think she's looking for a job. She might have seen something."

He was interested enough to fish a notepad and pen out of his pants pocket. "Did you get her name?"

"I know she said her first name was Pandora, but I can't remember her last name. She said she was a Mercer student."

"Pandora?"

I laughed a little. "Yeah. I wondered if she'd just made it up."

"And she said she wanted a job?"

"Ummhmmm." I gestured with a hand to the shop. "But, as you can probably tell, I don't have enough business to justify hiring anyone."

He nodded. "I'll see if we can't find this Pandora. Maybe she knows something." He eased further into the shop and leaned against the front counter. "Since I'm here, I guess you'd like to know we called APD and you checked out fine. They said they'd rehire you in a heartbeat."

"Yeah, I know. Kaminsky told me."

He wandered around the front of the store, stopping here and there to look at a book, as if it were the middle of the work day and he had a few minutes to waste. "I heard how your husband was killed."

I suppressed a sigh. I should have known he'd want to hear about it from me. It was a subject that was still awfully hard for me to talk about. Maybe he'd be satisfied with the condensed version. "Yeah, we were only about two blocks from our apartment. This guy came up to us – I found out later he was only fifteen years old. He pulled a gun and Donald – that's my husband – Donald handed over his wallet right then. Then the guy wanted my purse." I took what I hoped would be a calming breath. I was no longer in Chapter and Verse. I was standing on an Atlanta street corner on a stifling July night. "But my gun - my service pistol - was in there and . . I . . the idea of giving it up . . I was a cop and I decided I should act like one. So, when I was handing over my purse, I pulled the gun out." I blinked hard, trying to keep the tears from my eyes.

"You don't have to explain anything to me."

"No, it's okay." I'd gone this far. I had to finish now. "You should know just what happened. To this day, I don't understand why I did that. I know now, hell, I knew then, that the only smart thing to do during a robbery is to give the bastard what he wants and hope he doesn't hurt you. . . but I pulled out that gun. I pointed it at him and shouted to him to drop his weapon. He didn't, of course. He just . . . he lost it. He started shooting and screaming at us like a lunatic. I don't think he was really aiming at anything, but two of the bullets hit Donald in the chest."

I turned a few degrees away from him, not wanting to have to see pity in his face. "They told me later that I'd fired at him and missed as he ran away, but I don't remember doing it. All I remember is my husband dying in my arms." I squared my shoulders and tried to wrap up the story quickly. "They caught him a few days later and charged him as an adult. But he was still a kid. They knew they'd have a hard time getting a jury to convict him of murder. He entered a plea—first degree manslaughter—and got ten years to serve. With good behavior, he might be out next year."

I always wondered if one of the reasons the DA had taken his plea was to avoid putting me on the stand. I was so whacked out over Donald's death that they couldn't have had much faith in me as a witness.

"I'm sorry," Ballard said, his voice heavy with sympathy. "I can't even pretend to know how terrible that was for you."

He sounded as if he might be prepared to say more, but I didn't want any more condolences. And I'd had enough advice about moving on and time healing wounds to last me a lifetime.

"Yeah, I appreciate that." I stepped behind the counter and

switched off the computer. "Well, it's time for me to get out of here."

At the front door, I put my hand on the knob and glanced back at Ballard. "You parked out front?"

"Yeah."

"I'll let you out before I lock up."

He ambled toward me, then stopped. "How about a late supper? Nothing special, I mean, but you need to eat just like I do. We could go somewhere quick. Barbecue or the Waffle House?"

I didn't want to deal with this tonight. I used the first excuse that came to mind. "I better not. I need to get home and feed the cat."

"You haven't found it a home yet?"

I shook my head. "No. I don't suppose you want it, do you?"

"I don't know. I might – if I got to know it. I've always liked cats. We had a great little Siamese when I was growing up. Her name was Rosebud. She slept with me every night."

Hope rose in my heart. "Really? This kitten seems to be awfully sweet."

"Male or female?"

I had to admit I didn't know and he advised that such information could have some bearing on his decision. That's how I ended up with Ballard driving behind me up High Street to my house. I unlocked the side door and flipped on the kitchen light. Once we were inside, I had to tug on the door handle to get it to close properly.

The cat was nowhere in sight.

"I don't know where it is," I told Ballard. "It usually comes running as soon as I walk in."

Just when I had counted on it to demonstrate that it was a real people-loving animal, the silly thing was going to blow it by hiding. We finally found it curled up on the dining room table. It opened one eye when I turned on the overhead light.

"Must be tired," I said.

Ballard scooped up the little creature with no hesitation, turned it on its back and held it like a baby. He rubbed under its chin with his fingers and I could hear the purring clear across the room. "He's still a baby. He needs a lot a sleep."

I raised my eyebrows. "He? So it's a male."

"Sure is. He's a fine kitten. What's his name?"

"He doesn't have a name. I mean, I don't want to name him.

That's for his owner to do."

He set the cat on the floor with a gentleness I wouldn't have expected. "He ought to have a name."

"Well, if you take him, you can call him anything you want."

"We'll see." He walked out of the room, patting his leg with his hand. "Come on, hot shot."

It took me a second to realize he was calling the cat, not me. And, bless him, the little tabby ran after him towards the kitchen. I figured it – he – was only running in that direction in hope of finding something in his food bowl, but Ballard didn't know that and I sure wasn't going to tell him.

Thinking it might do cat and man a measure of good to spend some time together, I invited Ballard to stay for a supper of sandwiches, cheese, fruit and, of course, beer. I served Jamaican Red Stripe with the meal. I liked the beer and loved the stubby little bottles it came in. While I fixed the food, Ballard found a piece of string in the laundry room and dangled it in front of the cat. The young animal attacked it with tiny paws, battling furiously.

We ate at the kitchen table and didn't discuss the murder. Instead I told him about my remodeling plans.

"It's a good-sized room, but it's outdated and inconvenient," I said, stating the obvious. "I mean, it's over fifteen feet from the refrigerator to the sink. And storage and work space are awfully limited. I have to keep things like the blender and food processor in another room. Some modern appliances would do wonders for the place, too."

He shared a tiny piece of cheese with the cat. "You could use some better lighting, too. The corners are kind of dark."

"You're right. And glass-fronted cabinets might brighten it up, too." I told him about the island I hoped to have and the pot rack I wanted.

He smiled. "You must be quite a cook."

"I do all right, I guess." And I did. I could hold my own in the kitchen. But having a convenient place to cook wasn't the only reason I wanted the kitchen redone. I was ready to indulge myself. I wanted a modern, cutting-edge kitchen that looked really good, and stainless steel appliances and a professional grade gas range. I was tired of being surrounded by old, worn-out things.

The cat must have sensed that Ballard was a serious contender. He did his best to be adorable. When we'd pushed back our plates, he climbed into Ballard's lap, circled a couple of times and promptly fell asleep. His relaxation must have been contagious. Over a second beer, the lieutenant unbent enough to answer some questions about the progress of the investigation.

"Well, we're just getting started. It's usually slow this early in an investigation. You know that."

"Was it robbery?"

He shrugged. "It might have started that way. If that's what it was, something spooked the guy before he could take anything. Money was still in her purse and she had on a ring and a watch." He rubbed the bridge of his nose with a thumb and finger and I realized he was probably close to exhaustion. Murder investigations aren't nine to five propositions. "Maybe she panicked and tried to run. Or started to scream and he killed her to shut her up."

"Did you find a weapon?"

"Nah. Looks like manual strangulation."

I digested this information, hating the picture of hands around Glynnis's neck as the life was choked out of her.

"Anything under her nails?" I asked. "Surely she must have fought him." He shook his head. "She hardly had any fingernails. They were bitten down to the quick. The lab's hoping to get something, but I'm not real optimistic." I remembered seeing Glynnis chew on her fingernails. It always struck me as a painful habit.

"We did find one thing in her purse that was a bit odd," he said, interrupting my recollection. "A handwritten note – and it's her handwriting. We checked. She wrote 'Tom Clancy, Red October, Navy, and first edition.' Got any ideas?"

"Just the obvious. Tom Clancy is a writer and *The Hunt for Red October* was one of his books. The first one, in fact."

"Yeah," he said dryly, "even I know that."

"Of course," I said quickly. I hadn't meant to sound patronizing. Then something jogged my memory. "You know, Glynnis was talking about Clancy on Tuesday – at the work session. Somehow she'd got it in her mind that the Navy published Red October. Marian Saxby corrected her. It was the Naval Institute Press that first published it – a small run. Then it took off, of course, and was picked up by a major publisher.

"But that first printing, the one the Institute did, those books are hard to find and can be very valuable, maybe as much as $700 or $800. It would depend on the market at the time."

He shifted forward in his seat, causing the cat to change position, too. "Just what did Glynnis say about it? And who did you say she was talking to?"

I tried, but I just couldn't dredge up a clear picture of the incident. "I know she was sitting at one of the tables with a couple of other people, but I couldn't say who. I don't think Marian was part of the conversation until she heard Glynnis's comments. You know, in a group like that you hear bits and pieces of what's being said all over the room. I was talking to someone else and I just vaguely remember overhearing something about Clancy and the Navy." I shrugged. "I just wasn't paying attention."

He drank some beer. "Sounds to me like that's why she was coming to see you, to talk about the Clancy book."

"Maybe so." An idea came to me. "You don't think she had a Clancy first edition, do you?"

He shook his head, but I was warming to the idea.

"You know, that would explain it. Maybe she actually had a copy of the book and wanted me to appraise it – or even sell it for her."

"Could be. We didn't find anything like that with her, but I'll check with her mother."

I got up and started clearing the table. "Even if she did have one, it wouldn't make any difference, would it? I mean, when is the last time you heard about someone being killed for a book? I don't see how her coming to see me could have had anything to do with her death – except that it put her in the wrong place at the wrong time."

He had no comment for that. Instead he got to his feet. The cat jumped down and went over to check out his food bowl.

We were standing only a foot or so apart and I was suddenly, acutely, physically aware of this large, attractive man in my kitchen. For just a minute, I thought he was going to kiss me and I was trying to decide how to handle what could be an awkward situation, but instead he stooped down and scratched the cat on the head.

"I guess I'd better get going. Thanks for feeding me."

"I enjoyed the company." I took a deep breath and mentally crossed my fingers. "So, do you want the cat?"

"He's a cute little fellow. I'd love to have him, but I'll have to check with my apartment manager first."

"You live in an apartment?"

"Yeah. Why not?"

I opened the side door and turned on the outside light. "Oh, I don't know. I guess I just assumed you'd live in a house."

His laugh was bitter. "You mean, considering my age? Yeah, well, I used to. Before the divorce. I've been in this apartment for over five years now. Hell, it's almost like home."

When I climbed into bed a couple of hours later, the cat was right there beside me. I stroked his back and he slitted his eyes in pleasure. "You did good tonight, hot shot. I think he's falling for you. We may find you a home yet."

As I drifted into sleep, Glynnis McCullough's face suddenly flashed into my mind. I sat up, dislodging the cat from the crook of my arm. Common sense said a street criminal had killed her, but my mind wouldn't let it go at that. What if that wasn't what happened. If she hadn't been a robbery victim, then someone killed her deliberately. I felt foolish even considering it. She was a most unlikely victim for premeditated murder. Most killings were the result of fear, hatred, or greed. A middle-aged woman with a penchant for pettiness and gossip, the strongest emotion Glynnis had been likely to inspire was dislike. Still murders had been committed for some strange reasons.

If it were personal and not random, could her coming to my shop have had anything to do with her death? I didn't see how unless the knowledge of where she'd be later in the day gave someone an opportunity to meet her, persuade her to go back in the alley with him, and kill her. Her destination hadn't been a secret. Obviously anyone at the work session could have heard her say she'd be coming to see me, but the Friends didn't have exclusive knowledge that she planned to be downtown. There was no telling what she'd done or who she'd seen between leaving the library and arriving on Cherry Street.

CHAPTER SIX

Harold Edelman was a renovation expert, at least that's what his Yellow Pages ad claimed. And he certainly looked the part. In pressed jeans, a trim flannel shirt, and a Braves baseball hat, he strode into my kitchen as if it were already a work site. The cat had gone into hiding at the first clomp of his work boots. We sat at the table in the same chairs where we'd sat a week before when I'd explained what I wanted done.

I'd told him my grandmother had had some work done there in the sixties. "And the stove and refrigerator have been replaced since then, but nothing else has been touched. I want new cabinets, new appliances, oh, and a new floor."

He'd measured the room with a tape that retracted at the touch of a button. He'd opened cabinet doors, looked in the pantry, switched the lights off and on, and made a lot of notes on his clipboard. Then he'd delivered a little sermon.

"We can do a lot with this room. It's a good space. But what you end up with in here – the final product – that'll be up to you. If you go for the bargain basement stuff, it might look okay, but you'll know it's junk. And personally I wouldn't feel right about putting cheap stuff in this fine old house." He'd rapped a knuckle on the door frame. "This place is solid. It was built with quality materials by craftsmen who took pride in their work. I wouldn't want to put anything less in here. I believe that, if you and I can work together on this project, in the end you'll have a kitchen that you'll be proud of every day of your life."

We'd gone over his collection of catalogs and brochures and I'd made my choices. Today he was back with the design he'd developed. He reached into his briefcase and pulled something out with a flourish.

"There's your estimate, Miz McClatchey."

I'd expected a sheet of paper, maybe two, so I'm sure I looked surprised when he handed me a half-inch thick booklet with plastic covers and a spiral binder. I had to hand it to him, it was a slick presentation. The entire project was spelled out step by step and there were three separate computer-generated pictures of how my glamorous new kitchen was going to look. It was gorgeous, complete with a butcher-block center island, glass-fronted cabinets, and a wrought iron pot rack.

A timetable outlined every phase of the project and the proposed date of completion for each one. (I knew from my earlier experience with the shop renovation that such projections should be taken with a very large grain of salt.) Finally there were four pages showing the itemized cost for each phase of the job. At the bottom of the last page, in bold print, was the total estimated cost: $18,650. The figure took my breath. Below that figure was one last note: Cost of appliances not included.

"Well," I said. "Well."

"I know it may seem high," he said smoothly, "but it will be top quality work. You'll notice here, in the addendum at the back, that's my guarantee of complete customer satisfaction. You won't be unhappy when it's all done."

Maybe not unhappy, I thought, but I'd be considerably poorer. "I'm sure I wouldn't, Mr. Edelman, but that is a great deal of money."

"And worth every penny."

I told him I'd have to think about it. "I'll let you know as soon as I can."

"The sooner the better," he said. "I always like to get right to work on a project that interests me as much as this one does."

I opened the shop on time that morning, but had to close again less than three hours later to attend Glynnis McCullough's funeral. The weather continued fine and I walked, wishing my destination was anywhere else. The gun in my purse was inappropriate for the occasion, but I wasn't ready to return it to the closet just yet.

The First Presbyterian Church on Mulberry Street was only a few blocks away. Glynnis's family had been in Macon for generations and her father had been especially well known. The sanctuary was crowded when I arrived ten minutes before the service. I saw a lot of familiar faces as I made my way down the aisle. Cassie and her husband were seated far to the left. She looked uncomfortable and he seemed bored. Marian Saxby was right down front, still and upright, hands calmly clasped in her lap. The president of the Chamber of Commerce had an aisle seat on the left and I spotted the choir director from St. Paul's a few seats away from him. I slipped into a pew about halfway down on the right side, slid across the smooth wood and took a deep breath, steeling myself for what was to come.

Ever since Donald's death, I'd tried to avoid situations that might make me weepy. I could no longer count on keeping my emotions in check. A greeting card commercial or a sentimental song might trigger tears and one or two tears could develop into a flood over which I had no control. An occasion like this was almost guaranteed to upset me, but I was determined it wouldn't happen today. I was ready to retake control of myself. To assist with that, I avoided looking at the family members when they took their seats. I didn't want to see their grief, fearing it would be contagious.

From the first strains of "Amazing Grace" until the family finally filed out of the church, I was hammered with memories of the day Donald was buried. The pain of that loss and the depth of my responsibility for it were as fresh and raw as they had been three years ago. I tried to tune out what was going on around me and concentrated on seeing how many of the fifty states I could name. I only came up with forty-six, but it didn't matter. By then the service had ended.

As I left the sanctuary with the other mourners, I found Reg Anderson in the aisle next to me. He put an arm around my shoulders and squeezed.

"Dixie, this is so sad. Did you see her poor mother? The woman is completely devastated."

"It's terrible," I agreed. He, too, appeared to have found the funeral stressful. Emotion emphasized the age lines in his handsome face.

"Has there been an arrest yet?" he asked.

"Not that I've heard."

We walked in silence the rest of the way out to the narthex, the heavy strains of the organ filling the air. He gave my shoulder a last squeeze.

"You take good care of yourself, Dixie. I'll see you soon."

He bent to give me a quick kiss on the cheek, then ducked out the side door, leaving me alone in the crowd. I looked around for familiar faces and saw Carlton and Mary Mabry near the bulletin board.

Carlton was a loveable bear of a man. Just being around him made you feel like things were bound to get better.

"Hey, how you doing, honey?" He wrapped me in a huge hug and I relaxed in his arms.

"I'm okay. How about you two?"

Mary shook her head, eyes red. She hugged me, too. "I just can't imagine losing a child like that. I don't think I could stand it. That poor woman." Tears welled in her eyes and she blinked them away.

"I haven't seen you in a while, Mary," I said. "What have you been up to?"

Carlton smiled his thanks for my changing the subject. "She's got me putting in our first garden. Never had time for anything like this before and we're having a ball."

Carlton had single-handedly built a small printing company into one of the largest office supply houses in the city. Now that he'd retired and his oldest son was running the business, he and his wife were trying some new things.

"We're going to have tomatoes, beans, squash, and cucumbers," Mary said, her smile back in place.

"And peppers," Carlton reminded her. He put an arm around her shoulders and pulled her close to his side. "And now she wants an herb garden. I don't know what in the world she's going to do with one, but when we leave here she's dragging me halfway to Milledgeville to an herb farm."

She gave him a playful nudge. "Oh, hush, you old grump. You'll love it. It's a beautiful place and we'll get everything we need for the garden. You might even find some things that interest you."

He shook his head in mock dismay. "You're going to have us so covered up in this gardening stuff that we won't be able to get away for the Boy Scout jamboree in May."

Mary chuckled. "That'll be the day." She gave me a wink. "He'd rather be with those little fellers than eat when he's hungry. Started working with them when Junior was a scout and just never quit."

They left the church arm in arm and I felt a twinge of envy. Donald and I might have achieved that kind of timeless affection if we'd only had the chance.

I wasn't sure I could manage the graveside service, so I went back to the shop. But the residue of Glynnis's funeral hung over me for the rest of the day. It was all I could do to muster up a smile for the few customers who came in during the afternoon. When I looked up to see Pandora slouching into the store, I was actually glad it was she. Since I knew she wasn't a serious customer, I didn't feel the need to manufacture a show of good humor.

"Hi." She glanced at the recently relocated local writers, but made no comment. Today she'd topped her jeans with a loose, gauzy blouse and dangling peace sign earrings. She was embracing the Sixties with the kind of fervor reserved for those who hadn't actually lived through the decade.

"A policeman came to see me this morning. He said you told him to."

"Well, not exactly. I just told him you'd been here Tuesday afternoon and might have seen – "

"Oh, I didn't mind," she said quickly. "I've never talked to a real detective before. It was kind of interesting." She sighed. "He wanted to know if I'd seen the lady who got killed but I didn't. At least, I don't think I did. I mean, there were a bunch of people around. I didn't notice anybody special. I think he was disappointed."

I hid a smile. "I wouldn't worry about it. The police are used to being disappointed."

She looked over her shoulder at the ranks of bookshelves, then turned back to me, long hair swinging around her face. "Do you have books on music?"

"Back left corner." I put on a Diana Krall CD and Pandora spent the next twenty minutes in the music section. When she came back to the front counter, she had a battered Judy Collins songbook in her hand.

"Look what I found! I love her music! My mama has all her old albums. I played them over and over when I was a little girl. I bet I know every song in here by heart. And it has the guitar chords, too. I have to have this."

I checked the price penciled on the inside of the back cover and calculated the tax. "That's eight-forty."

She dug in her shabby backpack and eventually came up with eight crumpled one-dollar bills. Another dive into the bag produced a handful of change. She carefully picked out three dimes and two nickels and handed them to me.

I slipped the book into a plastic bag and held it out to her. But instead of leaving, she stood there a minute, her teeth worrying her lower lip.

"Are you sure you couldn't use me around here? I just want to work here so bad."

The refusal had already formed in my mouth, but for some reason I didn't voice it. She was so young, so vulnerable and, in spite of everything I'd said to her, pathetically optimistic. My meager profits didn't justify the expense of an employee, but I rationalized it might be worth it to have someone available to watch the shop when I needed to be away. And it probably wouldn't make much of a dent in my savings. After all, it would only be temporary. The school year would end in a couple of months and she'd be off to wherever it was she belonged.

"I can give you ten hours a week at seven dollars an hour – that's all. Just from now till school's out."

"Sweet!" She acted like she'd won the lottery. "Thank you so much! You won't be sorry, Ms. McClatchey. I promise. When do I start? I could start right now if you want."

I put up a hand. "Hey, slow down. It's only ten hours. And you'll have to call me Dixie if we're going to work together."

"Sure," she grinned. "I'm just so excited. See, the tarot said this job would be something special for me and – "

"Whoa! Let's not have any of that. I'm the one giving you the job, not some deck of fortune-telling cards."

Eyes wide and solemn, she nodded. I felt like I'd just told a small child that there was no Easter Bunny. "Yes, ma'am. I won't talk about it anymore. And I'm really grateful to you. I knew the minute I walked in here that this was where I wanted to work. You see, I just love books – reading them, just being around them." She lowered her eyes shyly. "I do some writing myself. So you can understand why I want to be here."

I wasn't sure I did, but it was too late to worry about it. "Okay. You can start Monday. Let's say two hours a day, Monday through Friday. Ten till noon? Except Tuesdays. I don't open till noon on Tuesdays. Does that work with your class schedule?"

"That'll be great for Monday, Wednesday and Friday. But I have a ten o'clock class on Tuesday and Thursday."

"Then come in at noon on those days. Okay?"

"Yes, ma'am! I can't wait! I'll be here at nine-thirty sharp Monday morning."

I laughed. "Well, if you are, you'll be by yourself. Ten is early enough."

She grinned. "Okay. You won't be sorry. I promise."

I thought I probably would. No good deed goes unpunished, my old sergeant used to tell me.

Ballard called late in the day and the news wasn't good. "I checked and my complex has a No Pets rule. I never knew about it 'cause I never asked. So I'm sorry, but I can't take the little cat."

I said the right things and thanked him for letting me know, but inside I was fuming. I didn't have time for this nonsense. Why couldn't I find someone to take the damned cat? I could, I knew, take him for a ride out to the animal shelter and make him someone else's problem, but that option didn't appeal to me. I decided to vent to Edward.

I loved visiting his shop. Bright paintings – the best of which were his own – were expertly framed and hung on the walls. He changed them out every few weeks, so going there was like visiting a gallery with an ever-changing show. The artist himself stood behind the framing table that afternoon, fitting an M.J. Venrick abstract into a metallic frame. From time to time he glared at what seemed to be a parade schedule laid out beside him.

He wasn't unhappy to be interrupted and listened with poorly concealed amusement as I ranted about my trials finding a home for the cat. When I finally ran down, he laughed out loud.

"You might as well face facts, sweet pea. You're now the proud owner of a kitten." His voice took on a theatrical timbre. "You were alone. He was alone. Now you've found each other. It's fate, pure and simple. Call it Kismet."

I repressed the urge to smack him and reflected that he was the second person to suggest fate had brought that cat into my life. I was getting tired of hearing it.

By the end of the day, I'd run out of people to call and surrendered to the inevitable. Fate, bad luck or whatever was to blame, I'd been beaten. A quick detour on my way home took me to PetsMart. I spent quite a while in the big store where I loaded my cart with an assortment of cat food, cat litter, and a bright blue, covered litter box. They carried a mind-boggling array of toys and treats especially for cats, not to mention the padded beds and carpeted climbing perches. By the time I finally left the store, I'd dropped over a hundred dollars on a nameless cat.

There were two messages waiting on my answering machine. The first was from my mother, who sounded delighted when she discovered I wasn't home on a Friday evening. I decided to wait until the next day to call her back. She'd have been disappointed to learn my big night out was a shopping trip for cat supplies.

The second message was from Delia McCullough.

"Can you come see me in the morning?" she asked when I called her back. "I need to talk to you. It's important."

"What is it?"

There was a sharply expelled breath. "I don't think I can get into it on the telephone."

I couldn't imagine why Glynnis's mother wanted to see me, but she was grieving and she seemed to believe it was important. It would only cost an hour or so of my time.

"I can't come in the morning. The shop is open until one on Saturdays. But I could come after I close."

She gave me directions and said she'd expect me about one-thirty.

Once the new litter box was set up at the back of the hallway, the cat needed no coaxing. He paid it a visit only minutes after its arrival. He also gobbled down the new cat food with the same relish he'd shown for the old. But the puffy pink and green cat bed left him cold and he completely ignored the three toy mice I arranged so attractively on the kitchen floor. However, he did spend a while batting around the package that they'd come in.

The weather held warm. Around eight-thirty, I settled on the screened porch with a book – not Sidney Lanier this time, but Sharyn McCrumb. I was happily immersing myself in the two-hundred-year-old tale of a woman who escaped from her Indian captors and ran all the way home when the doorbell rang.

Ballard had come, he said, to apologize. "I hate that I can't take that little guy. I really like him."

He'd brought gifts – a bottle of wine and a package of catnip. I opened the wine and filled a glass for him, but stuck with beer myself. It was Harp lager tonight. We took our drinks onto the porch and watched the cat roll ecstatically around in the catnip Ballard had sprinkled on the floor for him.

The lieutenant was definitely more informal tonight. In jeans and a tee shirt, and leaning back in the wicker chair, he seemed ready for a nice long talk. And while I'd have just as soon spent the evening alone, I was prepared to make the best of the situation. He hadn't mentioned the murder, so I didn't either.

"Tell me something about yourself, Lieutenant."

"Only if you can call me Steve."

"Okay, tell me about yourself, Steve."

"I'm afraid I'm not a very interesting guy. I work, I go home, I sleep." He shrugged. "That's about it."

I drank beer from the bottle. "Come on, even a dull guy would have more to say than that. And I don't think you're dull."

He gave in a bit and I learned he was a Macon native and a University of Georgia graduate. "Football scholarship," he explained, as if to make sure I didn't think he was giving himself educational airs. After school, there had been four years in the Army. "I was an MP. When I got out, joining the police department was the next logical step."

I nodded. "You told me you'd been married. Was she from Macon, too? High school sweethearts?"

"Not hardly. Nanci was a television reporter. I met her nine years ago when she moved here from North Carolina to take a job with WMAZ. I was a rookie detective working my first homicide and the station sent her to cover the news conference after the arrest. I thought she was the most beautiful woman I'd ever met."

He sprinkled a bit more catnip on the floor and the cat leapt on it with wild guttural noises. "He's got the makings of a junkie," Ballard observed.

"Come on, get on with the story," I said. "What happened next?"

He sat back down and grinned. "I thought she was sophisticated and glamorous and I guess she believed I was some sort of romantic, hard-boiled cop." A self-conscious smile warmed his face. "Fact is, we were both way off base. She was a small town girl who'd won a beauty contest and ended up on television. She loved the excitement and the attention. And going to parties and the theater and fancy restaurants. That was what she lived for – that and being recognized everywhere she went. And me," he gave that bitter laugh again, "I was just a hard-hearted son of a bitch who'd rather spend time arresting bad guys than taking her all the places she wanted to go."

There wasn't anything to say to that. I just waited and, after a minute, he went on.

"It took us three years to finally admit the whole thing had been a mistake."

"Do you have children?"

"One. A girl. She's six." He didn't do a very good job of hiding the pain. "She lives with her mother."

I remembered he'd mentioned losing the house in the divorce. "Do they live close by?"

"Not anymore. Nanci got a job offer up in Nashville last year. So

71

she and Lauren moved up there." He sighed hard and stood up. "Think I'll get a refill."

I figured he didn't need company right then, so I stayed on the porch. After a minute, I stood up and went to stand beside the screened wall. When Steve returned, I said, "Listen to that. Do you hear it?"

It was a bird of some sort, singing like it was daybreak instead of ten o'clock at night.

"Mockingbird," he told me as the sweet, liquid notes hung in the air.

I looked hard, but about all I could make out in the moonlight were the indistinct shadows of trees and bushes. I certainly couldn't have seen a bird, much less determined what kind it was. "How do you know?"

He moved closer. "That it's a mockingbird? They're the only ones who sing in the moonlight. Spring is nesting time. When a male hasn't yet attracted a female, he can't rest. He keeps singing, all night long if he has to, trying to lure a mate."

"How sad."

"It's only sad if it doesn't work."

He'd moved so close that I could feel his breath on the back of my neck. I should have moved away right then, but I didn't. A moment later it was too late. If he'd grabbed at me or tried to kiss me, I might have pushed him away. But he didn't. He slipped his arms around me and began a gentle nuzzling along the back of my neck that sent waves of pleasure through my body.

By the time his lips had, very slowly, inched their way around to my throat, any thought of resistance was long gone. Our first kiss was a slow, soft exploration, but the pace soon picked up. I was as much to blame as Steve was for the hungry crush of mouths and bodies. I'd been alone for so long and, like a starving person suddenly presented with a banquet, I wanted everything at once. The taste and feel of him was intoxicating. After only a few frantic minutes, I led him up the stairs, stopping every few steps for another caress or kiss.

There was no show of false shyness, no declaration that I usually didn't do this kind of thing. Our coming together was a whirlwind that, once set in motion, would not be stopped. No conversation or explanation was necessary. We were awkward at first, unsure of each other's wants and moves, but our needs soon overcame that and we moved together in perfect accord. Afterwards, we lay in a damp jumble of limbs and sheets, our breathing slowly returning to normal.

Steve traced the contour of my back with his hand and I snuggled closer to him. I could see his profile in the half-light from the window. He looked more peaceful than I'd seen before. Small wonder. I felt considerably more peaceful myself.

Lovely as it was to lay there together, I knew he'd have to go soon. I wasn't yet ready for a man to stay overnight. But I was so totally relaxed that I had to close my eyes for just a few minutes more to enjoy this new serenity.

The cat woke me by butting his little head against my hand, a gesture I'd come to recognize as a demand for attention. I reached out, sleepy but obedient, to pet him and realized I was naked. Then I remembered Ballard.

I sat up in bed. The early morning light showed I was alone, but I could hear water running in the bathroom. I pulled on some clothes, stopped in the hall bath to wash my face and run a brush through my hair, then went on downstairs. By the time Ballard joined me in the kitchen, hair still wet from the shower, I had fed the cat and had the coffee maker going.

"Well, good morning." He gave me big grin and a quick kiss. I was grateful he didn't feel obligated to make a clever comment about the night before.

"Good morning. Coffee will be ready in a couple of minutes."

I expected awkwardness, but there was very little. He went out and got the paper and we sat companionably at the table, drinking coffee and scanning the headlines. The cat, after winding between both sets of legs, decided on Ballard. He jumped into his lap, turned around a few times and fell asleep.

"So," he finally asked, laying the sports section aside, "what are your plans for the day?"

"Just like every other Saturday – working in the shop. What about you?"

"I've got a long day ahead of me. I'm driving to North Carolina."

"Why?"

"Nanci's visiting her parents up there and it's closer than Nashville. I can go up and spend some time with Lauren." His smile held a trace of the bitterness I'd glimpsed the night before. 'If I'm lucky, she'll be able to stay overnight with me in the motel."

"How far is it?"

He shrugged. "A couple of hundred miles. Should take about four hours to get there."

A few minutes later, he was ready to leave. I walked with him to the front door. As I reached for the knob, he bent forward and kissed me very sweetly on the lips.

"I'll talk to you Monday."

"Have a safe drive."

His steps as he walked out to his car were almost jaunty.

I closed the door and considered what had happened. I tried to feel embarrassed about going to bed with a man I'd known for less than a week, but I couldn't. Instead, a quiet kind of excitement like a low voltage electrical current coursed through my body. Maybe, just maybe, this was how it felt to start living again.

CHAPTER SEVEN

Twenty minutes later, I'd showered, dressed, and made sure there was food and water left out for the cat. Now I was ready to take on the day. As soon as I stepped out of the house, I noticed the smell. Local wisdom held that when the sickly sweet odor of the paper mill drifted up from south of the city, it brought with it a good chance of rain. More often than not, the prediction was accurate. It was at least as reliable a forecast as the one printed in the paper or pronounced on television. I went back inside for an umbrella.

Saturdays are slow downtown. Most of the stores are closed and the restaurants' business doesn't really start until mid-afternoon. Only a few people ventured into my shop and the morning passed slowly, but I didn't mind. I was too busy reliving the previous night to worry about book sales.

Closing early was looking like a real possibility until, just before one, a nervous woman with big hair and perfect makeup came in. She wandered around pulling books off the shelves and shoving them back in the wrong places. When she finally left, conspicuously devoid of any purchase, it was ten after one.

The delay didn't concern me. Few locations in Macon were more than fifteen minutes apart.

The rain had started around noon. It now fell steadily, straight down. But the drive out to Bass Road was still enjoyable. Spring had arrived, seemingly overnight. Bright patches of color spotted the wet landscape. Azaleas glowed pink and red and white everywhere. Seeing Macon this time of year, you'd think there must be an obscure law on the books requiring every yard to have at least one azalea bush that was visible from the street. Even the cherry trees were beginning to bloom and most homes showed signs of recent yard work. Pink bows adorned mailboxes and many front doors sported colorful wreaths. Macon always spruced up at Cherry Blossom time.

The McCullough house was relatively new; built of brick and beige wood, it stood anonymous in a subdivision of similar structures. Daffodils in a bed beside the front porch waved and bobbed in the gentle rain. Delia opened the door only a second after I rang the bell.

She was dressed in black slacks and a neatly tucked-in white blouse. She had her daughter's dull brown hair, but where Glynnis was round and soft, Delia was all sharp angles. Her eyes were red and swollen, but she managed a weak smile.

"Thank you for coming, Dixie. Please come in." I followed her down a long hall toward the back of the house, past a curio cabinet that displayed a collection of tiny teapots and into the kitchen.

"Would you like something to eat?"

It was more than a casual question. The breakfast table and the center island were loaded down with food. Cakes, cookies, foil and plastic wrapped sandwiches, and pies were everywhere. I knew the refrigerator would be crowded with casseroles, fried chicken and, most likely, a HoneyBaked Ham.

"No, thanks."

A worried expression crossed her face. "I just don't know what I'm going to do with all this food. People keep bringing more and more. Poor Glynnis, she just loved sweets and . . . and now, with so many different things here . . . and she can't enjoy any of them."

She teared up and turned away. I could see her shoulders heaving, but she never made a sound. After a minute, she pulled a tissue from her pants pocket, resolutely blew her nose and turned back to me. "Well, if you won't have anything, we might as well go sit down."

I followed her into the sunroom. The view of the backyard through the floor-to-ceiling windows was all fresh green and pink, gleaming in the rain. Delia indicated an overstuffed love seat. I stepped around a cardboard box that seemed out of place on the terrazzo floor and sat on one side of the small sofa. A lazy-looking dachshund occupied the other end. He opened his eyes and issued a low growl.

"Oh, don't mind Fritzie. He doesn't bite. He's just old and grumpy." She took a deep breath. "I appreciate you driving out here in this awful rain. When poor Glynnis died, I knew I had to do something, but I was so upset that I didn't know what. I thought and thought and finally decided you were the person I should talk to."

"Why?" The question popped out before I could think of a more tactful way to ask.

"Because of your background, of course. Anyone who investigated murders in a city like Atlanta shouldn't have any trouble doing the same thing in Macon. I mean, I know that you left the police force when your husband was killed and everything." She reached to pat my hand. "You can't be blamed for what happened. After all, you weren't the person committing a crime. Besides, it's been several years now. I expect you're ready to get back to it by now. And I really need your help."

"How do you know all that about me?" I had deliberately kept my past in the past. I hadn't wanted sympathy or questions. Except for Deannie and Edward, no one in Macon knew the details of Donald's death or how I made my living in Atlanta – at least, I hadn't thought they did.

"Oh, Glynnis talked about you a lot, Dixie. She admired you so much. And, of course, once I thought about calling you, I checked your file."

That didn't make any sense at all, but I'd come back to it in a minute. We had to get something straight first. "Mrs. McCullough, the police are investigating Glynnis's death. I'm sure they're doing everything they can to find out what happened. You just have to give them a little time."

"The police? They haven't done a thing." She made a disgusted sound in her throat. "Have you met that obnoxious little man? What's his name? Kanetsky? Kaminsky? Yes, that's it, Kaminsky. If you ask me, he's more concerned about keeping his hair styled than he is in finding out who killed my baby." The tears came again and I waited until the spasm passed. When she was able, she continued. "No, I want you to do it. And don't worry, I'm prepared to pay you well for your work. Money is no object where justice for Glynnis is concerned."

I shook my head. "Mrs. McCullough, I don't do that kind of work. And when I did, I didn't work for private individuals. I run a bookstore. If you don't trust the police, maybe you should hire a private investigator, someone that investigates things for a living. But not me."

It was like explaining quantum physics to a Pekinese. She went on as if I hadn't spoken at all. "You're the one I need. You were her friend. And Glynnis knew you were a great detective. She showed me newspaper clippings about your cases up in Atlanta. I always thought Glynnis should have been a detective herself. She was a whiz at research." Pride strengthened her voice. "And the way she kept her files – she was a master of organization."

"Mrs. McCullough, what are these files you keep talking about?"

"Oh, my Glynnis had files on just about everybody."   She reached over to open the cardboard box and pulled a manila folder from it. "See? This is yours. Now you can't tell me that's not complete and well organized."

My name was neatly printed in black ink on the tab. When I opened the folder, I was presented with a chronicle of my own life in newsprint. In addition to the few newspaper articles that had appeared in the *Atlanta Journal-Constitution* about murder cases I'd worked, Glynnis had somehow located clippings from my high school days when I'd been a very lackluster member of my school's basketball team. She even had photocopies of pages from my high school yearbook. There was a copy of our marriage certificate, as well as Donald's obituary.

But the real gems of the collection were the clippings that dealt with Donald's murder. She had it all – from the initial report the day after it happened to the arrest and trial, and the official inquiry into my own actions that night. I didn't want to read the report of the findings – I knew it by heart – but I couldn't keep my eyes away. 'Sgt. McClatchey, while acting in a less than prudent manner, did not violate any laws of this state or any departmental regulations. It is regrettable that her actions may have contributed to the death of Donald McClatchey.' I turned the clipping face down on the stack and looked at the next item.

Glynnis had also acquired a copy of the deed my grandmother signed when she gave me the High Street house. And to top it all off, there was a series of snapshots of me. One showed me standing at the door to the shop and another out for a morning run. She even had a picture of Deannie and me sitting at a table outside Chimera. I was so flabbergasted at what I saw, and the knowledge of how much work it took to accumulate it, that it was a few minutes before I trusted myself to speak. Then I wanted answers.

"Why would Glynnis have a file on me?"

"Like I said, she had one on most everybody she knew." She waved a hand at the box. "She was a very smart girl, my Glynnis. She really should have gone into business.   With her brains and determination, there's no telling what she might have accomplished. I told her that plenty of times, but she was just such a good daughter." She stopped to take a shaky breath and dab her eyes. "She felt she had to stay with me, to take care of me after Hurley died. Have you ever known anyone so selfless?"

I wasn't interested in nominating Glynnis for sainthood just then. "I still don't understand about the files."

"Well, she never really said why exactly, but I always thought she did it because she needed something to keep her mind sharp." She smoothed the fabric of her slacks with unsteady hands. "She started with the genealogy, of course, and she was very good at that. Why, she traced our family back to the Norman invasion of England. Can you imagine that? But I don't believe that was enough of a challenge for her. I think she decided to research the people she knew, just to see what she could find out.

"She enjoyed it so much. I can't tell you how many times she told me, 'Mom, you'd be surprised at the secrets the most ordinary people have'." Delia smiled at the memory. "And now. . . now I can't help but wonder if her little hobby might be what got her killed. People don't always understand women like Glynnis. She was absolutely brilliant, but not everybody saw that. And people can be so cruel!"

This time she started sobbing in earnest. She got up and walked out of the room. The dachshund hopped off the love seat and followed, toenails clicking on the stone floor. I was left alone with the box of files, trying to take in what I'd been told. What would possess Glynnis, or anyone else for that matter, to do background investigations on her acquaintances? What possible use could the information have been to her?

I went over to the box, lifted the lid and looked inside. There must have been twenty folders there. I could see only three names from where I stood. Two were vaguely familiar, but the third was Alexandra Michaels.

"So," Delia said briskly when she returned some minutes later and took her seat, "I want you to take these files and look into it."

"But Glynnis was killed in a robbery," I tried to tell her. "It was one of those random things that just happen."

"Nonsense. My daughter was not a fool. If some street thug had tried to rob her, she'd have handed over everything she had that very minute. We've talked about that so often. No possession is worth getting hurt over, she told me many a time. And the police said she still had her purse over her arm and nothing was taken." Her mouth tightened with certainty. "No, it was no robbery."

I thought I understood what was happening here. Delia didn't want her daughter's death to be a random occurrence, a tragic accident. She needed something more. If Glynnis's murder was precipitated by her own brilliance, it might be easier for her mother to accept. And who was I to tell her it hadn't happened that way?

"Mrs. McCullough, if these files could be related to Glynnis's death, the police should have them, not me."

"After the way they behaved? I might have given them the box if they'd just been polite. Instead, that little sawed-off detective showed up here with a search warrant and demanded to search Glynnis's room. They spent a long time in there, pawing over her things." A crafty look came into her eyes. "I knew they wouldn't find anything there. Glynnis kept all her research in the office next to the laundry room. But they didn't even ask. So I didn't tell them.

"Now, I do believe there might be something in one of those files that could lead to finding the person who killed my daughter. But it would only be one person, wouldn't it? I mean, it stands to reason that only one person is responsible. So, if I gave all of them to the police, what about the people in those other folders? There are some ugly things in some of them, things most people would be terribly ashamed of. I'm sure Glynnis would never have wanted her research to hurt anyone. I'd hate for that information to leak out. It could ruin someone's life. And I don't trust that Kaminsky person to be one bit discreet."

She'd never know it, but that last statement made my decision for me. I didn't want to see the files, much less take them with me. But I couldn't help wondering if they contained information that would damage innocent people. There was no way to know what "ugly" might mean in Delia McCullough's vocabulary. While painful to relive, the information in my file couldn't do me any real harm. But others might not be so fortunate. Was I ready to take responsibility for all those secrets being handed over to the police?

I thought about Alexandra Michaels and what might be in her folder. There had been rumors that she was having an affair with the tennis pro at her club. In fact, Glynnis had made some snide remarks about that at a sorting session. For all I knew the rumors were true. But true or not, Alexandra wouldn't have killed Glynnis to keep that quiet.

The police, however, wouldn't know that. They'd have to look into it. The odds that they could do so without involving Alexandra's husband and family weren't good. I shared Delia's distrust of Kaminsky. I thought he would take delight in spreading scandalous information all over the place. So in the end, I agreed to take the files with me.

But I did make one last attempt to explain my reasons. "Mrs. McCullough, I am not going to investigate your daughter's murder. I want to make sure you understand that. What I will do is examine these files for anything that seems like it could be connected to Glynnis's death. And if I find something, I'll take it to the police. Otherwise, I'll bring this box back to you and you can decide where to go from there."

She shook her head, tears welling in her eyes again. "I don't want any of them back. I trust you to know what to do with them, Dixie."

She walked with me out to the Blazer where she stood silently, arms crossed, as I stowed the box in the back. She continued to stand there while I backed out of the drive and left the subdivision.

I put together a quick dinner of pasta and vegetables and reflected again just how inconvenient my kitchen was for food preparation. Even a meal this simple required a lot of walking and backtracking around the room. Edelman's renovation estimate lay on the table, tempting me with visions of spacious countertops, state-of-the-art equipment, and more storage space than I'd ever need.

While I ate, I read and reread the booklet, weighing the pros and cons of having the work done. On the plus side, it would make my life easier and much more pleasant. The changes would also boost the value of the house in the event I ever wanted to sell it. The minuses were the enormous price tag and the certainty that my life would be disrupted for weeks. I made up my mind with the last bite of pasta. My savings would take a hit, but it would be worth it in the long run.

Edelman had placed his business card in a little plastic sleeve inside the back cover. I pulled it out and dialed the number. He didn't answer – not surprising for a Saturday night – but I didn't let that stop me. I was primed for commitment.

"Mr. Edelman," I told his machine, "this is Dixie McClatchey on High Street. I've thought it over and I want you to go ahead with the kitchen."

I replaced the phone in the receiver and took a deep breath. The decision was made.

The kitchen table was the logical place for examining Glynnis's files – bright, overhead light and a place to spread everything out. What I hadn't counted on was the cat. He seemed fascinated by my every move. He perched on the edge of the table and watched me. Every time I laid down a file, he eased over and stretched out on top of it. I spent almost as much time relocating the kitten as I did reading.

In between files, I'd lean back in my chair and wonder about Ballard. Was the visit with his daughter going as he'd hoped? How difficult must it be to see your only child so infrequently? And did he have any time to think about me?

There were eighteen folders in all. Four contained information on people I'd never heard of, but I recognized the names on the rest of the tabs. I pulled out the files on the five Friends volunteers first. It was unpleasant work. While no earth-shattering secrets were revealed, most of the folders contained information that the subjects wouldn't enjoy being made public.

As I'd halfway expected, Glynnis had found confirmation of Alexandra's affair with Denny, the tennis pro, complete with photos of the lovers together. Reg Anderson's file held some items that suggested he might be removing valuable books from donations to the Friends and selling them himself.

While those two folders contained current information, what Glynnis had collected on the other Friends was ancient history. Comparing a marriage license and a copy of a newspaper birth announcement, I gathered that Cassie Waycaster's oldest child had been born only six months after her marriage. But who cared? The same went for Carlton Mabry's 1978 Driving Under the Influence arrest. The supposed scandal in Marian Saxby's file dated back to before she was born. I couldn't believe any of them would be concerned with this stuff now.

After the Friends' files, I moved on to the others. There was one for Edward Swanson that held no surprises and one for Deannie Vandeusen that did. Glynnis had garnered unpleasant information on everyone from the assistant director of the Visitors Bureau to the president of a local garden club, but there was nothing anywhere serious enough to have caused her murder. Around eleven I called it quits.

I opened a Saranac Black and Tan and took it to the side porch.

A soft rain was falling once more and I welcomed it. Here in Georgia we'd experienced so many years of drought or near drought that no one, except for the occasional TV weather bimbo, dared complain about rain. I listened for the mockingbird, but heard nothing. Had he found a mate after all or did he just not sing in inclement weather?

The cat climbed in my lap when I got comfortable on the love seat.

"Hey, Hot Shot, how you doing?"

He was adjusting well to what we both now accepted was his new home. I stroked his fur as he obviously thought I should and, when he turned over on his back, paws kneading the air, I scratched his stomach as well. His purring was loud and satisfied. At least one of us was happy.

The morning's elation was gone. I felt dirty and depressed. I never wanted to know all those petty little shames and secrets, but now I did. Would I ever be able to look at any of those people the same way again? My position was impossible. Were the files evidence in a murder case? I didn't think so, but they could be, and I couldn't just destroy them as long as the possibility existed. Withholding any information from the police in a murder investigation went against everything I was and had done in my life. And yet I couldn't bring myself to hand all that dirt over to Kaminsky.

I was furious with Delia McCullough for involving me in this and even more furious with Glynnis for gathering the information in the first place. And then there was the guilt I'd felt when Delia referred to me as Glynnis's friend. There'd been no friendship – not that I knew anything about. She had admired me, her mother told me, and my only reactions to her had been irritation and dislike. Why couldn't I have spent some time getting to know the woman? She must have had some good qualities. Everyone did. Perhaps if she'd actually had some friends she wouldn't have felt the need to pry into other people's lives.

I pondered the situation as I drank my beer and stroked the cat, but in the end I could only come up with one way out of the mess. I'd try to quietly eliminate as many of Glynnis's victims as I could. Maybe it wouldn't be so difficult after all. If they could be accounted for during the time she was killed, I could justify not turning their files over to the police.

Of course, that brought up another little problem. When had Glynnis died? I didn't know and I doubted if Kaminsky would be eager to share that detail with me. Ballard might, but that would have to wait until Monday.

CHAPTER EIGHT

Saturday's rain had moved on, leaving behind a clear, cool Sunday morning. I skipped church, figuring I'd already put in enough pew time that week. Ordinarily Chapter and Verse is closed up tight on Sundays, but today was the Cherry Blossom Parade and I opened at noon, hoping to take advantage of the influx of parade goers into downtown. I propped open the front door with a small bookcase to invite customers and fresh air into the shop.

A lot of people milled around the streets even though the parade was three hours off. Chapter and Verse attracted a number of browsers and quite a few actual customers. The theme of the day was anything Southern. Local books were my biggest sellers, along with some coffee table editions featuring Southern cities and gardens.

Edward's shop was closed, of course. He'd been in the parade staging area since early that morning. But several of the other stores had opened up, their doors and windows decorated with pink ribbons and streamers. Even the streets were decorated. Huge cherry blossoms were painted here and there on the pavement and pink stripes had been added to the yellow center lines. The city was infused with a fine, festive atmosphere and it made me glad I lived there.

As parade time drew closer, my business dwindled and finally disappeared altogether. Everyone had gone to secure a good spot on the edge of the sidewalk. Drumbeats boomed in the distance. I locked the front door and joined the crowds lining Cherry Street.

The parade began right on schedule. Brightly colored floats, bands, baton twirlers, horses, clowns, jugglers, and dignitaries in convertibles streamed past. It lasted nearly an hour and I enjoyed every minute of it. It was probably as close to a Norman Rockwell experience as I was likely to get. When it was over, the satisfied crowd began dispersing and Edward had another success under his belt.

Across the street I spotted a couple of familiar faces. Carlton and Mary Mabry were making their way through the throng of parade-goers. I waved, but they didn't see me. A small boy of seven or eight, in shorts and a bright Spiderman tee shirt, walked between them.

Mary had his hand firmly gripped in her own and his little face was creased by a frown as he dodged the people walking the other direction. I couldn't remember being that small, but I imagined it must be a scary to be three feet tall and surrounded by a sea of legs. I crossed the street to meet them.

"Hey, sugar," Carlton said. "Quite a parade, wasn't it?"

"It was great," I smiled a greeting at Mary. "Is this young man your grandson?"

She beamed as befitting a proud grandmother. " This is Josh. He's Danny's youngest boy."

"Hey, Josh."

The child raised wide, brown eyes at me, but didn't speak.

"Come on, little guy," Carlton said. "Come out here and say howdedo to Miss Dixie." He put a big hand on the boy's shoulder and gently moved him to stand in front of me. "Now say hello."

I had to strain to hear his faint, "Hello."

He looked absolutely terrified of me, so much so that I didn't offer to shake his little hand. Although I've never been particularly good with children, this was the most extreme reaction I'd ever gotten. Usually they just stare at me as if I were some species they'd never encountered before. As soon as Carlton released him, the boy scurried back to Mary's side.

"He's just real shy," she said. "And he used to be the most outgoing child. I believe it must be a phase he's going through."

"Don't worry about it," I told her with a laugh. "There are plenty of days when I don't feel especially sociable."

Tena Roberts, who ran the Italian boutique across the street, called to me as I returned to my shop.

"You gonna be open tonight? The blue grass concert ought to bring in a bunch of people."

"I don't think so. But I hope you have good luck."

In my experience the crowds who came down for the outdoor evening concerts were more interested in food, beer, and music than they were in shopping for books. I'd stayed open through a couple of concerts during last year's festival and not made a single sale. My evening would be much more constructively spent catching up on housework.

There was a message waiting from Harold Edelman when I got home. He'd left his home phone number and I called him back.

"Glad we're going to be doing the job for you, Ms. McClatchey."

"Me, too." I looked around the big, inconvenient room. "I'm really looking forward to a new kitchen."

"Well, we don't want you to wait any longer than you have to. If it's all right with you, I can bring the contract around for you to sign first thing in the morning."

"Tomorrow?" It was sooner than I expected.

"Yes, ma'am, if that suits you."

Well, why not, I thought. The sooner the better. "Okay, that'll be fine."

"Great. See you about eight-thirty."

I told him I'd be waiting.

"We'll try to get started Wednesday – might even make it by Tuesday afternoon," he said as he hung up.

Suddenly the project was real. An idea I'd toyed with, something I'd thought of as a possibility, was actually going to begin Wednesday, maybe even Tuesday. What in the world had I started? How would I manage having workmen in the house all day with Hot Shot? Would they rip out the kitchen first thing? How long would I have to manage without a stove? Would the work spill over into the rest of the house? These were, I realized, all questions I should have already asked.

I took a deep breath and stopped myself before I surrendered to panic. People had kitchens renovated all the time and did just fine. So would I.

The call came around eight that evening. I'd finished the chores, with the cat's dubious help, and was trying to decide between a salad and a can of soup for dinner.

"Dixie? Are you . . . ? Where's Dixie? Can you hear me?"

"Deannie?" She sounded far away and loud music almost drowned out her words. "I can hardly hear you."

"That better?" Her raised voice blasted my ear.

"Yeah."

"Dixie, can . . . come over . . . I . . . it's late I guess but. . . need . . . can you come over?"

What was wrong with her? Was she sick? Or drunk? I'd never known Deannie to have more than two glasses of wine in a single evening. "What is it? Are you okay?"

"Please . . . please . . . now." I couldn't be sure, but I thought she was crying.

"I'm on my way."

"Hurry. Please."

It was only a five minute drive, but it took me a while to find a place to leave the car. People had poured into downtown for the outdoor concert. I finally found a spot on Mulberry and half ran the three blocks back to Martin Luther King, Jr. Drive. My heart pounded – not from the exertion, but from fear. What had happened to Deannie?

I could hear occasional snatches of music in the distance and merrymakers crowded the sidewalks, but no one paid any attention to me. Deannie's loft was on the third floor of a renovated warehouse. When there was no answer to my knocks, I tried the knob and opened the door.

The loft was usually a meticulous, minimalist masterpiece – exactly what the developers had hoped for when the revitalization of the area was begun. Tonight it looked like the leavings of a tornado. The two standard poodles that shared Deannie's space met me at the door, turning in frantic circles. There was a faint smell of dog waste in the air and I wondered when they'd last been taken out. Dirty plates and take-out containers were piled haphazardly on the kitchen counters. Clothes and newspapers were strewn across the furniture and floor. In a far corner, the bed was a tangle of sheets. Music blared from a box near the front door. I turned it off.

Sprawled on a low gray sofa, Deannie herself was a mess, too. Her white man-styled shirt was stained with what might have been tomato sauce and only half tucked into her jeans. Her beautiful, caramel-colored face was streaked with mascara-stained tears and her braids were a wild tangle around her head. She'd been crying and I didn't need to see the almost empty bottle of lemon-flavored vodka on the coffee table to know she'd done a lot of drinking. When she saw me, she struggled to her feet. Once upright, she lurched across the room, threw her arms around my neck and burst into tears.

I was so shocked that, for a minute or so, all I could do was hold the sobbing woman and try to reconcile this emotional wreck with the Deannie Vandeusen I'd known for two years. I'd never seen her even a little out of control. She was the most disciplined person I'd ever met. But tonight she was a basket case.

I led her to the sofa, murmuring what I hoped were comforting words. "It's okay, honey. It's okay. Everything's going to be all right. Try to get hold of yourself and tell me what's wrong."

The tears slowly subsided. She took some deep shuddering breaths, then wiped her eyes with the back of her hand. "Iss ruined." Her voice was hoarse. "I'm goin' lose everything. And . . . nothing I can do."

I put a hand on her arm. "What are you talking about?"

"That bitch Glynnis!" She jerked away from my hand, eyes blearily searching the room, as if looking for a place to run. "Dead, but she won't leave me alone. And . . . " The last sentence was so slurred that I couldn't tell what she said. I started to ask her to repeat it, then decided there was no point.

"Just sit here for a bit." I kept my voice low and calm. With my hands on her shoulders, I gently pushed her back against the cushions. "I'm going to get you something to eat – "

"Ah, God, I don' want food! … don' unnerstand – "

"You can explain it to me in just a minute. Right now I'm going to fix you some food. You stay here and try to calm down."

She covered her face with her hands, crying again. "Don't unnerstand! It's bad, bad."

There was a Stouffer's lasagna in the freezer that I popped in the microwave. By the time it was done, I had a pot of coffee going, the trash deposited in a can, and most of the dishes in the dishwasher.

When I called her, Deannie obediently came to sit at the table. She surprised us both by digging right into the lasagna, hardly stopping to breathe between bites. When had she last eaten? I poured a Diet Coke over ice for her and, when she drained that in about thirty seconds, I brought her another.

While she was occupied with the food, I cleaned up the dogs' accidents. Their leashes hung on a coat rack near the door. I clipped one onto each collar and slung my purse, heavy with the added weight of the gun, over my shoulder. "Back in a bit," I called to Deannie. She barely looked up from the food to nod.

There was a small park just a block up the street. Orange, high intensity streetlights illuminated the area. The dogs, ecstatic at being outside, jumped and pranced along the sidewalk. When we reached the green space, they took care of their needs quickly, then began happily sniffing the bushes and examining benches and trash cans. They'd have spent hours there, but I hurried them along. We were entering the door to the loft ten minutes later.

Deannie was back on the sofa. While the food had helped a little, she was still agitated and her speech was still less than sharp. I brought her coffee, which I'd made extra strong, and insisted she drink it. She started to balk, but then gave in. When the first cup was down, I poured her another.

"Are you feeling better?"

She nodded, although she didn't look much better. She didn't seem to notice that her hair was hanging in her eyes. Sagging back against the cushions like an inflatable doll that was a pound or two low on air, she apologized.

"Sorry about this, Dixie. I just had to talk to somebody."

"Then I'm glad it was me." I fetched myself some coffee and took a chair across from her. "Now tell me what's wrong."

"Glynnis was . . . there are some things in my past that I wouldn't want . . . " She gulped some coffee. "Oh, what the hell. You might as well know – everyone's going to soon enough. Have the pleece … police said anything about me yet?"

"Nothing." I'd told her that before.

"Well, they will." She sounded as if she might cry again, but got it under control. "Glynnis had the proof. I know. I saw it. Police'll get to it eventually."

"Proof of what?" Surely she didn't mean she'd had a hand in the woman's death.

"Of my past, Dixie, that's what. Who I really am."

I knew what was coming. I'd seen her file.

She was sitting a bit straighter now and spoke very deliberately. "I think I told you I was in school at the Southern Culinary Institute in

Atlanta? I don't know how much you know about that place. It's very expensive – a two-year course of study is over $20,000 – but it's worth every penny. Completing the course work just about guarantees you a job with a first class restaurant."

As she told her story, forced to organize her thoughts and put them into words, Deannie began to sound like her old self again. "Even though I had a partial scholarship, I still had to work the whole time I was there. In different restaurants around town. Mostly kitchen work, but I waited tables some, too. For a few months there I was working three jobs at once. But it was never enough. Atlanta's not a cheap place to live and I wasn't very smart about money back then. The bills kept piling up and I was getting in deeper and deeper. Plus I never got enough sleep. I was a zombie most of the time and my work at school was starting to suffer."

She gave the vodka bottle on the table in front of her a look. Instead, she got up and refilled her cup with coffee, picking up her story as she walked back to me.

"Then this guy I knew – he showed me how I could make a lot more money, not have to work nearly so many hours. It sounded, I don't know, kind of daring. I even thought it was glamorous. God, I was stupid!"

She settled back on the sofa, then looked hard at me. "I became a whore." Her eyes dared me to be shocked. I stared back without expression and waited. "I didn't call it that, of course. When I called it anything, I said I was a professional escort. That sounded more respectable. I mean, I was way too good to stand on a street corner. I worked through an escort service. My . . . ummm . . . professional name was Stormy. Real sophisticated, huh? Oh, and I didn't have johns. I called them clients. But, you know, honey, bottom line I was a whore—just one more stupid black chick turning tricks. And I knew it, too, even if I didn't admit it to myself."

There might have been tears in her eyes, but she blinked them away. "For about six months it seemed to work okay. I just about managed to convince myself that it wasn't immoral, told myself that most women traded sex for what they needed – marriage or security or children or whatever. So what I was doing wasn't any different, was it?

And I had plenty of money – more than I'd ever had before. I was doing great in school. But then it turned bad real quick." She closed her eyes for a minute and I thought she must be seeing the woman she'd been years ago. "It always does when you're not doing right, doesn't it?

"I got arrested for prostitution. There was this man that – oh, it doesn't matter how it happened. I got busted. Shit, I got the full, four-star treatment – photographed, printed, and put in a cell. I paid a fine and spent three months on probation."

She shook her braids back. "After that, life changed big time. Everybody found out about it, of course. People I'd thought were my friends just disappeared." Her lips curved into a pained smile. "Could have been worse, I guess. I only had a month of school left. I stuck it out, but it was miserable – the longest month of my life. No one talked to me, but they all sure talked about me. The minute school was over I got the hell out of Atlanta. Never wanted to see the place again."

I reached out to squeeze her hand. She squeezed back and gave me her first real smile of the night.

"I ended up in Charlotte. Found a job with a restaurant in one of the big downtown hotels. If they knew about my past, they never let it show. I had a hole-in-the-wall apartment and, for two years, I worked like a dog. I've never worked harder in my life. I hardly spent a dime. No friends, no social life, nothing. That's when I really got into the stock market. Learned how to trade online. I studied hard and made some good investments."

One of the dogs wandered over and cocked his curly white head at her. Deannie patted the cushion beside her and the poodle hopped up on the sofa, snuggling in as close to her as he could get.

"Finally I'd made enough money and I was ready to make my move. I had some old friends here in Macon. You know them, I think – Dee and Andrew Stewart over in Shirley Hills? They told me about a restaurant that was for sale down here. Research – a lot of it – showed that the place had real potential. And I bought it. That was four years ago. You know the rest."

I could only imagine the sacrifices she'd made to get where she was now.

"I was doing so good here, Dixie. I really was." Her eyes were wet again. "Terrific staff. And business has been good almost from the first day. But now it's all going to end."

"Why do you keep saying that?"

Her voice hardened. "Glynnis. She knew. I don't know how, but she knew. She came in for dinner one night last year. I think it was the first time she'd ever been inside the place. She was by herself and, after she ordered, she asked to see me. We'd run into each other several times over the years. You know how Macon is, really still a small town in a lot of ways.

"Anyway, they called me out of the kitchen. I was ready to do that 'make nice to the customer' thing. But when I walked over to her table, the bitch looked up at me and said, 'Hello, Stormy.' Then she smiled like she was real proud of herself."

She shook her head so violently it set her braids snapping around her head. "I swear to God, it was completely unreal. She just sat there grinning. It was all I could do not to slap her nasty face right then. But I didn't." Her smile was mocking. "I was pleasant to her. Even when she said she'd accidentally left her wallet at home. I told her not to worry, that the meal was on the house. Oh, yes, I was pleasant."

"She blackmailed you for a meal?" It was hard to imagine even Glynnis being that petty.

Deannie gulped some of the coffee that must have been cold by then. "Oh, that was just the beginning. She was back again the next week and that time she brought a copy of my . . . what do they call it? . . . mug shot? Yeah, well, she brought a copy of that. Gave it to me right there in the restaurant and said she didn't think it was a very good picture of me. What a vicious person she was! I'm glad she's dead."

I went to sit beside her, putting an arm around her shoulders. I wasn't sure she even noticed. "How long did this go on?"

"Six or seven months, I think. At first it was just the food. Then she started ordering a glass or two of wine with the meal. The last few times, she brought her mother, for God's sake! Introduced me to her like we were old friends! And there wasn't a thing I could do about it. She was just mean enough to go to the newspapers with the story if I didn't give her what she wanted."

"Did you ever try to talk to her about it?"

"What good would that have done? You could tell she enjoyed it!" She sighed and her anger drained away as quickly as it had come. "And now, who knows what's going to happen. If the police haven't already found the stuff she had about me, they will soon." She smiled again. "You know, I'm not even scared they'll think I killed her – I almost wish I had been the one to do it. She deserved exactly what she got! But I was in the restaurant all that afternoon and night. There are eight or nine people who can swear I never left. Not to mention all the customers who must have seen me."

"You don't have anything to worry about, honey," I told her. "No one is going to find out about your past."

But she wasn't listening to me. "I know they won't arrest me, but once they find out about me and Glynnis, I'll be part of the investigation. And then word will get out, just like it did in Atlanta. Everyone will know. Everyone will talk about me and no one will want to eat at the whore's restaurant!"

I pulled her closer to me, trying to quell her rising panic. "You can stop worrying. I promise you that no one is going to find out about your past, at least not from the information Glynnis had. I have her file on you. In fact, I have her files on everyone."

She was looking at me as if I'd just declared I planned to stand on my head in front of city hall while reciting the periodic table.

I quickly gave her a condensed version of my meeting with Delia McCullough. "I didn't want them, but I was afraid if I didn't take those files she might give them to the police after all."

She frowned. "So you already knew? About me, I mean?"

"Well, just about the arrest itself. You made me understand what happened. And I'd never have said anything to you about it if you hadn't brought it up yourself."

Deannie's eyes filled with tears. "You must think I'm some kind of trash."

I gathered her into an embrace. "All I think that you are is my dearest friend. Nothing else matters. And I promise you that everything in that file will be destroyed."

Relief, combined with the food and residual vodka, acted like a strong sedative on her. I could actually feel the tension leaving her body. The hands that had been either gesturing wildly or clinched into tight fists the whole time we'd talked were now relaxed and still.

"I don't know what to say."

"Don't say anything. You're exhausted. Just get some sleep now. We'll talk tomorrow."

I was feeling pretty satisfied with myself on the drive home. I had succeeded in protecting a friend and, even though I had to verify her alibi, it shouldn't be all that difficult. When I got home, I opened a beer and dialed a number I knew by heart. Although Chimera was closed on Sundays, at least one person was usually there, trying out new dishes or working on the books. Claude Mason picked up on the second ring.

"Yeah?" It was well known that he didn't like being interrupted when he was working.

"Claude, it's Dixie McClatchey."

"Ummmhmmmm." He wasn't a man to waste time on small talk.

"I wondered if you can tell me if Deannie was at the restaurant last Tuesday afternoon and evening."

"Tuesday? Yep, she was here."

"Are you sure? The whole time?"

"Open to close. We were slammed – had a twelve top with a six o'clock reservation. And they all ordered chocolate soufflés for dessert. Damn near didn't get them all done on time."

I thanked him and hung up. There was no need to manufacture an excuse for calling. He wouldn't care and his mind, I knew, was already back on the recipe of the moment. Even if he said something to Deannie about it, she would understand my checking her alibi. Knowing her as I did, this verification was just a formality, but I wanted to make sure that I did everything by the book.

I had just settled on the living room sofa for some mindless television when a disturbing thought occurred to me – it was one that shouldn't have taken so long to rise to the surface of my mind. I had the paper copies of the files, but Glynnis had a computer – Delia had told me so. What were the chances that the same information was loaded onto that machine? Considering she was such a "master organizer," it was a no-brainer. I didn't feel so smug anymore. If the police decided on another search and came back for the computer, they'd have the same information I was trying so hard to protect.

A bird, presumably a mocking bird, sang in the tree beside my bedroom window but I didn't think it would keep me awake. I kind of liked the sound. It reminded me of Steve Ballard. I climbed into bed just after midnight and was piled up under the covers with a book and a sleepy cat when the phone rang.

"Hello?" I was ready to let loose on whoever was inconsiderate enough to call that late, but I wasn't prepared for the anger that poured through the receiver.

"This is Teddy McCullough, Miss McClatchey. I've heard about your little arrangement with my mother and I want to get things straight right up front! She's an old woman, but I'm here to look out for her. You're not going to make money off her grief. I'll see to that."

"You don't understand. I'm not – "

"No, you're not! I'll be damned if some fast-talking scam artist is going to swindle her out of the money my father left her. She doesn't need a private investigator and I'm warning you to leave her alone. If you don't, I'll go to the police. If I can't stop you, maybe they can!"

Then he hung up on me, leaving any explanation I could have made unspoken. I thought about calling him back and explaining that I didn't want his mother's money and that I wasn't a private detective, but given his state of mind, it wouldn't have done any good. I decided to just get another beer instead. But even with the alcohol, my anger kept me awake a long time that night.

Harold Edelman was all smiles Monday morning.

"Here it is, Ms. McClatchey," he said, contract in hand. "All we need is your signature."

We took care of the business necessities back at the kitchen table. After I wrote out a check for one third of the job cost as an advance, he stood up, a satisfied smile on his face.

"So, you think you might be able to start Wednesday morning?"

"Or even sooner!" He seemed about to burst with good humor. "Tell you what, you might want to go ahead and clear everything out of here today. If I can manage, I'll get a crew in here tomorrow afternoon to start taking out these cabinets."

He left a few minutes later with a key to my house, promising I'd hear from him very soon. I was left in his cheerful wake, wondering how I'd ever have the kitchen ready by tomorrow and what it was going to be like having workmen in and out of my house at will? This, I realized, was the time to panic.

Pandora was still dressed like a latter-day flower child, but she arrived right on time that morning. She surprised me by approaching her work in a businesslike manner, listening attentively as I gave her a quick overview of the operation and asking the right questions. She even made a few notes in a little notebook she carried in her jeans pocket. I set her up on the computer for her first task and, within fifteen minutes, she was entering information into the inventory file like she'd been doing it for years.

Delia McCullough called while I was packing an order for shipment.

"Before you say anything, Dixie, I want you to know I've had a very serious talk with Teddy. He told me what he said to you last night and I'm so sorry. He wasn't raised to behave like that. But he won't be bothering you anymore. You have my assurance of that."

"That's fine, but it's not surprising he was upset, Mrs. McCullough. Somehow he got the idea I'm a private investigator." I didn't accuse her of telling him that, but the implication was right there. "I'm not a private investigator and I have no intention of acting like one."

She expelled an impatient breath. "I never told Teddy that you were. He's always been bad to jump to conclusions. I just explained that you were investigating Glynnis's death.

I tried again. "It's not an investigation. I've read the files, like I said I would, but that's all. I don't think there's anything there to account for what happened to Glynnis. I'll still do what I can just to be able to reassure you and myself that none of those people had anything to do with the murder – I've already started doing that – but you should know that I still believe the most logical explanation is that Glynnis was killed during a robbery."

"Nonsense. Robberies don't happen in downtown Macon. Maybe

out on Riverside Drive or on Gray Highway, but not on Cherry Street."

There was more I wanted to say, but a customer came in and approached the counter where I sat. I told Delia I'd get back to her.

At eleven-thirty, I walked up Cherry Street to Bert's for sandwiches. I got a chicken salad croissant. Predictably, Pandora had asked for the vegetarian special. Ten minutes later I was on my way back up the street, carrying our lunches in a plastic bag.

There was one customer in the store when I returned – Harriett Black. But instead of poring over the genealogy section, she was seated at the signing table. Pandora was perched in the chair across from her and, on the table between them, a number of brightly colored cards were laid out in a cross-like pattern. She glanced over her shoulder at me and then back at the table.

"You're covered with the three of pentacles, right here, see?" Pandora was saying. "That means you're in the early stages of a rewarding work situation."

Harriett nodded as if that actually made some kind of sense.

I couldn't believe the girl was doing a tarot reading in my shop after I'd made it clear I didn't want to have anything to do with such nonsense. But I couldn't say anything with Harriett there. I stood at the front counter and fumed as Pandora went on and on about death reversed and resistance to change and the fool representing Harriett's environment.

"And this, the three of wands, this is your outcome card. Reversed this way, it indicates overconfidence. You shouldn't try and do things all by yourself. Attaining your goal may be impossible unless you swallow your pride and accept help from other people."

Pandora stopped speaking and Harriett sat looking at the cards for a minute. Then she said, "Well, that was certainly interesting, my dear, and I can see how it might very well apply to me at this time in my life. Thank you very much. Now what do I owe you?"

"Oh, no," Pandora said with a hard shake of her head, "I couldn't take money for a reading. I just hope it was some help to you."

She gathered up the cards and wrapped the deck in a brightly colored silk cloth while Harriett got to her feet and noticed my presence for the first time.

"Why, hello, Dixie. How are you? I guess you know you have a treasure in this young lady. It's all so very interesting."

"Ummmm." I hoped I didn't sound as furious as I was.

Harriett did visit the genealogy section then. She picked up the book on immigrants to Pennsylvania – the same one she'd examined and discarded last week. This time she brought it with her to the counter and handed over the money.

When she'd left with her purchase and we were alone in the store, I was finally free to tell Pandora what I thought about the tarot readings. "I'm not running a fortune telling parlor here. What you do on your own time is up to you, but I won't have you doing that here during business hours. I'm very disappointed in you, Pandora. The minute I left you alone, you did something you know I disapprove of."

She bit her lip and, for a minute, I thought she might cry.

"I'm sorry, Dixie. Really. I was just doing a quick reading for myself – I'm kinda worried about my mother. See, she's got to have some tests and . . ." She must have noticed my lips pressed together in impatience. "Anyway, that's what I was doing when the lady came in and she saw the cards and wanted me to do a reading for her. And I got a good vibe from her. You know, a real sincere feeling. I . . . I didn't want to hurt her by saying no. But I won't do it again. I promise."

"Okay," I relented. "I just want you to know how I feel about it. Now come get your lunch. You need to eat before you go to class."

Pandora left to pursue higher education shortly after noon and I phoned Deannie. There was a good chance she'd be home – Chimera was closed on Sundays and Mondays, like many Macon restaurants.

"Did you get some rest?"

"Yes, Mother." She laughed. "You could say that. I slept almost twelve hours!"

"Good. That's just what you needed."

She apologized for the previous night. "I can't believe I lost control like that. You must think I'm insane."

"I think you are just fine," I told her. "And I want you come to dinner tonight."

"I'm eating, I swear. Just finished lunch. You don't have to keep feeding me."

"It's not that. I'd like the company." And I wouldn't mind the opportunity to pick her brain a little about Glynnis's files.

She agreed and we settled on eight o'clock. That gave me time enough to get home and make a big batch of my mother's potato soup.

I heard from Steve Ballard late that afternoon.

"Let's go out for a meal," he suggested. "We'll even get a doggy bag – or should it be kitty bag – for the cat."

I couldn't help smiling. "I'd love to, but I've already made plans to have dinner with a friend. You know, girl talk."

I hated to sound so coy and girly, but I wanted him to understand that the friend was female. What was wrong with me? I was acting like a high school girl with her first boyfriend.

"Enjoy your girl talk. Maybe we can get together later in the week."

"I'm sure we can. And you can tell me all about your trip to North Carolina."

"That won't take long," he said dryly. "But I'm sure we can find something else to talk about."

"Then it's a date."

CHAPTER NINE

My mother's potato soup recipe is simple – potatoes, onions, butter, cream, salt and pepper – but with a salad and crusty French bread, it makes a rich, satisfying meal. I made a big pot so there would be some left over to take to Mr. Pryby in the morning. When Deannie arrived, she sniffed the air in the kitchen appreciatively.

"No wine?" I asked, noticing her empty hands. She doesn't share my fondness for beer and usually brings her own wine when she comes for dinner.

She gave me a sheepish grin. "I'll stick with water tonight. I've had enough alcohol for a while."

I smiled. "How bad did you feel this morning?

"Oh, bad. Really bad. 'Set-me-adrift-on-an-ice-floe-and-just-let-me-die' bad."

I laughed with her. That was the only reference either of us made to the night before. She met Hot Shot and pronounced him a fine cat. He sat on the floor near the stove, content to watch as we ate. In the cat world, potato soup evidently didn't rate very high on the begging scale. After the meal, I cleared the table and set Glynnis's files where our plates had been. Deannie watched with a puzzled frown.

"I need some help with this stuff."

Her frown deepened. "What is that? Are those her files? The ones you told me about?"

"Yes and I need some help." I put the same lilt in my voice that you'd use trying to interest a child in an educational exercise. "Now, what I want you to do is look for something I missed. I don't see anything here worth killing Glynnis over. I know some of these people, but not all of them. You might know those that I don't. If you could tell me something about them – what they're like, their temperaments, what they care about – maybe it will help me understand them."

"Why me?" she asked with an edge of suspicion in her voice.

"You're the one person I know I can trust with this stuff."

"Because I'm one of the bitch's victims?"

I looked her in the eyes. "Because you're my friend. Because I trust you and I know that you aren't going to share anything you see here with anyone else."

She looked at the names on the tabs. If she was surprised by any of them, she didn't show it. "Where's mine?"

"I burnt it in the dining room fireplace last night."

She got up, took her glass to the sink, then turned back to me. "I don't think I like this, Dixie. You're asking me to help you find the person who killed Glynnis McCullough. Why should I do that? I don't want him to be caught. Why punish someone for a public service?"

"It's not like that," I tried to explain. "I can't really believe any of these people were involved in her death. If I can eliminate them completely – satisfy myself that they didn't have anything to do with the killing – then I won't have to give any of these files to the police."

"Why not just get rid of 'em now? You already said you don't think these people were involved. We can burn all their files in the fireplace. If we start now, we'll be done by ten."

But it wasn't that simple. "I want to, believe me, I do. But if one of these," I tapped the stack of folders, "turned out to be evidence of a crime and I withheld it – or worse, destroyed it – I don't think I could stand the guilt."

She still wasn't convinced. "Maybe that's important to you – you've got some cop code of honor or something – but not to me."

In the end she gave in, probably not because I convinced her I was right, but for the sake of our friendship. She didn't want to read the dirt Glynnis had dug up, but, bless her heart, she did it. She read them all. When she looked through the folder with my name on it, her eyes filled with sympathy.

"Oh, Dixie, it must have hurt you, seeing this."

"It did," I admitted. "But there was nothing there that I'd have paid blackmail to keep secret."

She grinned, trying to lighten the mood. "It's a good thing. Otherwise you might have been giving Glynnis free books."

We worked steadily, comparing our impressions of the people involved and trying to decide how important the information in the folders might be to them. Nothing new turned up and Deannie didn't provide any startling insights. After two hours, all we had to show for our time and effort were stiff necks and, at least in my case, the beginnings of a headache.

"You're right," Deannie declared as she laid the last folder on the stack. "There's nothing. Even if Reg Anderson has been taking the odd book here and there, and Marian Saxby has skeletons in her family closet, I haven't seen anything worth killing to keep secret."

She left at ten, reminding me that I now owed her big time.

It had been a long day, but my evening's work was just beginning. I stood in the kitchen for a minute, nearly overwhelmed by the task ahead. Hot Shot twined around my legs. He knew it was getting close to bedtime.

"Sorry, buddy, not yet."

He curled up on the quilt near the stove and watched me until he fell asleep – about a minute and a half. It took just under three hours to remove everything from the kitchen cabinets and pile it in the dining room. I stacked things so high on the sideboard that they nearly obscured the Ginger Concepcion still life I'd bought for myself at Christmas.

I couldn't believe that I owned so much stuff – more than half of which I hadn't even seen since I moved it to Macon. There were also a lot of things my grandmother had left behind – bowls, cooking utensils, even an old Mixmaster that might still work. A major sorting and throwing away was in order, but that would have to wait until another day.

I suppose Hot Shot joined me in bed some time that night, but I couldn't say for sure. I don't even remember turning over. When the alarm sounded at eight, I couldn't believe it was already time to get up.

After a quick run and breakfast, I took a plastic container of soup next door to Mr. Pryby. Before leaving the house for the day, I carried Hot Shot's food, water, and litter box up the stairs to my room. Then I went back for the cat. I closed him in my bedroom and taped a note on the door. 'CAT INSIDE. DO NOT OPEN.' I hoped that would keep him safe if the contractor did show up. He wasn't happy with the situation. I could still hear his howls of protest as I left by the kitchen door.

The Friends of the Library volunteers met that week as usual, but we were a smaller and more subdued group. Cassie had stayed home with a headache and, of course, Glynnis wasn't there.

"I know that this is a sad time," Marian said once we were all gathered in the work room, "but Glynnis would have wanted us to go on with our work."

I had the uncharitable thought that Glynnis would have preferred we shut the project down. She'd never wanted anyone to have anything that she didn't have. But I kept those thoughts to myself.

Marian got right down to business, assigning us each to specific tasks. Carlton and I would do the original sorting, separating the newly donated books into general categories. Then those stacks would go to the others for pricing. Reg's responsibility was, predictably, popular fiction and Alexandra was given all the cookbooks. Carlton took the few children's books that came in and Glynnis had usually been given the self-help books. I'd always wondered if that was Marian's version of irony. Today all the books in that category were stacked in a corner without comment.

I plopped down on the floor beside the box Carlton had just carried in and used my pocketknife to slice the tape across the top. As always, I experienced a tiny flutter of excitement when I folded back the flaps. You never knew what you might find in a box of donated books. But this one held no surprises. Most of these were paperbacks and more than half were romance novels with garish covers and titles in which the words 'wild,' 'desire,' and 'passion' were prominently featured. They weren't my cup of tea, but they were some of our most popular items and boasted a diverse readership. Even our own sensible Marian Saxby devoured them like candy bars when she was taking a break from more learned works. I knew from experience how quickly they'd go at the next sale. Little thought was required in valuing this batch. I stuck fifty-cent stickers on most of them and moved rapidly through the box.

We worked mostly in silence, the usual chatter replaced by somber expressions and a seemingly unanimous agreement to avoid talking about the murder. Alexandra Michaels was surrounded by the cookbooks she loved. It looked as if we'd gotten in a whole box of them. I tried not to think about her affair with the tennis pro and instead made myself concentrate on the good things I knew about her.

Alex was easily the most athletic of all the volunteers. She ran, she swam, and she played tennis several days a week – A level, she'd told me. I was ignorant of the finer points of the sport, but gathered that meant she was pretty accomplished. She was also an exceptional cook, famous for her dinner parties, and a stunning woman. In her early forties, tanned, blond, and trim, she was the only woman I knew who could look chic anywhere at any time, even in this morning's outfit – a shapeless denim dress over a plain white tee shirt.

The wife of a successful doctor, she had two perfect children and a designer house. It would have been easy to envy her to the point of dislike if she hadn't been so genuinely nice. She never refused to pitch in for a good cause and always did it with grace and enthusiasm. In addition to the Friends, she was a big supporter of the symphony and regularly took part in building projects with Habitat for Humanity.

I wondered if my companions knew about the information Glynnis had gathered about them. They were quieter than usual that morning and Reg was jumpy and distracted. Even when I asked about his upcoming trip to Austria, he only gave one-word answers.

I think we were all relieved when Marian dismissed us an hour early. I couldn't help watching Reg as we left the library. Regardless of what he might have done in the past, he certainly didn't steal any books that morning.

The Cherry Blossom Festival was now in full swing. Musical performances and concerts were held every day in Third Street Park. Thousands of visitors filled the streets, waiting in lines at the museums and the historic houses. Horse-drawn carriages and little green trolleys carried tourists through the historic district, free cherry ice cream was served on downtown streets during the lunch hour, and every morning the Krystal out on Vineville Avenue served pink grits with their breakfast meals. With all the extra people in town, I was busy from the moment I unlocked the door.

Steve Ballard and Pandora arrived within seconds of each other just before noon. I was taking money from a pleasant couple who'd told me they were in town from Tennessee.

"Hey, Lieutenant," Pandora greeted him with a big smile.

"How you doing, hon?"

You'd have thought they were cousins.

"Just great! I got the job here after all!"

"Well, congratulations. You making any progress with that statistics course?"

She made a disgusted sound deep in her throat. "I still hate every minute of it."

I gave the couple their change and wished them a good morning. Pandora went to the back of the store to help a woman locate a book and I offered Steve a cup of coffee.

"Looks like you're busy."

I laughed. "Yeah, isn't it great? I wish the Cherry Blossom Festival lasted a month." I handed him the cup. "So how was North Carolina?"

A long sigh preceded his answer. "It was a long drive just to spend two hours with my daughter, but I guess it was worth it."

"The overnight visit didn't work out?"

"No. They had plans."

"Well, it's good to see you back," I told him. And it was. My heart rate had been elevated since he walked into the shop. "Are y'all making any headway with the investigation?"

He shook his head. "Not much. We've looked at Glynnis six ways from Sunday, but there doesn't seem to be anything in her personal life worth following up on. I still believe that it was a robbery gone bad. Strangulation is kind of strange for a crime like this, but there isn't any other explanation."

My conscience gave me a guilty poke. "You're probably right." What was I doing withholding those files?

He shrugged. "We'll get him sooner or later. You know how it goes. Most of these guys just aren't that smart. You can bet he's already told at least a few people what happened. When one of his buddies gets popped for something, he'll give up our killer in a heartbeat, just to get out of his own jam."

He was right about that, I knew. There's no code of honor among criminals. I once cleared a string of twenty-six business burglaries because the thief's brother-in-law was trying to bargain his way out of a DUI.

"Have you determined a time of death?" I asked. Might as well find out what I could.

"Yeah. Well, a block of time anyway." He finished his coffee and put the cup on the counter. "We know it happened sometime after she left her hairdresser about five and the time you found her."

I nodded, silently congratulating myself on getting that information. Now I had a starting place. Not only that, I could eliminate another person. Edward Swanson had been well occupied by his Parade Banquet during the time of Glynnis's murder. Even though I never really considered him a suspect, it was nice to know I could burn his file, too.

"So how's the kitten doing?"

"Oh, he's fine. He seems to get into something every few minutes, but we're getting along okay."

I glanced at his hands and suddenly remembered them on my body. I felt heat rise in my chest and into my face.

"Does he need more catnip?"

"What? Oh no, the supply's holding up pretty well."

I knew he was angling for an invitation and there was nothing I'd rather do than welcome this man back into my house and my bed, but I didn't rise to the bait. Even now I could remember the feel of him against me and his lips on mine – but I couldn't let myself dwell on that. The knowledge of those files was like a huge stone hanging over my head. I felt so guilty about withholding them that I could hardly stand to be in the same room with him. I had to finish up with them soon – so that I could get back to concentrating on Steve Ballard and what just might become an important relationship.

"Maybe you can come over later in the week and see him for yourself," I said, trying not to discouraging him, but still keeping my distance until I could get out of this mess with the files. "He's really doing great – even if I do have him locked up this week."

I told him about the renovation and the security arrangements I'd had to make for the cat. He was still smiling when he left.

"You guys would make a great match," Pandora said after he'd gone. "You're really compatible. He's an old soul. The t— " She snapped her mouth shut before any reference to tarot cards, or any other variety of divination, could slip out. She turned around and continued dusting the shelves. I switched on some music.

"Hey!" Pandora commented. "Little Richard. We play his stuff all the time in the dorm. He is so good."

I smiled to learn that one of Macon's favorite sons was known by the current college set. Richard Penniman had grown up in this town and come to musical prominence here. His music always made me feel good and today I was especially in need of a boost in spirit.

The best way I knew to assuage my guilt about keeping the files from Ballard was to get on with the task of eliminating the people in them. But first I needed to call Delia McCullough. I'd been so frustrated when I talked with her earlier in the day that I'd forgotten to ask her an important question.

She was way ahead of me. "Her computer? No, the police didn't take it. I told you, they never even went in her office."

"But they might come back and search again."

She snorted. It was very ladylike, but it was definitely a snort. "Well, it won't do them any good if they do. I had my nephew come pick up that computer the day you were here. He took it over to my sister's house. Since I have my own investigator working on the case, I sure don't want any of Glynnis's research to fall into the hands of that Kaminsky person."

I sighed and dropped my head toward my chest. What had I gotten myself into? In spite of everything I'd said, Delia was still thinking of me as her very own investigator. Trying to make her see reason was more than I could face right then. I told her I'd call if I had any news and turned my attention to my own computer.

Working online during business hours wasn't a problem since I could stop any time customers needed attention.

Reg Anderson's transgressions were the most serious ones in Glynnis's files, so I started with him. The information she'd collected suggested that he'd been selling books on the Internet. And she'd discovered the name he used in his online dealings. It was RegRider. To the heartening strains of "Good Golly, Miss Molly," I began my search.

I was no stranger to eBay and some of the other auction sites, but this was the first time I'd used them for investigative purposes. It turned out to be quite simple. I began with the Find Members section and there he was: RegRider. He'd been a member of that web site since November of 1999.

Checking to see what items he had available for sale, I was rewarded with a lengthy list of books. Among others, I saw a Thomas Harris first edition of *Red Dragon* and an early Patricia Cornwell. And, as I'd suspected based on the note in Glynnis's purse, there was the 1984 Naval Institute Press first edition of *The Hunt for Red October*.

I took my time looking over his offerings, but couldn't specifically remember seeing any of the titles among our donations. And there were three or four books there that I was positive had never gone through our sorting and sale procedure. They were valuable enough that I'd have remembered them. Of course, Reg could have taken them early in the sorting process before anyone noticed them. There would be no way to prove that.

For a while I wasn't sure Glynnis had made much of a case against Reg Anderson. Then I saw the last book on his list – a 1660 copy of *The Anatomy of Melancholy* by Robert Burton – and I was convinced my friend Reg had, indeed, been stealing from the Friends. The presence of that book also cleared up a strange little incident that had happened back in January.

Cassie Waycaster had caused quite a stir at one of our work sessions.

"There's a book missing!" she declared, standing in the big room where we stored those books that had already been sorted and priced. "It was here last week, but I can't find it now."

"What book are you talking about?" Marian had asked her.

Cassie gave an exasperated huff. "I can't remember the title exactly. It was an old medical book, I think. Maybe about depression or something? Anyway, it was by Richard Burton. You know, the actor? I didn't look at it too close, I mean, we were real busy last week. I just priced it at five dollars and stuck it in with the science stuff. But I got to thinking about it later. The cover might have been leather. And if it was, it would make it more valuable, wouldn't it? Anyway, I wanted to find it this morning and ask y'all if you thought I priced it too low. But now it's not here."

We all tried to help her – making a search of the storage area. But we weren't very effective since we had no idea what we were looking for. At any rate, the book was never found. Now I believed I knew what it was and where it was. Reg must have seen her with it the day she priced it.

How hard must it have been for him to hide his excitement when he realized what she had. He must have grabbed it as soon as he had the opportunity. It would have been a temptation for any collector. Even without the opportunity to examine it, I'd put a conservative value on the book at $900 to $1,500. At auction it might go for considerably more.

If the information Glynnis put together on Reg was to be believed, he'd made a tidy little sum selling books over the last four years. And she'd compiled a corresponding list of expenditures – trips he'd taken, a new Miata sports car and a boat he kept in a marina over on Lake Oconee.

Although his file, coupled with the information I found on the web, suggested illegal activity, I didn't believe it was enough to provoke murder. The Reg I was sure I knew wouldn't have harmed Glynnis or anyone else. Still I was going to have to talk with him.

I checked my Rolodex and found his number. No answer. But my investigative juices were running high now. I flipped through the cards and dialed again. If I couldn't talk to one, I'd try another. Alexandra Michaels sounded puzzled when I said I wanted to see her, but she invited me to stop by her house late that afternoon.

Edward says people come to the Cherry Blossom Festival with money they are prepared to spend. And that day a good number of them were ready to spend it in Chapter and Verse. Remembering Edward's words made me realize I hadn't seen him in a couple of days. I called his shop, but got no answer. When I poked my head out the front door, I saw the Closed sign displayed in his window. I knew he'd be back soon. He wouldn't dream of missing the business brought in by the Festival.

I was busy with another customer around one when I noticed a tiny woman with close-cropped black hair come in and approach Pandora at the front counter. They exchanged a few words, then a few more. Finally Pandora's voice rose with emphasis.

"I told you I can't do that here. I'm sorry."

"But Harriett Black said you did. She said you helped her make up her mind about a promotion. It was very important. Now I've got a question, too."

Pandora smiled placatingly. "Look, I'm really sorry. I just can't do readings in the shop anymore. If you'd like to meet somewhere later, I'd be glad to – "

"Why can't you do it now?" The woman's voice grew shrill. "You did it for Harriett right here. Why not me?"

The situation was becoming strained. With a resigned sigh, I intervened.

"Go ahead, Pandora. It's okay."

The girl raised her eyebrows and I nodded confirmation. Five minutes later, the cards were again spread on the signing table and the little woman was listening with rapt attention as Pandora spouted her drivel. Several people came in and out while this was going on, but no one paid the two much attention. I concentrated on the computer and tried to ignore the whole thing. When the woman left twenty minutes later, she was smiling and had bought a $65 book about antique furniture.

"I'm so sorry about that," Pandora told me. She hung her head like a child waiting to be scolded. "She had a really angry aura."

"It's okay. There wasn't much else we could do. I was afraid she'd throw a hissy fit if you turned her down again. But let's make that the last time. Okay?"

She smiled. "Okay. I promise."

An estate sale was scheduled for that afternoon in Milledgeville. Although I'd had several weeks' notice and the flyer promised a diverse selection of books, I had decided to skip it. Closing the store again, especially during the Cherry Blossom Festival, was not a smart thing to do. But watching Pandora charm an elderly man as she guided him through the reference section until he found a thesaurus that pleased him, I reconsidered. She'd been right on top of things all day long, assisting customers and ringing up sales like she'd done it for years.

"Do you have any classes this afternoon?" I finally asked.

"No, nothing till eight in the morning."

"Would you be able to work a few extra hours today? Say till four or four-thirty?"

"Sure." Her face lit up. "Anything you need, Dixie."

Highway 129 runs east from Macon to the small town of Gray. There you pick up Highway 22 for the twenty-mile drive into Milledgeville. As soon as I'd left the congestion of Macon behind me, I could feel myself beginning to relax. The drive was just what I needed. The countryside rolled out, fresh and green, on either side of the road. As I sped on past fields, farms, and the occasional country church, I could almost forget the murder and my own dilemma. The air was clean and the sky was remarkably blue.

That deep blue sky was one of the things that had most impressed me about middle Georgia. In Atlanta, a clear, dark blue sky was a rarity reserved for only a few days each October. But down here away from the smog it was so common that no one but I seemed to find it noteworthy.

The Washburn house was two miles down a narrow two-lane road, just south of Milledgeville. Five or six cars were parked in front of it. The house dated from the early 1800s. Unlike the antebellum Southern plantations popularized in books and films, there were no columns here. The sharply pitched roof of the single-story house dipped low over a wide front porch. It was a basic sort of design, with six square rooms, three on either side of a central hall. There had been an addition on the back some time in the twentieth century, but it began as, and still was, a simple house. The people who'd cleared and worked this land and built this house had neither the time nor the inclination for a ballroom or a sweeping verandah.

Pieces of heavy furniture and boxes of clothing and linens were set out under oak trees that had been growing in the same soil since before the Civil War. Several outbuildings were filled with tools and yard maintenance equipment. Everything was tagged with a price. Inside the house more items were displayed for sale. Pots and pans, stuffed animals, appliances, computers, bicycles – a lifetime of possessions laid out for strangers to examine. I didn't know who had lived there and didn't want to. That story, coupled with the fact that there was no one left to love and care for all these things, was likely to be a sad one.

The books were in the front room and I spent a pleasant hour going through what was there. At the end of that time, I located the sale manager and made an acceptable offer. By three-forty-five my purchases were packed in boxes and loaded in the back of the Blazer, and I was on my way back to Macon. I walked in the back door at Chapter and Verse at four-twenty-five.

It looked as it had when I left. Little Richard sang at a sedate volume and there was no indication that anything unusual had taken place during my absence. Pandora happily recounted the details of every sale she'd made.

"And I didn't do a single tarot reading, Dixie. I swear I didn't."

I wondered if I'd been too harsh with her. "Look, Pandora," I said gently, "I don't have anything against your doing tarot readings. It's just that our customers are of all ages and from all walks of life. If word gets out that fortune telling is going on at Chapter and Verse, some of those people will never set foot in the store again."

"Hey, I completely understand," she told me. "And I really won't do it anymore here. It's just that, ever since I was a little girl, I've had this . . . ability. I know things. My mother and grandmother have the sight, too. And the cards seem to help me clarify..." She caught herself before launching into some kind of metaphysical explanation and neatly changed the subject. "Listen, do you know anything about statistics? I'm having the worst time getting a handle on this course."

I realized I'd probably been more worried about the tarot ban than she had. And I had to confess to her that the one statistics course I was unfortunate enough to take had left me totally mystified. "If you want help there, you're asking the wrong person."

She grinned and slipped her arms into the straps of her backpack. "Oh, well, it was worth a try. See you tomorrow."

Edward's tan Volvo was parked behind his store, but there was no answer when I phoned and his Closed sign was still posted out front. I felt a faint stirring of uneasiness. I locked my own shop, slipped out the back and knocked on his door. No answer. But it wasn't locked so I went on in. I made my way through the darkened workroom and peeked into the front of the shop. Edward stood at the back counter, working on a frame.

"What's going on with you?" I demanded, coming out into the

shop. "What's wrong? Why won't you answer your phone? If I weren't so secure, I'd think you were trying to avoid me."

Then he lifted his face and I gasped. An ugly bruise, tinted shades of red and purple, covered most of his left cheek. His left eye was discolored and swollen nearly shut.

"Oh, my God. Edward, what happened?" I rushed to him, hand out, but he stepped back to evade my touch.

"I'm okay," he said, sounding annoyed at my concern. "Just a little mishap." He returned to the matte in front of him, deftly cutting a square from the center.

"A little mishap? Your face looks like you were in a fight." I drew in a quick breath. "Was it George?"

He kept his eyes on the counter.

"It was, wasn't it? George did this to you, didn't he?" He still wouldn't look at me. "Goddamn it, Edward, talk to me! What happened?"

When he finally met my gaze, the one eye I could see was wet with tears. "Yes," he said fiercely. "It was George. He gets crazy when he drinks. He'd had a really bad week. He lost two clients. I knew that I shouldn't have served two bottles of wine with dinner, but I was so excited about the parade being over. I should have known better – "

"Don't you dare try to take any of the blame for this! Where is he? Have you called the police? That son of a bitch is going to jail."

He shook his head wearily. "He's gone. He left yesterday morning. I doubt if he'll be back, especially not after taking the money."

"What money?"

He covered his face briefly with his hands, then turned to me with an expression of pure despair. "The money I collected for the auction. I showed it to him earlier in the day. I was so proud of myself." His voice broke and he cleared his throat before continuing. "There was nearly five thousand dollars."

"And he took it? He stole the money?"

Edward swallowed as if it were painful to do so. "He . . . after all this happened," he indicated his ruined face with a wave of his hand, "he was still furious! He told me that I was the reason he was losing clients. He said that he couldn't concentrate with me living down here, that if I'd just move up there to Atlanta . . ." I waited as he took a couple of calming breaths. "He broke some of my things before he left and then went to the desk and took the money. He said I owed it to him for the aggravation."

Edward tried a smile, but it was a failure. "At least he only took the cash. He left the checks."

"How much?"

"Right at twenty-four hundred dollars."

"You did call the police, didn't you?"

"Oh, sure," he said sarcastically. "What a good idea. Why didn't I think of that? That way I can be humiliated all over again when some Neanderthal cop falls on the floor laughing at the fag who got beat up by his boyfriend."

"That wouldn't happen, Edward. They'd get a warrant for him and he'd go to jail – where he belongs. Besides, you've got to get that money back."

"No, no. I can't go through all that. I'll just make up the loss myself."

"That's insane. The man is a criminal and we have to do something."

He shook his head. "I just want to forget this ever happened."

"Then what about a doctor?"

"No! I'm okay, Dixie, just leave me alone. That's all I want. Just leave me alone." He didn't sound angry, just terribly tired.

I tried to think of something he would let me do for him, but couldn't. As much as I hated leaving him, it was obviously what he wanted. After a couple of minutes standing awkwardly there beside him, I gave up.

"Call me if you need me," I said at the door. He didn't answer.

Alexandra Michaels lived in a subdivision of oversized brick houses bordering a sprawling golf course. Her home would have been a natural for any of the glossy decorating magazines on the newsstands.

Alex, in a spotless white tennis outfit, greeted me at the front door with the news that her husband and daughter were out.

"I've only been home a few minutes myself." A wave of her hand explained how she was dressed. "Tennis at the club. The match went longer than I expected."

She led me down a hall past several exquisite Sterling Everett watercolors. A vase full of bright, yellow tulips graced a narrow mahogany table. I got quick glimpses of perfectly decorated rooms through open doors. I didn't spot a single thing out of place. The kitchen was so filled with stainless steel that it put me in mind of a high-tech operating room, but the breakfast nook where we settled was cozy enough. As I sat down, she offered me a martini.

"I'm having one myself," she said, gesturing with a short tumbler full of ice and clear liquid. "I'd never had a martini until a few months ago. What a discovery!" Her silvery laugh rang out. "Now I just love them – especially on the rocks."

"Thanks, but I'm driving."

"What about tea? Or a soft drink?"

"No, nothing, thanks."

She settled in a chair across the glass table from me. "So, what did you want to see me about?"

I hated this. It was nothing like it had been when I was a police officer. This woman wasn't a witness or a suspect. She was a friend. And I found myself in a very uncomfortable situation. What was the best way to start? Nothing seemed right. Finally I just took a deep breath and blurted out what I knew.

"Glynnis McCullough did what she called research on the people she knew. She kept files and even took pictures sometimes." I pulled a manila folder from my canvas carryall. "This one is yours."

CHAPTER TEN

I watched as her tanned face went ashy gray. I'd never seen anyone go that pale that fast.

"She kept files?" It was barely a whisper.

I handed over her folder without another word. She took her time, examining every item Glynnis had collected about her. When she came to the photographs of herself and the tennis pro in a passionate embrace at his apartment door, she drew a quick breath, but she didn't utter a word.

Finally she closed the folder and raised her eyes to mine. Her face was still pale, but anger now hardened her expression. There were lines on either side of her mouth and at the corners of her eyes that hadn't been there before.

"Why are showing me this?"

This was the moment I'd been dreading all day. I wished it was over and I was back home.

"Glynnis's mother gave me the all the files she made. She's got some wild idea that Glynnis was killed because of something in one of them." I sighed. Talking to someone who just glares at you is not easy. "Look, I think Glynnis was killed in a robbery and these files didn't have anything to do with it. But that's not what Delia believes. She wants me to look into the...the contents and see if there's any evidence that would point to Glynnis's killer. She didn't want all this to go to the police; she was afraid innocent people might get hurt."

She continued to glare and I hurried on. "I only agreed to this because most of what's here doesn't need to be made public. But I can't just throw it all away until I know for sure that these people weren't involved in her death. Once that's done, I'll get rid of everything. No one will ever know the files existed."

My explanation didn't go very far in defusing her anger. "Why you? Who the hell are you? Nancy Drew?"

I tried again. "Well, I'm better than the police at this point, Alex. Some of the stuff in those folders could do real damage if it came out."

"You could say that, I guess," she said dryly. "So, Dixie, what do you want to know? All the juicy details about me and Denny?"

"No," I said hurriedly. "Nothing like that."

"I want you to know that I don't appreciate you bringing this," she shoved the folder across the table to me, "into my home."

I bit my tongue. Nothing would be gained by pointing out that it was her own behavior that had made the file possible in the first place. We both already knew that.

I tried again to smooth the waters. "I want to get this over with, probably as much as you do. It may not be any comfort, but you're not alone. Glynnis researched a lot of us, me included. And it looks like she was using the information she unearthed to get favors from people."

She gave me a blank look over the rim of her glass. "What kind of favors would that be?"

"I don't know. Different things. Didn't she ever ask you for anything?"

"You mean like money or something? No, never." She gave her watch a meaningful glance, but I wasn't going to be rushed. Now that I was here, I wanted to finish.

"She never asked you for anything?"

She sighed. "Well, back some time . . . maybe February? . . . she started hinting around that she'd like me to take her to the club. I never really acknowledged her – thought if I ignored it, she'd get the idea. But it didn't work. One day not too long ago she came right out and suggested we have lunch there." She turned up her glass and drained it.

"Did you?"

"Of course not." Her mouth narrowed with distaste. "It's not like we were friends or anything. I wasn't about to spend any of my social time with someone as unpleasant as Glynnis McCullough. And after some of the things she said to me after I told her no, I was right to refuse."

I thought that might explain the way Glynnis needled Alexandra that last day, making snide comments about her tennis game. Alex hadn't come across with what she wanted – namely entree to the country club – and she responded by flexing her blackmailing muscles. Had she lived, I was sure Glynnis would have approached Alex again, armed this time with proof of the affair and a more pointed demand. Would Alex have dared to refuse her then?

"Did she ever show you the stuff in the file?" I asked, remembering Deannie's account of her session with Glynnis.

"No! I had no idea she . . . She never showed me a thing, Dixie. I didn't know anything about her disgusting snooping until right now." She narrowed her eyes. "Is it a hobby you might take up as well?"

My cheeks were burning now with anger. I shouldn't have been surprised that the idea crossed her mind, but I was. She was scared and angry, I knew, but I this was no picnic for me either. "It's not like that. I told you why I was here."

"Ummmm." She was unconvinced. She stood up in one quick motion. "So now what? Do you give the files to the police or are you going to keep them for your own amusement?"

My head was beginning to ache. "No, Alex. Once I'm satisfied you had nothing to do with the murder, I'll destroy this thing. No one else will even know it existed."

"So you get to be the judge as well as the detective?" At the kitchen counter, she dumped ice, gin, and vermouth into her glass with an efficiency of motion that testified to much practice. "And how are you going to do that? Satisfy yourself, I mean."

"Well, we could start with where you were last Tuesday. I know you were at the Friends' work session in the morning. Then what?"

She stirred the mixture with a spoon and took a healthy sip. "I was in Snellville – on the other side of Atlanta. My tennis team had a match up there at four. A country club called Summit Chase. We played the match, stayed long enough for a bite to eat and then came home. I dropped the others off – Rose Ackley was the last – and I was back here by nine o'clock. Would you like the names of all the people on the team?"

I shook my head and she went on.

"I didn't go out again after that. Peter wasn't here, so he can't provide me with an alibi, if that's what you want. He was in Chicago for one of his never-ending conferences." She looked to me for a reaction, but didn't get one. "But Regina was home, I think. She's fifteen, you know, and doesn't pay much attention to anyone but herself and her friends these days, but I'm pretty sure it was Tuesday evening that she announced she was going to get a tattoo. We had quite a discussion about that. I expect she'll remember." She took another sizable gulp of martini. "Would you like to interrogate her, too?"

"No, I don't think it's necessary to talk to Regina."

Regina might or might not remember. No matter what Alex believed, I really didn't want to do anything to embarrass her. And teenagers were notoriously unreliable witnesses anyway, but it probably wouldn't matter. If she were telling the truth, Alex's whereabouts were accounted for during the critical time. Besides, I thought I had a way to verify her story without having to approach her family.

Clouds had moved in to obscure the sunset when I left my still angry, probably former friend for the drive home. The spring warmth still softened the air, but the humidity had been building all day and fog was now collecting in the low areas along the road.

My thoughts kept returning to Edward and his poor, battered face. George Bennett was no stranger to violence. Last week Edward had had bruises on his arm where George had grabbed him and at Christmas he'd broken a bone in Edward's hand during another drunken rage.

This time George had added theft to assault and the thought that he might get away with what he'd done, leaving Edward to repay the missing money, infuriated me. Even without involving the police, there had to be some way to get that money back.

There was more than money at stake here. What if he came back to Macon? Would Edward see him? Would he take him back? I'd worked my share of domestic abuse cases in my other life and I knew just how persuasive a repentant lover could be. I also knew that abuse had a tendency to escalate. It wasn't beyond the realm of possibility that, if the relationship was resumed, Edward could be seriously hurt or even killed.

There was no sign that Edelman's crew had even set foot on my property that day. I wasn't surprised. I hadn't really believed the work would start as soon as he'd said. If past history with contractors was any indication, dates and schedules were only suggestions in that profession. They probably wouldn't show up until a week before my next payment was due.

The first thing I did was climb the stairs and open the bedroom door. Judging by Hot Shot's enthusiastic welcome, he hadn't enjoyed his imprisonment. After a couple of passes around my legs, he dashed out of the room.

Several dresser drawers were open and the vanity doors in the bathroom were ajar. For just a moment, I wondered if I'd left them that way. My next thought was that the contractors had come to the house after all and one of them had plundered through my bedroom. But no intruder would have gone to the trouble of closing the door after leaving the drawers wide open. No, this was an inside job and the culprit was a small gray and white cat. I'd have to keep a much closer eye on him if he was this talented.

I picked up the food and water bowls and carried them downstairs, but I didn't move the litter box, figuring the imprisonment would have to continue the next morning. In the kitchen, I refilled the bowls and Hot Shot fell on the food like a dieter ending a week-long fast.

My own appetite was gone. Poking around in other peoples' dirty laundry had left me feeling soiled as well. I found an Abita Turbodog, a souvenir of my last trip to New Orleans, at the back of the fridge, wrenched off the cap and drank. It slid down my throat, cold and smooth. Bottle in hand, I looked through the mail, pulled out the only bill and tossed the rest.

I wandered out onto the side porch. A little daylight still lingered. Only a few distant bird songs disturbed the quiet neighborhood. In the park across the street, the fog hung back in the trees like a thief waiting for full dark before approaching the house. I shivered even though I wasn't cold.

I was angry – with myself and the circumstances. When I agreed to look into the files for Delia McCullough, I'd somehow thought I could just ask people where they were when Glynnis had been killed, they'd tell me and that would be the end of it. I'd envisioned myself eliminating everyone in two or three days. But it didn't work that way in the real world. No one appreciated my asking embarrassing questions or suggesting that they needed to provide an alibi.

The hour I'd spent with Alex showed me that this was going to be a difficult task and might end up costing me some friends. But what was the alternative? Even if I was willing to do so, I couldn't turn the files over to the police now. The time for doing that had been when they first came into my possession. It was too late now. Besides, I still felt somehow responsible for protecting people I cared about. I was trapped and there was no easy way to extricate myself. I finished the beer and went to find the phone.

Rose Ackley was the personnel manager for a large Macon manufacturing company. She and I had served together for over a year on a United Way committee and I hoped a call to her would confirm Alex's whereabouts on the evening of the murder.

"I thought I'd call and say hello, Rose. We haven't talked in a while, although I saw you going into Bert's last week – Tuesday night. I called to you, but I guess you didn't hear me."

"Last Tuesday? It wasn't me, honey. I was up in Atlanta at a tennis match. It was after dark when I got home."

That told me what I wanted to know, but I couldn't very well end the conversation there. So I asked how her tennis team was playing this year – a question guaranteed to prompt a flood of information. When we hung up fifteen minutes later, I was sure of two things: we'd chatted long enough to keep her from wondering why I'd called and her tennis team would make the regional playoffs if Sandra Gillespie would just get the lead out of her butt and hustle.

Before it got any later, I called Marian Saxby and asked if she would meet me for dinner the next day.

"Why, I suppose I could," she said, sounding more than a little surprised by the invitation, "as long as we can make it early. I don't like driving after dark anymore."

Resigning myself to an early closing, I agreed to meet her at five-fifteen at the TaylorMade Grill off Riverside Drive. The hour was early for me, but I couldn't fault her choice of restaurant.

I was on a roll. I got in touch with Cassie Waycaster next.

"Tomorrow?" she asked distractedly, "no, no, there's no way I can meet you tomorrow. We're right in the middle of science projects and . . . " A crash and a wail interrupted her. "You two go to your rooms right this minute! Dixie, I can't talk to you right now. Can I call you sometime later in the week?"

All I could do was agree.

My last call of the night was to Edward. He didn't answer, but I left a message on his machine. "I love you and I'm here for you. Call me when you feel like it."

I'd done what I could. Before I went to bed, I took Alex's and Edward's files into the dining room, knelt in front of the fireplace and burned them to ashes.

I slept alone. No mockingbird sang outside my window and Hot Shot had forsaken me and my bed as if he knew that I'd been meddling in other people's lives and didn't want any part of it. Or maybe he was just avoiding the site of his recent incarceration.

I desperately missed Donald. He'd have understood what I was doing and why. With a mix of sadness and almost unbearable longing, I remembered the long evenings when he patiently listened as I obsessed over an open case. He never hurried me and never criticized my actions or ideas. He just listened with all his attention until I'd talked myself out. Then he'd ask questions and, more often than not, offer at least one suggestion that might help. If only he were here to do that now.

I shifted around under the covers, trying to find a comfortable spot. There were times like this when Donald's absence was an almost physical thing. I could remember the mass and warmth of his body beside me in bed. I could almost hear the rhythmic rush of his breathing. But he wasn't there and never would be again. I felt as alone as I ever had in my life.

Sometimes the best ideas come when you least expect them. During my Wednesday morning run I'd struggled with Edward's problem to no avail. Without police assistance, no real solution presented itself. My initial impulse had been to rush up to Atlanta and somehow force George Bennett to return the money, but that wasn't a rational course of action. I'd met the man. He was big, muscular, and obviously not afraid to get physical. If I approached him on my own, I'd need a weapon to get the money back. Unfortunately, doing that would be considered armed robbery. I wanted to help Edward, but I wasn't willing to risk five-to-twenty years in prison to do so.

It wasn't until fifteen minutes later when I was standing in the shower, shampoo lather and hot water sluicing down my body, that the answer came to me. It was so easy that I couldn't believe I hadn't thought about it before. I stood still, struck by the simplicity of it, until the suds stung my eyes and I had to get on with the business of bathing.

I pulled on gray slacks and a V-neck cotton sweater in a shade of pumpkin that I'd always believed was somewhat flattering. I told myself I wasn't hoping to see Ballard, but I was lying.

Then I put in a call to an old friend in Atlanta and set everything in motion. Once that arrangement had been made, I started looking for Edward. He wasn't home – at least he didn't answer the telephone. I decided I'd drive to the shop and, if he wasn't there, I'd go on out to his house. One way or another, I was going to find him that morning.

I locked Hot Shot in the bedroom again and drove to town. The Volvo was parked in its usual space in the alley behind Edward's shop. I didn't even stop at my door, but went directly to his. Today the shop was open for business and Edward was there, hanging a lush gardenscape by Carol Pope on the back wall.

"Good morning, sweet thing." His face was still horribly bruised, but at least he was smiling. "I would have called you back last night, but I was just too exhausted."

"You seem much better today," I said and gave the painting he'd just hung a critical look. "Needs to come up about half an inch on the left."

He made the adjustment. "I am much better today, thank you. I'm also wiser and about to be considerably poorer."

I hoisted myself up onto the back counter and sat there, legs dangling. "That's what I want to talk to you about. I'm going up to Atlanta this morning to get your money back from George, but I need your help."

His good humor vanished in an instant. "I won't do it, Dixie. I don't ever want to see him again and I will not humiliate myself further by begging him to give that money back."

"Who said anything about begging? And what makes you think I want you to go with me?"

"You don't?"

"No, I definitely don't."

"What are you planning?" He sounded torn between concern and hope.

I started to explain, but thought better of it. Edward couldn't veto what he didn't know was going to happen. "All you need to know is that I'll bring your money back." I'm a firm believer that positive thinking and speaking contribute significantly to success. "But I need some information from you."

Ten minutes later, I opened my own back door. In my purse I had the name of George Bennett's interior design firm, which he operated from the ground floor of his home, and directions to its Morningside location.

It was only five after ten, but Pandora was waiting at the front door. She wore a skirt and blouse of Indian design today. I hoped she wouldn't be burning incense later. Her backpack lay beside her feet and she was leaning against the doorframe watching the morning activity on Cherry Street. I opened the door and flipped the sign.

"Good morning, Dixie," she said, sliding into the shop. "It's such a beautiful morning. The forces of the universe must be in perfect balance."

I didn't care if the forces of the universe were singing "On Moonlight Bay" in four-part harmony. I had to get moving.

"Listen," I said hurriedly, "I've got to go to Atlanta today. It's really important. I know you only signed on to work two hours a day – and that's fine. I'm not asking you to do more than that."

"Oh, but I'd be glad to stay," she said. "I can be here all day if you want."

"I'm not sure how long I'll be gone," I said, "but I really appreciate your taking care of things here." I fumbled in the counter drawer and came up with a key. "Just stay as long as you want, then lock the place up and leave."

She took the key. "I'll stay all day, Dixie. You can count on me." Then she frowned. "Be careful, okay? I just got a ... a flash of some kind of problem."

On impulse, I gave her a quick hug. "I appreciate your concern, but I'll be fine. Thanks for staying today. I owe you."

An hour and a half later I was on Interstate 85, just north of the Atlanta skyscrapers. Traffic was heavy, even at noon. The congestion and exhaust fumes reminded me of how happy I was to be living in Macon. I exited onto Monroe Drive and, minutes later, pulled into a parking place in a small shopping center on Piedmont Road. The directions had been good. I found The King and I with no trouble. When I saw it was a Thai restaurant, I knew why Dennis Brown had chosen it. He was addicted to spicy food.

There might have been a little more gray in his hair and a couple more pounds around his middle, but all in all he looked much the same as he had the last time I'd seen him – a tall, rangy man with rust-colored hair and kind blue eyes. After we'd hugged, exchanged pleasantries, and ordered lunch, I congratulated him on his recent promotion.

"Thanks. Yeah, I was real excited about it for a while there, but now it's, oh, I don't know, like any other job, I guess. I never get out on the street anymore. Spend all my time putting out fires. I swear, Dixie girl, employees are a pain in the ass.

"Last week I had to suspend Bobby Jenkins – you remember him? He was visiting his girlfriend while he was on duty. I mean, really visiting her, if you know what I mean."

"Yeah, old Bobby always was one for the ladies."

"Well, he hasn't changed and I doubt that a four-day suspension is going to make a new man of him. But we do what we can." He gave me a critical look. "Now, what's going on in Macon that has the cops down there asking questions about you?"

I told him about Glynnis's murder, but didn't mention the files. I knew what his reaction to that situation would be.

A young Asian girl, who lowered her eyes and giggled when I tried to make conversation with her, served the food. I took a bite and was pleased to find it light and flavorful. Watching Dennis, I was glad I'd ordered a relatively mild dish. His first bite had enough heat in it to bring sweat to his forehead. He swallowed, gulped sweet tea, and sighed with pleasure.

"Mmmmm, delicious. I don't get to come here much. Hell, I hardly ever take time for lunch these days. And Terry won't eat Thai food," he said, referring to his wife of more than twenty years. "Nor Mexican either. So this is a treat." He laughed. "Especially since you're paying for it."

I waved a fork. "It's the least I can do. I figure I owe you – or I will by this afternoon."

Over the meal we tried to catch each other up on the last three years. I told him about my shop and how much I liked Macon. When he announced that his son, Sean, had been accepted at Georgia Tech, a big smile spread across his freckled face.

"Boy's got a good head on his shoulders. He's made his mama and me real proud."

With the check came the time for serious talk. I handed my credit card to the shy waitress and she hurried away with it.

"Now, tell me again what it is you want me to do," he said. "You know as well as I do that I can't do anything for your friend officially – not unless he makes a complaint."

I'd told him about Edward and his problem during our telephone conversation earlier that morning. "I know, Dennis, it's nothing like that. I just want this guy to see you. That's all. I'll take it from there."

When we left the restaurant, I climbed into Dennis's city car. It was unmarked but, like its driver, few people would mistake it for anything other than police property. For me, it was like stepping into a time machine. Everything about it – the radio, the worn fabric-covered seats, the computer, even the smell – was familiar and brought back a flood of memories from that other life.

To distract myself, I pulled Edward's directions from my purse. "Turn right on Monroe," I told Dennis. "Then we make a left on Yorkshire."

He followed my directions without comment and I took in the scenes of my former hometown. Atlanta is only a hundred miles north of Macon, but the distance made a significant difference in the arrival of the seasons. Spring was just now appearing here and the yards in the old Morningside neighborhood were only slowly coming to life.

We had no trouble finding Bennett's house on North Highland

Avenue near the Morningside Drive intersection. It was a two-story brick structure positioned close to the road. An understated wooden sign beside a massive magnolia tree in the front yard identified the place as George Bennett Creations/Interiors with Style. Dennis pulled into the drive and, as I asked him to do, stopped there instead of driving on around back to the parking area. We both got out. I walked up the cracked cement walk while he remained there in the warm sunlight, leaning back against the car with his arms crossed over his chest. He couldn't have been more easily recognized as a city cop if he'd carried a sign with a two-foot high badge on it.

What had once been the front parlor of the old house now served as the reception room. It was amply furnished in lavenders and burgundies, and decorated within an inch of its life.

The bell that signaled my entrance brought George Bennett hurrying to the front of the house. He wore jeans, a tweed jacket, and a starched white dress shirt open at the neck. He was just as hard and muscular as I remembered. He'd perfected the persona of a designer who didn't mind getting his hands dirty. His face was creased with a welcoming smile – at least it was until he saw me and registered who I was.

"You're that friend of Edward's with the stupid name, aren't you?"

"Yep. Dixie McClatchey."

"Oh, yes, Dixie. How very antebellum. And what is it you want?"

"I came for Edward's money."

He stared at me a minute, then his heavy, handsome face dissolved into laughter. He was genuinely amused and it was several seconds before he was able to speak. "You have, have you?" He used his fingertips to wipe the tears of laughter from his eyes. He didn't deny the theft. "And just how do you propose to do that?"

I wondered if he was conscious of flexing his chest and shoulders or if it was just an atavistic instinct to make himself appear larger to an adversary.

"Well, today, Georgie, I thought I'd just ask you for it. The total comes to $2,360." He laughed again and I ignored it. "So if you'll just hand it over, I'll be on my way. And if that doesn't work, the police can handle it."

He moved a few feet closer to me. "Oh, please, you don't expect me to believe that Edward is going to prosecute me, do you? He's a rabbit; he's scared of his own shadow. He sure as hell isn't going to take a chance going up against me."

"Oh, did you think I meant he was going to prosecute?" I asked, feigning surprise. "No, no, he won't have to do that. I'm afraid he'd find the whole business distasteful." I stepped to one side so he could see out the window where Dennis lounged against the car, smoking a cigarette and watching the passing cars. "I have a lot of friends up here in Atlanta and some of them owe me favors."

"And that's supposed to scare me?" He laughed again, but this time I thought there was a trace of nervousness in it. "You can have every cop in the city in your hip pocket, but without a victim, there is no crime. You see, I know the law, too."

"That's what I'm trying to tell you. Edward won't have anything to do with it." I wandered across the room to an ornate wall shelf where a collection of tiny glass figurines was displayed. I picked up a delicate dragonfly and turned it over in my hand. "See, if I don't get the money today, we'll just take it out in trade – $2,360 worth of annoyance and inconvenience."

His eyes followed the figurine as I gently tossed it from hand to hand, but I knew he was listening to what I said.

"The really exciting part is that you'll never know exactly when to expect it." I gave him big smile. "Let's take today as a for-instance. When I leave here, I might go meet with some guys I know in Narcotics. And I might tell them how, while I was here with you, I saw you toking on a joint or maybe that you offered to sell me a dime bag. They could have a search warrant in a couple of hours and then come and take this place apart. By the way, have you ever seen a house after it was searched?" I shook my head sadly. "All I can say is that hurricanes leave less of a mess behind."

"You didn't see anything of the kind," he said indignantly. "That would be an out and out lie."

Now it was my turn to laugh. "Oh, Georgie, don't tell me you expect me or the police to play by the rules. You don't. Why should the rest of us?"

"It doesn't matter." He was smug. "I don't use illegal drugs. They wouldn't find anything here."

"Maybe not the first time." I smiled.

He tried for a sneer, but couldn't quite pull it off. "Just what would you tell your friends when they don't find anything?"

I shrugged. "I don't know. I guess that you moved it before they got here. It wouldn't be the first time they came up dry on a drug search. Happens all the time."

"And when I tell them you set me up?"

I laughed again. "Oh, Georgie, who do you think they'll believe, you or me?" I put back the dragonfly, making sure it clattered a bit when I set it down. George winced and I picked up a stylized pig. "Anyway, they can always search again. They have a number of what they call confidential informants. You know about CI's, don't you? Those are the people that cops get information from – about drugs or stolen goods or child pornography. And, because the CI's are usually involved with the criminals, the police don't even have to use their names to get the search warrants. That's what makes them confidential. There's no way to check on them or prove whether or not they're telling the truth."

I replaced the pig on its shelf and moved farther around the room, fingering a lampshade here and a vase there. I was really getting into my performance now. I almost believed it myself. "Just because they come up empty the first time doesn't mean they will every time. How many people come through here in a month? Customers, delivery people, salesmen? How hard do you think it would be to get someone in here to leave a bag of marijuana in a drawer or, even better, some kiddie porn?" I raised my hands in a who-knows gesture.

"Then the next time they search the place, they just might find something, " I said, keeping my voice bright and upbeat. "Not that it matters all that much. The publicity alone will probably ruin your business. You know how the TV stations in this town love crime stories. Why, the cops might even let a reporter and cameraman come along for the ride. That way, the search of your little business here would be splashed all over the six o'clock news.

"So you have to decide how much it's worth to you to avoid all that. What do you think, Georgie? Is $2,360 too much to pay for peace of mind?"

I must have been convincing. He was quiet for a bit, chewing on his upper lip, evidently considering the implications of what I'd threatened. Finally he expelled an angry breath and glared at me.

"All right. Whatever. I'll give the little fag back his money, but I don't have that much cash here. I'll send it – "

"Don't bother. I'll take a check," I interrupted. "Make it out to Edward and write on there that it's for the repayment of a loan."

He stalked into the next room and I followed. At an elaborate writing desk, he pulled out a checkbook. I stood close by as he wrote and contemplated the absurdity of taking a check from a thief. But I was fairly certain it wouldn't bounce. George Bennett didn't want a visit from the police. When he gave it to me, I looked at it to make sure it was correct, then put it in my purse.

"You can tell that son of a bitch Edward Swanson that I don't ever want to see him again. Understand?"

"I'll be sure and tell him," I said sweetly.

"And you can get the hell out of here!"

That last comment was unnecessary. I was already out the door.

"You get what you wanted?" Dennis asked as we drove up North Highland Avenue.

"Right here." I patted my purse.

"What happened in there?"

I reached over to squeeze his arm. "Nothing you need to know about. But I do thank you for the help."

He laughed. "Well, it was the easiest lunch I ever earned." Then he gave me a quick look. "This isn't going to come back and bite me on the ass, is it?"

"No. I never even used your name. Just the sight of you standing there – a big, beautiful example of Atlanta's finest – was enough." I laughed. "You should have seen his face."

The lunch rush was over and few cars remained in the restaurant's parking lot. Before I got back into mine for the trip home, Dennis gave me a final hug.

"You take care of yourself, you hear? And don't be such a stranger. Terry wants me to invite you to come and visit us. You could come up for a weekend. We've got plenty of room. We'll get together with some of the old gang from Homicide. I know the guys would love to see you. It'd be fun."

"I'll try to do that some time soon," I said, but I knew I wouldn't. That was part of a life I didn't want to revisit. "Give Terry my love. And thanks again."

CHAPTER ELEVEN

I arrived back in Macon just in time for my dinner date with Marian Saxby. In fact, I was a couple of minutes early getting to the restaurant. The hostess settled me in one of the upholstered booths along the back wall. I ordered a Samuel Adams and wondered if I should call the shop. But then I realized that whatever might have happened there on Pandora's watch would be over by now. I'd deal with it in the morning.

The TaylorMade Grill hadn't changed since my last visit a few weeks before. A boutique of a restaurant, it was one of my favorite places to eat. Decorated in a sort of middle Georgia-meets-Tuscany style, the colors were understated earth tones and the atmosphere casual. Vibrant Teresa Griffith and Debbie Anderson paintings adorned the walls and a Lilliputian bar with six stools was tucked into one corner. The room held only fifteen tables. Additional seating could be found on the small outdoor deck, but in late March the temperature dipped along with the sun. Only one brave couple sat there tonight and I could tell from the way the woman clutched her cardigan close to her body that there was already a bite in the wind.

The best feature of the restaurant was, of course, the food. Even Deannie, who was hypercritical of all eating establishments, conceded that this was a fine place to dine. We'd shared a table here more than once and the only criticism she could find was the size. "With food this good, they should double their seating," she'd pronounced.

Marian Saxby walked in the door at exactly five-fifteen. A petite woman with short, iron-gray hair, tonight she wore a tailored blue shirt-waist dress with a matching sweater draped around her shoulders. Her bag and shoes were unadorned black leather. Her eyes made a quick inventory of the tables. When she spotted me, she waved. We smiled at each other as she slid into the booth.

A waiter materialized at our table by the time she'd put down her purse. Marian greeted him familiarly. "Good evening, Ricky. How is your mother?"

"Oh, much better, Miss Saxby. She should get the cast off next week."

"Well, that's good news." She asked him for a glass of white wine and, after a quick glance at the menu, set it aside. Then she turned serious brown eyes to me.

"I taught both Ricky and his mother, you know. She was an excellent student." She smiled indulgently. "Ricky, on the other hand, was best known for his genial manner. I believe he's chosen an appropriate profession." Her manner turned businesslike. "Now, what's so important that we have to meet for dinner? Don't misunderstand, my dear, I do consider you a friend and enjoy spending time with you. And I'm always pleased to have an evening out, especially here. They do such a good job with this place, don't you think? But you've never asked me to dinner before. You must have a good reason."

"I do."

Before I could tell her, Ricky returned with her wine and took our orders. When he'd gone, I explained the situation to Marian. By the time I'd finished, her lips were pressed together so tightly there were white marks at the corners of her mouth.

"And you've seen these files?"

"Yes, all of them."

She nodded, eyes down. "So you've seen mine." It wasn't a question. "And you know about my parents."

"Yes." I knew this had to be awkward for her.

When she began speaking, her voice was so soft that I had to lean forward to hear her words. "My parents were the sweetest, most loving people you could ever meet. Both of their families had been in Macon for generations. When Daddy married that first time, he was staying up in Jackson, all by himself. He'd gone there to work in his uncle's store. It was the first time he'd been away from home. I think he must have been terribly lonely. He met a young woman and they married within just a few months. I'm afraid it was never a happy match. Within the year, she went back to her family and he came home to Macon. He never went back to Jackson. A few years later, he and Mother met and married."

"But there was no divorce from his first wife?"

Her mouth tightened again. "There was no divorce."

Ricky brought the salads and set them before us with a small flourish. He wielded a large wooden pepper mill like a majorette's baton. "Fresh ground pepper?"

We both declined and he left us alone. Marian continued her story.

"I don't know why he did it that way. Divorce was a scandalous thing in those days, of course. Perhaps he wanted to avoid that or it could be that his first wife refused to consider it. We'll never know now. I don't know when Mother found out about it either. I lived most of my life not knowing the secret and my brother still doesn't know. Mother told me just days before she died – a deathbed confession, I suppose you could call it. She felt she'd lived in sin for so much of her life and was praying for forgiveness."

I nodded. "I'm sure it was hard for her to tell you."

"Yes, but she knew it was important that I be told the truth."

I took a bite of salad, then said, "I've come across some evidence to suggest that Glynnis might have been using the information she found to pressure people into giving her things."

Marian sighed. "What a tactful way of saying she was a blackmailer." She moved her salad around with her fork, but never lifted any to her mouth. "I suppose you want to know what she got from me."

I nodded. "If you don't mind telling me."

"She hinted around for a while about my sponsoring her for membership in my garden club. When I didn't do what she wanted, she showed me the same things you probably saw in the file. The copies of the marriage licenses, newspaper clippings, census records showing both my mother and the woman in Jackson as married women whose last names were Saxby." She shrugged. "So I did what she asked. I despised doing it, hated every minute of it, but I did it."

A piece of a puzzle fell into place. "That's why you nominated her for vice president of the Friends."

She nodded. "It's not something I'm proud of."

A lesser woman might have shed some tears, but Marian wasn't the sort to give in to emotion in public. Her breathing had remained even and slow. Her hand as she lifted the wineglass was steady.

"Why was it so important, Marian?"

"What?"

"I don't mean to sound unfeeling, but what difference would it make if the information did come out? After all this time, who would care one way or the other whether your parents were legally married?"

"I would. I'm a Saxby. I've been a Saxby all my life." Her voice was still low, but was now shot through with a kind of ferocity. "Family is important. Without family, a person is rudderless. There are no roots. My father's family goes all the way back to seventeenth century Virginia.

It was, and still is, a respected name. I'm a Saxby, my brother's a Saxby and so are his children. I could not take a chance on that being destroyed. So I gave in to her silly little demands. It wasn't as if she were asking for anything really important."

Yet, I thought.

Over our entrees, I asked as tactfully as I could where she'd been the night Glynnis was killed.

She looked up from the pork medallions she was eating with obvious enjoyment. Clearing the air had certainly improved her appetite. "Are you asking for my alibi?" There was a spark of humor in her eyes.

"Yes, I guess I am."

She smiled. "Then I'm delighted to provide you with one – at least for some of that day. There was the book sorting in the morning, of course, and I had a doctor's appointment at three, down at the Medical Center. Dr. Revis Parker. As usual, I had to wait. Some people never learn to keep to a schedule. It was after four before I even got into an examining room and ten to five when I finally left the office. I was almost late meeting Joyce Schafer and her daughter for dinner – right here, as a matter of fact." She inclined her head in the direction of the bar. "We sat at the table in the corner there. I told you I liked this restaurant."

She raised her hand a few inches and our waiter hurried over.

"Yes, ma'am. What can I get for you?"

"Do you remember when I was here last week?"

He frowned for just a second, then nodded. "Oh, sure. On Tuesday with Mrs. Schafer, wasn't it? Yes, ma'am, I remember."

Marian shot me a triumphant look. "When did we get here?"

"Five-fifteen, just like always."

"Do you remember how late we stayed, Ricky?"

"How late?" He looked uncertain, as if this were a test he hadn't studied for. "Uh, seven, seven-fifteen? I'm not absolutely sure, but I know it was just about dark when you left."

She smiled. "Thank you, Ricky."

And that was that. I told Marian I'd destroy her file when I got home. "And I won't tell anyone what's in there."

Her eyes crinkled. "Why, I never thought you would, Dixie." She reached across the table and patted my arm. "You're a good friend to go to this much trouble."

That attitude made the rest of my dinner much more pleasant.

Marian's acceptance and understanding of what I was doing went a long way to improve my outlook on the drive back downtown. For the first time since I'd begun, I believed that I just might be able to complete the task I'd set for myself. I drove in a mindless way, hands and feet moving automatically while my brain went over and over what I'd learned so far. I was satisfied that Marian, Edward, Alexandra, and Deannie could all be eliminated from consideration, but getting to this point had taken more time than I'd expected and I'd barely scratched the surface. A lot of people remained on the list.

I was on Riverside Drive when, instead of turning onto College Street, I yielded to an impulse, pulled into Rose Hill Cemetery and drove on up the steep drive. I stopped the car beside the huge rose garden and leaned back against the headrest.

It was best in early summer when most of the roses were in bloom, but I loved this spot any time of the year. High on a hill, it was a wonderful place for watching sunrise or sunset, and, more important tonight, clearing your mind. Along the road, the cherry trees were in full bloom. To the south, Macon's few tall buildings thrust up through the greening trees. Farther west I could see the law school cupola and a few church steeples.

The cemetery itself, which dated to 1840, spread out to my left over the steeply pitched hillside that ran all the way down to the river. Rose Hill is quite large – almost seventy acres – and is on the National Register of Historic Places.

Narrow paved lanes twist through this city of the dead, making it an intriguing setting for a peaceful stroll. It was, however, much too late in the day for that now. The gates would close at sundown.

While I sat watching the sky change from blue and gold to pale purple, a familiar-looking car scooted up the drive and disappeared through the white brick arch. Reg Anderson and his little red Miata were unmistakable and I was more than a little surprised to see him there. In the years I'd known him, Reg had never impressed me as a cemetery fan. He'd never shown the slightest interest in Rose Hill or any other historical site in the city. In my mind, he was a man firmly anchored in the present. My curiosity was definitely stirred.

I shifted into drive to follow him, but before I could, a beat-up blue van rattled out through the entryway and stopped. The man at the wheel sported shaggy, graying hair and a matching beard. His companion was a middle-aged woman whose haggard face was framed by long, lank, brown locks. They were recognizable as aging hippies and I had a pretty good idea why they'd visited the cemetery.

The history of the Allman Brothers Band is entwined with that of Rose Hill. Based in Macon during the early part of their career, the band had once practiced in the lower part of the cemetery, down where the Ocmulgee River runs past the older graves on its slow southward journey. And legend said that several of their most famous songs were composed there. The long, haunting instrumental classic "In Memory of Elizabeth Reed" was so titled because her grave, which dated back to the thirties, was located in their practice area. In an ironic twist of fate, two of the band members, guitarist Duane Allman and bass player Berry Oakley, were buried in Rose Hill after being killed in motorcycle accidents a year apart.

Even now, some thirty years after the band's heyday, fans still made pilgrimages to the musicians' graves. It wasn't uncommon for them to leave small offerings – flowers, poems, beer, or marijuana. I thought it likely that the couple in the van, now moving slowly down the drive, had been to visit Duane and Berry.

When the way was clear, I steered through the narrow entrance and stopped at the top of the hill. Marble monuments of every shape and size rose around me like a giant stone garden, but the Miata was nowhere to be seen. I drove down the main road, then south along the river and back past the Confederate soldiers' section to the entrance, but never even got a glimpse of Reg or the red car.

Darkness was rapidly overtaking the daylight and, in spite of my own rational self, the surroundings made me a bit uneasy. Towering markers stood tall against the deep purple sky and a chilly breeze blew in the open window of my car. I could hear a whispering noise that sounded like a low insistent voice, but was probably only the rush of the river. There were several side lanes crisscrossing the hillside that might have led me to Reg and satisfied my curiosity. But they were narrow and twisting and looked forbidding in the fading light. I didn't want to drive down any of them. And there was more than one way out of Rose Hill. Reg might not even have been there any longer.

Darkness was beginning to press in on me. I made my way back out to Riverside Drive and headed home.

This evening there was no doubt. Even in the deepening twilight,

I could see that the contractor and his crew had been to my house. The lawn beside the driveway was rutted with tire tracks, a metal Dumpster had been set up in the back yard, and a sign declaring the place to be an Edelman Construction work site was stuck in front of the mailbox. But the real proof was in the kitchen. More than half the cabinets had been prised off the wall and were now in a jumble in the middle of the floor. Demolition, I realized, had begun.

I hurried up the stairs and released Hot Shot from the bedroom. He didn't bother greeting me this time, realizing, perhaps, that I was responsible for his being locked up in the first place. He took off down the stairs. By the time I'd shut drawers and cabinet doors, changed clothes, and returned to the first floor, the kitten was stepping cautiously around the debris in the kitchen floor.

I fed Hot Shot in the center hall, right beside the refrigerator the workmen had moved there. I was relieved to see they'd plugged it back in. I rummaged through the jumble in the dining room until I found the microwave, which I set up on a table beside the refrigerator. Since the stovetop was now covered with a big, blue tarp, any meal preparation would have to take place here.

I reached in the refrigerator for a Tennant's Scottish Ale. It took several minutes to locate a bottle opener, then I called Edward, impatient to give him the good news that I'd gotten his money back. His response wasn't what I'd expected.

"Yeah, I know." He sounded cold and distant. "George called me, said he thought it was so cute that I had a woman to fight my battles for me. He called me a lot of names . . . and asked why I hadn't come for the money myself."

"Screw him! Did he tell about the six-foot-two cop that stood in his driveway while we talked?"

"You had the police with you?" He sounded alarmed.

"Not officially, no, but a friend of mine went along – in his city car. That's why George gave back the money. I threatened to sic the APD on him."

As I told the story, he gradually thawed. And by the time I got to the part where I told George we would plant contraband in his house, Edward actually laughed out loud.

"Sorry, Dixie," he said before we hung up. "I am grateful. Really. It was just that George made it sound like you went up there and . . . and . . . "

"And played Jane Wayne? Come on, give me some credit. I wouldn't go after George alone. He's built like a rugby player and mean as a snake. Hell, he'd mop up the floor with me. I'm not crazy, you know."

"Well, you probably are," he said with a smile in his voice, "but I love you anyway."

"I'll get the check to you first thing in the morning. You probably ought to get it in the bank before George has too much time to think about it."

I sipped a second beer and returned to the problem of the files. At least there were only three Friends left to eliminate and I was anxious to get it done. I called all three and didn't get a single answer. Maybe I could find them in the morning, if I started early enough.

The remaining files presented me with a whole different set of problems. I knew some of the people, but none very well. Approaching any of them was going to be delicate work. It would take some time to figure out the best way to do it.

On the bright side, there was the chance that I wouldn't have to. Over a week had passed since Glynnis's murder and the police had been steadily working the case. They might make an arrest at any time. If that happened, the files would be history and I'd be happily out of the investigation business.

The telephone rang shortly after eight. It was Steve Ballard. I was almost embarrassed at how glad I was to hear from him. I declined his offer of a movie, but agreed to meet him for dessert at Adriana's.

The café on Third Street wasn't busy and we took a table by the window. Steve wore jeans and a soft blue sweater that made me want to snuggle up to him. Instead, I sat properly across the table and ate cheesecake and drank coffee.

"I stopped by the store this afternoon, but Pandora said you were in Atlanta."

"Just a quick business trip. She wasn't conducting a seance or anything was she?"

"Nope, and no sign of tarot cards or tea leaves either."

"How was your day?"

"Okay. No major bumps."

"Any developments on Glynnis's case?"

He shook his head. "Nothing. It's like whoever did it just dropped off the radar. There aren't even any rumors going around about it. Did you hear about the reward?"

"No. Who put up a reward?"

"The folks at Jackson-Connover, the investment firm. Ten thousand dollars."

"Why would they do that?" I asked.

"Seems her father was on their board of directors. They must have thought a lot of him."

Or Delia got to them, I thought. If she'd decided that needed to be done, she'd have badgered them until they agreed.

He put down his cup and reached across the table to take my hand. He stroked the palm with two fingers and my legs felt jittery and weak. What was it about this man?

"I've been thinking about you a lot."

I smiled into his eyes. "I've thought about you a lot, too."

We talked for over an hour, sharing childhood memories and present-day frustrations; comparing opinions on music and books, people and movies, likes and dislikes, religion and politics and art. We touched the surface of most of the important things and I wished there were more time. There was so much I wanted to know.

We were the only customers left in the restaurant and the staff was growing impatient. The floors had been swept and two of the waiters were stacking chairs on the empty tables.

"I guess we'd better go, huh?" Steve got to his feet.

I stood up. "Yeah, I need to get home and get some sleep. The construction has started on my kitchen and the crew will be there bright and early."

He walked with me to where I'd parked and kissed me before I got in the car. But he didn't suggest following me home and I didn't invite him back to the house. I knew I'd never be able to have him there and not tell him about the files.

Hot Shot was unusually active that night, running through the house at breakneck speed. It was probably a reaction to being locked up all day. Every now and then, he'd leap at something I couldn't see, screech at the top of his lungs, then take off again. Once he made an abrupt 180-degree turn and bounced back in my direction, back bowed and tail fluffed like a raccoon's. Since he didn't seem sick during the occasional breaks in this activity, I had to conclude it was normal behavior for a cat.

And he was entertaining.

Unfortunately, this normal behavior continued off and on through most of the night. At three-thirty it was much less amusing than it had been four hours before. After I'd been awakened for the fourth time by little feet, complete with claws, tearing across my bed and body, I closed the door to the hall, shutting Hot Shot on the other side.

Minutes after I got back to sleep his cries of protest woke me. I tried shooing him away, but he was a tenacious little thing. When the wailing alone didn't produce the desired reaction, he began throwing his body against the door. For such a small creature, he made a surprising amount of noise. I finally decided his mad dashes were preferable to the yowls and crashes, and permitted him access again. He settled down to sleep some time towards daybreak.

CHAPTER TWELVE

I didn't know what I might find when I opened the shop Thursday morning, but everything was in order. There was no trace of fortune telling paraphernalia and Pandora had left the balanced receipts for the day locked in the cash drawer along with a list of the items she'd sold. I made a quick trip next door to deliver the check to Edward, then came back and got the coffee going. A number of online orders were waiting and there was a steady stream of customers all morning.

When my new assistant arrived at noon, she was trying out a new look. Inspired, maybe, by her new job, she'd traded the bell-bottoms for a long, dark skirt and a demure blouse. Her hair had been tamed into a ponytail at the nape of her neck. But she was as cheerful and eager to work as ever. And she seemed really glad to see me.

"I'm so glad you're okay, Dixie. I was worried because…you know." I knew, but I wasn't going to get into a discussion about her feelings.

"I'm fine," I told her. I got her started shelving books.

I called Reg one more time and still got no answer. "I really have to talk to you." I told his machine. "It's important."

I'd leave Cassie and Carlton for after lunch.

Pandora had taken it upon herself to rearrange the window display. I hated to admit it, but her effort was much more eye-catching than the one she replaced. When I thanked her for taking care of the store so ably the day before, she brushed it off.

"No big thing. I enjoyed it and it's not such a tough job, you know."

She had brought an oversized veggie sub sandwich for lunch and offered me half, but I felt the need of something more substantial than bean sprouts.

"I'm going to get something up the street."

Reveling in the luxury of having someone to watch the shop, I walked the two blocks to Chimera where I ate a roast beef sandwich at an outside table. Deannie joined me there. The kitchen must have been operating up to her standard because she stayed for a full fifteen minutes.

"That cat kept me awake half the night," I complained.

She smiled a wise smile. "He's a kitten. You can't expect him to sleep through the night. Have you gotten his shots yet?"

"No." Here was something else I had to do.

"And he'll have to be neutered, of course. Unless you want him spraying all over your house."

"Thanks for that pretty picture." I chewed a bite of sandwich, then asked, "Isn't he a little young for all that?"

"He looks like he's three or four months old. I think that's old enough. Even if he isn't, you still need to have him checked out, make sure there's nothing wrong with him."

"What could be wrong with him? He's healthy as a horse. And he eats like one, too."

She shrugged. "Some cats are born with diseases like feline leukemia and they can pick up viruses and things when they're real little. It can be serious – even fatal."

Oh, great. Now I'd worry about him until I got him checked out. "Okay, okay. I'll do it. Just as soon as I have time and can find a vet."

She recommended a mobile veterinarian who would come to the house to examine the cat and insisted that I write down his name. "The dogs just love him. And it's so much less stressful for them than loading them in the car and taking them to an unfamiliar place."

While I ate, she entertained me with a rundown of her week so far. There were the usual problems with food suppliers and employees. She was also getting ready to teach a gourmet cooking class at a local college. It sounded remarkably busy, but then, Deannie's weeks always were. Last weekend seemed very far behind us now. In fact, when she made reference to it near the end of my meal, she seemed more concerned about me than herself.

"Listen, I know what you did for me. And I appreciate it. But I've been thinking about what you said, you know, about the police finding the killer." She frowned, creating a single line between her brows. "And I want you to know that, if you feel like you have to, you can tell them about me if you need to."

I smiled at her, knowing how much courage it took to say that. "I don't think it's going to be necessary. There just isn't anything in those files that's bad enough to be a motive for murder. I don't think having them would do the police any good at all."

I hoped I was right.

I'd only been back in the shop for a few minutes when Delia

McCullough telephoned.

"The police came back!" She shouted so loud I had to hold the phone away from my ear. "And this time they broke in the front door and tore the house apart!"

"Why would they . . . What did they say to you?"

"They didn't say anything to me. I wasn't here." She drew a deep breath. "I had a hair appointment. I just got home this minute and. . . Well, it was like this when I got here. I'm going to sue them, that's what I'm going to do! And I'll have that Kaminsky fired!"

It made no sense. "What did they put on your copy of the search warrant?"

"I don't know what you mean, Dixie."

"They didn't leave a copy of the search warrant?"

"They didn't leave anything but this mess. How could they do this after what happened to poor Glynnis?"

And then I knew, of course, that the police had nothing to do with it. She started crying, but there wasn't time to comfort her.

"Mrs. McCullough?"

The sobbing continued.

"Mrs. McCullough? Delia!"

She gulped. "What?"

"Where are you?" I was pulling my keys from my purse as I asked.

"What do you mean? I'm at home, of course."

"Delia, listen to me. I'm coming right now. I want you to go outside and wait for me in your driveway. Do you hear me?"

"Yes, but why on earth . . . "

"Just do it! And call the police! Tell them what happened."

I said a silent prayer of thanks for Pandora as I gave her a one-sentence explanation and dashed out to my car.

It wasn't unheard of for the police to conduct a second search of a murder victim's home, but I couldn't see anyone, even Kaminsky, breaking into the house to do it. I took the expressway to north Macon. Traffic was light and I pulled into the McCullough drive at one-twenty-five. Delia wasn't in the driveway, but she had heeded my word enough to be waiting for me in the shade of her front porch.

"Where are the police?" I shouted the minute I was out of the car.

"They're not here yet," she said as I started up the stairs. "What's going on?"

"I'm not sure." I put a hand on her arm. "Just wait here for a minute."

I slipped the gun out of my purse and she gasped.

"Dixie!"

"Just stay here."

I left my purse on the porch and entered the house. All the old moves and instincts came back. I went through Delia's house the same way I used to search a warehouse on an alarm call. I didn't really expect that anyone would still be in the house. After all, Delia had been there for a good half hour and a burglar wouldn't have waited around that long.

But someone had certainly been there. Shelves were emptied onto the floor. Every drawer and door had been opened. Closets were stripped of clothes. Even the food in the refrigerator had been tossed into the floor. Delia hadn't exaggerated when she called it a mess.

I went back to where she waited on the porch. There was still no sign of the police.

"They should have been here by now," I told her. "What did you say when you called?"

"I told them I wanted to register a complaint, that's what I told them, that their detectives had searched my house and torn things up." She sniffed. "The woman I talked to said a supervisor would call me, not come here, mind you, just call."

It was hard not to grab her and shake her, but I resisted the impulse. We sat on the front steps while I explained the situation.

"This is a burglary. The police didn't do this."

She gave me an uncomprehending look. I was sure she'd already rehearsed what she was going to say to the mayor. "Of course, they did."

I shook my head. "No. I don't care if it was Kaminsky or anybody else, no police officer would do this to a murder victim's home. I'm not even sure theft was the motive here. This looks more like vandalism."

"But they searched here before." She wasn't willing to give up her theory. "I thought they just came back."

"They might have, Delia. But even if they'd served a search warrant while you were gone, they wouldn't have destroyed the place. And they'd have left you a copy of the warrant. They have to do that. No, if it had been the police, you'd have found a copy of the warrant tacked to your front door."

"Then who – "

"I don't know. From the looks of it, I'd say some of the neighborhood kids would be a good bet. You'll probably find out that the only things missing are money and maybe food or liquor."

"There's no liquor in this house!" she bristled, but she couldn't maintain her outrage. Her shoulders rounded and her head hung forward. She seemed weighted down by despair. "But why did they have to tear the place apart?"

I could only shake my head. How could you explain the casual cruelty of youth? "Call the police again, Delia. This time tell them there's been a break-in. They'll come out and take a report."

I went inside with her while she did.

"They're sending a car," she told me when she hung up.

I hated to leave her there amid the ruin of her belongings, but the police would arrive soon and I'd neglected my business way too much lately.

"I've got to get back to the shop, but I can come back this evening and help you clean this up," I told her. I couldn't explain why I felt the need to make such an offer, but I was relieved when she refused it.

"No, no, Dixie. You've already got your hands full with the investigation. I'll call my brother – he and his family will come over and we'll take care of it."

I could have reminded her that I wasn't investigating anything, but since her belief that I was had given me a way out, I kept my coward's mouth shut. With any luck, she wouldn't mention the "investigation" to her brother and I'd be spared another nasty telephone call.

I entered the shop through the alley door and stashed my purse in the desk. Pandora was at the cash register. She had an odd look on her face.

"Is everything okay?" I asked. Nothing seemed to be out of place.

"Yeah, I . . . I guess so," she said slowly. "Isn't Reginald Anderson one of your library people?"

"Yeah, he is. Did he call back?"

She slowly shook her head. "No. But I turned on the radio after you left. The news ... They found a body in Rose Hill Cemetery and they said it was Reginald Anderson. It's not a very common name. Could that be the same man you know?"

My stomach gave a roller coaster lurch. I fished in my purse until I came up with the card Ballard had given me. My fingers were shaking as I punched in the numbers.

How could I have been so arrogant as to keep information from the police? I still didn't believe anything in those files was motive for murder, but that didn't matter anymore. Since when did I get to decide what was and wasn't important?

Who did I think I was? Now a second person – a friend of mine this time – was dead. With two members of the same very small group murdered within a short time, I couldn't pretend the deaths weren't connected. The theory of a robbery gone bad flew right out the window and Delia's burglary took on a frightening significance.

"Ballard."

"Hello, Steve. This is Dixie."

"Well, hello. It's good to hear your voice."

I thought that might be about to change. "I just heard about Reg Anderson. I wanted you to know that I saw him last night – at Rose Hill Cemetery."

"You were with me last night."

"It was before that, when I was on my way home from dinner."

"Are you calling from your shop?"

"Yes."

"Don't go anywhere. We're coming over."

But ten minutes later, Kaminsky alone walked through the front door. And he wasn't happy. One look at his scowling face sent Pandora fleeing to the back of the store. I wasn't lucky enough to escape.

"If you had information about this case, Ms. McClatchey, you should have called me," he said. His nostrils flared with anger. "Me, not my lieutenant. I don't know how it is in Atlanta, but down here, the detectives work the cases, not the supervisors. The supervisors supervise."

"I just wanted to let you know as soon as I could – "

"Yeah, yeah, whatever." He pulled a notepad and a pen from an inside pocket. "You want to tell me what you know about this?"

I explained that I was at Rose Hill the evening before.

"What were you doing at a cemetery?"

"Well, it's really more than a cemetery, you know. With the roses and the history, it's more like park. I like to go there sometimes. It's a good place to think."

He frowned at me. In Kaminsky's world, normal people didn't visit cemeteries to think. "And you saw Anderson there? What did he say to you?"

"He didn't say anything. I was at the top of the hill – where the roses are – and he drove past me and went into the cemetery. I doubt if he even saw me."

"Then what?"

I was tempted to leave out the next part, but I knew better. "I drove in after him – well, not immediately after him. Another car was coming out. After they left, I drove into the cemetery." I felt my face color. "I was just curious about why he was there. Reg isn't interested in history or anything like that."

He wasn't going to thaw just because I'd admitted to a human foible. "And?"

A customer came in about then and Pandora hurried up front to meet him and gently guide him back into the shelves.

"And?" Kaminsky repeated.

"And nothing. I drove down the main road all the way to the river, but I didn't see him again. I don't know where he went." I shrugged. "It was getting dark, so I left."

I retreated behind the counter, but he moved right along with me, effectively hemming me in the small space. "That's it? You've been in close proximity to two murders and you haven't seen anything and don't know anything? That's pretty hard to swallow, Ms. McClatchey. Just how do you explain it?"

"I don't see that there's anything to explain." My back pressed uncomfortably against the counter. I couldn't move any farther away from him.

"Doesn't it seem to you that this goes a little beyond coincidence? It's like you attract murders."

"That's not fair." I pushed past him and moved to stand in the open area near the door. "I didn't have anything to do with these killings and you know it."

Homicide detectives can conduct an investigation without being nasty – I knew that from experience – but it was a lesson Kaminsky had yet to learn. When he'd entered the store minutes before, I was ready to go ahead and empty the bag for him – the files, the people I'd talked with, everything. But now, I just couldn't do it. I'd make sure Ballard got the whole story later that day, but I wouldn't give this posturing little rooster another reason to belittle me.

He kept at me for half an hour, first rehashing the discovery of Glynnis's body, then going over and over my time at Rose Hill. He wrote down where I'd been and with whom before arriving at the cemetery and where I'd gone afterwards. His nostrils reached full flare when I related meeting Ballard for coffee, but he refrained from making any comment.

Several customers came in while Kaminsky was there, but even though Pandora came out of hiding to help them, they didn't linger.

Although I wasn't going to tell him everything right then, there was some information I knew he had to have. "Delia McCullough's house was burglarized today."

His eyes narrowed. "How do you know that?"

"She . . . she called me." I'd let him learn later on that I'd been to her house. "She thought the police had come back and searched the place again."

"We didn't do that."

"I know. I told her that. She called the police, so there'll be a report."

That covered about everything, I thought. But Kaminsky still had a surprise for me.

"Maybe now you'd like to tell me why you called Reg Anderson this morning. The message you left sounded like it was important."

There it was. I'd have to tell him the truth now, at least part of it. He had the message I'd left for Reg and by tomorrow he'd have spoken with Marian and maybe even Alex. One of them was sure to tell Kaminsky about the questions I'd been asking. How, I wondered again, had I gotten myself into this mess? I'd be lucky if he didn't lock me up for obstruction.

"I was . . uh . . . kind of looking into Glynnis's murder myself. I wanted to talk to Reg about that." I steeled myself for the reaction.

Kaminsky stared at me as if I'd gone stark raving mad. "You were what? You were 'kind of looking into the murder'?" he said in a mocking tone. "What the hell do you think this is? A game? You're way out of line here, Ms. McClatchey."

"I know." It nearly killed me, but I did my best to look and act contrite. "I was trying to help, but I see now how wrong I was."

At that moment, Steve Ballard came in the front door. He gave me a smile, then looked at Kaminsky. "You still here, detective?"

"Yeah, some stuff came up." He glared at me. "I'll fill you in later, Lieutenant."

"It's just as well you're here," Ballard told him. "I thought of something Ms. McClatchey might be able to help us with." He turned to me. "We spent quite a while at Anderson's apartment this morning. Guess what we found?"

He sounded too cheerful to be talking about my telephone message. I just shook my head.

"A copy of Tom Clancy's *Hunt for Red October*. A first edition. Just like the note in Glynnis's purse."

Again, he looked to me for comment and again I kept my mouth shut. If Kaminsky hadn't been there, I'd have told Ballard everything right then.

"And that's not the only book we found. There are lots of them. Looks like he was selling them – quite a few were packaged up, ready to be mailed."

Kaminsky shot his superior an incredulous look, horrified, I was sure, that the lieutenant was sharing those details with a civilian. Ballard ignored him.

"Now, you obviously know a lot about books, including first editions, right?"

"I know a good bit," I acknowledged. "And I know where to look for what I don't know."

He nodded. "I was wondering if you'd come over there with us. It's not that far and it might be a help if we had some idea of how valuable those books are."

Pandora had returned to the front of the store at Steve's entrance and had been standing nearby, listening to every word. When he issued his invitation, she volunteered to stay at the shop until I got back.

"I couldn't ask you to do that. You've already worked so many extra hours this week. Don't you have classes this afternoon?"

"Nothing important."

So I agreed to go look at the books. The afternoon was pretty much shot anyway. Besides, doing this favor now might go a long way toward the massive fence mending that lay ahead of me.

Kaminsky had other things to do, so Steve and I went alone.

"I had a great time last night," he said.

"Me, too. Maybe as soon as they finish the kitchen, you can come over and I'll cook you dinner."

He laughed. "I know about remodeling projects. They might not be finished before some time next year. I was hoping we'd get together sooner than that."

I looked over at him, eyes on the road and both hands on the wheel. I didn't want to wait that long either. "What about this Sunday? I can't promise a home-cooked meal, but Hot Shot and I would love to share a pizza with you."

He grinned. "That is a date. And I'll bring the beer."

Oh, this relationship had great potential.

I debated telling him about the files right then, but just couldn't bring myself to do it. Would one more day really matter? Maybe I could eliminate Carlton and Cassie as suspects. Then I wouldn't feel obliged to hand any of the Friends' folders over to the police. And maybe by then I could think of some way to make the explanation easier.

As we crossed Interstate 75 and joined the northbound traffic on Vineville Avenue, I gave Steve a brief, somewhat sanitized account of my conversation with Kaminsky.

"I'm sorry I meddled in something I shouldn't have, but I thought the other volunteers might feel a little easier talking to me. You know, off the record."

He took his eyes off the road long enough to give me a puzzled glance, but didn't say anything.

"Until today – until Reg, I mean – I really didn't think there could be any connection between Glynnis's death and the Friends," I told him. "I guess I was just, I don't know, kind of keeping my hand in."

Steve smiled. "Just can't get police work out of your system?"

"Yeah." I said, pretending to be just as silly as my explanation sounded. "That's right."

Reg Anderson had lived in one of the gated condominium communities on Rivoli Drive. Each building sat like a stucco jewel on a postage-stamp-sized lawn. Reg's unit was pale peach. Steve used a key on the heavy wooden door.

If the editorial staff of *Gentlemen's Quarterly* had collaborated with the AARP, they'd have produced the interior of Reg's home. The furnishings were elegant and expensive, even if the paintings on the walls were mass produced pieces chosen to complement the upholstery rather than satisfy the soul. The kitchen contained every gadget known to cooks. In contrast, an assortment of vitamins, over-the-counter nostrums and prescription drugs covered a sizable area of the bathroom vanity. A worn plaid bathrobe was draped over one of the bedposts and a heating pad, pressed and creased from frequent use, lay across the back of one of the living room's designer chairs.

Reg had turned the condo's second bedroom into a combination library and office. Two walls held nearly full bookshelves. The shiny, bright spines of the books made a colorful display against the white wall.

"There are one hundred and sixty-three of 'em," Steve said. "I know. I counted. Most of them seem new or almost new. I set that Tom Clancy there on the desk."

I nodded, but was more interested at that point in the other books. I stood before the shelves, bending my head at an uncomfortable angle to read the titles on the lower shelves. On the bottom shelf, lying flat by itself was *The Anatomy of Melancholy.*

"So, can you tell us what they're worth?"

I straightened up. "I should be able to give you a ball park figure after I've done a little research."

"We'll have an inventory made and get it to you," he suggested.

I shook my head. "That won't work."

"Why not?"

"The value of a book depends, in large part, on its condition. There may also be inscriptions or signatures." I nodded at the shelves. "I'll have to examine each one myself."

He wanted it done right then, but I had to turn him down.

"I had no idea there'd be so many books. This is going to take quite a while. I can't leave poor Pandora alone any longer. She didn't sign on as a full time employee and I think she's already missed one class today."

He nodded.

My conscience prodded me. "Look, I can come back after I

close up."

"Won't work. I've got a meeting at five that could go long. What about tomorrow?"

"Any time after six."

"Why don't I pick you up at the shop when you close?" Steve asked.

"Why don't I meet you here instead?"

CHAPTER THIRTEEN

I got back to the shop just in time to thank Pandora and close up.

"Are you sure you're okay, Dixie? You seem kind of frazzled."

"Yes, I'm fine. Sorry I left you here so long on your own."

"Oh, I didn't mind at all. I love being here." The quick smile was replaced by a sympathetic frown. "I'm so sorry about your friend Reg."

I hugged her. "Thanks. Why don't you take tomorrow off?"

"Oh, I couldn't do that. I'll see you at ten."

It was a five-minute drive home. More demolition had taken place during the day. Where cabinets once hung in the kitchen, holes now dotted the plaster. And more cabinets had joined the pile in the middle of the floor. Hot Shot must have heard me come in. His angry cries were loud enough to be heard in the kitchen.

I picked my way through the debris and hurried up the stairs. There I released the cat from his prison and went about what was becoming the daily task of closing the drawers and doors he'd opened. Should I invest in childproof locks? I reflected I should be grateful he was a kitten and not a puppy. Even though he'd pulled a few things out on the floor, at least he hadn't felt the need to chew them up.

I fed the cat and warmed up some leftover soup for myself. I watched the evening news as I ate. Reg's murder had replaced Glynnis's as the lead story. From Channel 13's report, I gathered the police were no closer to solving the second killing than the first.

It was already dark when I remembered it was Thursday – the night I had to roll the big plastic garbage bin to the front curb for early morning pick up. I pulled the plastic bag from the kitchen can, which I supposed was now the hall can, knotted the top and carried it outside. After I'd rolled the bin to the curb, I strolled slowly back up the drive, listening to the crickets and the distant hum of traffic. I did my best to embrace the peaceful evening, but it did nothing to calm my worries about Ballard and the files.

From the direction of the magnolia tree came a shower of liquid notes, sung over and over with ever-changing variations. I knew it must be the lonely mockingbird. In the limited light afforded by the streetlights, I tried to find him, my eyes darting from one part of the big tree to another, trying to follow the elusive song. But I never spotted the singer himself. I moved closer for a better look and the song abruptly stopped. The bird was silent as long as I stood there. After a few minutes, I gave up and headed back to the house.

Hot Shot was inching cautiously across the cement step toward the back yard.

"Oh, no, you don't." I scooped him up. "I'm not about to let you get out and get yourself hurt – not after what I went through saving you in the first place. You might as well accept the fact that you are a house cat."

I put him down in the kitchen, then turned my attention to the door. As was its habit, the latch hadn't caught when I'd closed it and this time I could have lost the cat. I shut the door firmly, pulling upward to make sure it was secure. I'd call Edelman first thing in the morning and ask him to move fixing the door to the top of his priority list.

Once again there was no answer at the Waycaster house. Leaving a message on the machine was the best I could do. But I got Carlton Mabry on the second ring.

"Sure, honey," he said when I told him I needed to talk with him in person. "You know I'd never turn down an opportunity to see you. I've gotta come downtown tomorrow anyway, having lunch with some fellas at the City Club. Want me to swing by your store in the morning?"

I told him that would be great and he said to expect him around eleven.

If his alibi checked out and I could eliminate Cassie as a suspect – and I couldn't realistically see her in the role of homicidal strangler – I'd have no more excuses for keeping the files to myself. I still hated the thought of turning Kaminsky loose on Glynnis's other victims, but I couldn't justify keeping information from the police any longer.

To underscore that resolve, I carried the box of Glynnis's files out to the Blazer. I stashed it in the back, covered it with an old blanket and locked the car. Now I'd have no excuse for not handing them over to Ballard the next day.

Hot Shot and I spent a quiet evening curled up on the living room sofa with the television remote. Before bed, I opened the door to the side porch and listened for a moment. The mockingbird's serenade had ended. Had he found love or just gotten sleepy? Everything had to sleep – even Hot Shot, as it turned out. Last night's wild marauding was only a distant memory. He snuggled up beside me in bed and didn't move until morning.

Friday was a noticeably cooler day. Springtime in Macon was living up to its erratic reputation. A light north wind held the potential of developing into a wicked blow. I passed over the cotton dresses in my closet in favor of wool slacks and a long-sleeved, celery-colored jersey. A short leather jacket completed my outfit.

Business continued to be brisk. The Cherry Blossom Festival would end Sunday afternoon and, as a merchant, I'd be sorry it was over. Customers came and went with satisfying regularity, but three of the people who stopped by weren't interested in looking at the books. All three were women, all three were young and white and all three came, at different times, in search of Pandora. Her reputation as a seer had spread through downtown Macon like fire ants in a pasture. She handled them well – tactful, friendly, and promising to meet them later in the day at a nearby coffee shop.

"You might be able pick up some extra money doing your readings," I said when the last woman had left.

Pandora's face showed shock. "Oh, I'd never charge for a reading. That would just be wrong, I'm sure."

"Oh." I hadn't known fortune telling was so fraught with moral pitfalls.

"My mama would die if she ever heard that I took money."

Her sharp eyes examined my face for interest. When she saw none, she returned to stocking shelves.

We didn't have many customers that morning and I took advantage of the lull to box up some Internet orders.

"I'm going to mail these," I told Pandora. "Be back in a few minutes."

I loaded the boxes into the back of the Blazer and drove the few blocks to the post office. There I stacked them onto a little hand truck, rolled them inside, and sent them off across the country. The Internet was definitely a blessing for my business.

Carlton Mabry was as good as his word. He was waiting at the store, a big bunch of daffodils in his hand, when I got back.

"Mary sent these, said she knew you loved them."

"I do. They're beautiful." I inhaled what I've always thought of as the very essence of spring. "I'll be sure to call her and thank her."

I went to the back room for a vase and he trailed after me. As usual, he was casually dressed in khakis and an oxford cloth shirt. He avoided suits and ties whenever possible. I knew he and his family were well off, but Carlton never strayed very far from his blue-collar roots.

"Now what did you want to see me for, honey? Is there something I can help you with around the shop?"

I arranged the bright flowers in the vase and filled it with water. "No, nothing like that. I'm just looking for some information."

I laid out the whole situation for him. My explanation, helped by repetition, was quicker and more concise this time.

"Well, I'll be damned," he said when I'd finished. He gave a little chuckle. "So that's what she was hinting around about."

"Who, Glynnis?"

"Yeah, pulled me aside after a work session a couple of weeks ago and said something about this DUI that I got back twenty, twenty-five years ago. I thought she was just being nosy. You know how she was – always into everybody's business."

I nodded. "That was the information in your file – the DUI."

He looked puzzled. "Well, who the hell cares about that? I'm not proud of it, but it's no secret. I mean, I was married at the time so my wife already knows all about it. I took some boys out after work one night and just had too many beers. Mary's never let me live it down."

I had to agree that a twenty-year-old DUI arrest was pretty poor blackmailing ammunition. "Did Glynnis ever ask you for anything? Ask for anything in exchange for keeping quiet?"

He gave a bark of a laugh. "Hell, no, and I'd have told her what I thought about it if she had. The only thing she ever asked me about was getting one of our puppies." I remembered that he and his wife had raised Brittany spaniels for years. "When I told her they were going for three hundred a piece, she backed off damned quick." He shrugged. "That's not what you mean about blackmailing, is it?"

"Maybe. From what I've learned, she never asked for anything very big. She might have thought keeping your past a secret was worth the price of a puppy."

He laughed again. "Then I guess she was disappointed."

"Just one more thing. I feel silly asking, but, like I told you, if I can eliminate everyone, then I can just destroy the files. So. . . can you tell me where you were when Glynnis was killed?"

"You serious? You want my alibi?" he asked with a grin.

A twenty-year-old DUI wasn't motive enough to snub someone, much less kill them, but I felt like I should be consistent.

"Yes, if you don't mind."

"Hell, I don't mind. Last Tuesday Mary and I went down to the campgrounds in Peach County – for the Boy Scouts, you know. A bunch of us go down there from time to time to do regular maintenance, keep the place nice for the kids." He gave his watch an unobtrusive look. "Is there anything else I can tell you?"

I shook my head. "No. I really appreciate your coming by." I reached up and gave him a quick hug. Then I picked up the vase. I'd put the daffodils up front where everyone could enjoy them. "You wouldn't believe the trouble I'm having getting in touch with everybody. Cassie hasn't returned my calls and Reg . . . well I tried to talk to him, but now . . . You know, it's so strange. I saw him the day he was killed, at Rose Hill Cemetery, but I didn't get to talk to him. I still can't imagine what he was doing there."

He hurried off to his lunch date. As soon as the door closed behind him, Pandora materialized out of the bookshelves on the far side of the shop. Her forehead was creased in a rare frown.

"What were you doing back there?"

She shrugged. "Just trying to stay out of the way so you and your friend could talk." She pressed her lips together, then added, "I got a weird feeling about that man."

I didn't think I could stand another lecture on psychic hunches. "Look, Pandora, I don't mean to hurt your feelings, but you seem to get vibes and feelings and such about everyone who walks in the door. But they don't really amount to anything, do they?" I sighed. "Could we just concentrate on the here and now and leave the clairvoyance for another time?"

"Sure," she said with a touch of anger. "I won't mention it again."

I knew I'd have to soothe her feelings, but I just didn't have the strength for it right then. The biggest concern of the moment was confirming Carlton's alibi.

Just the same as everyone else I'd talked to, I was sure Carlton hadn't anything to do with the murders. Still I wanted to touch all the bases. That way I could destroy the files in good conscience. Then I realized I had a ready-made reason for the call.

"The daffodils are beautiful," I said when I reached Mary Mabry by phone a few minutes later. "You were so sweet to send them."

"I was glad to do it, dear. I remember you saying that you were partial to them."

"How is the vegetable garden coming along?"

She prattled happily about soil preparation and planting while I tried to come up with the right words for checking on Carlton's actions. When it seemed right, I spoke.

"Carlton told me about how you all work down at the campgrounds for the Scouts. I was just wondering if it's something anyone can volunteer to do. I mean, would I have to be involved with a particular troop?"

"Oh, bless you, no. We'd love to have you." She laughed. "We're always needing extra hands. There's so much to do."

"Yeah, Carlton said y'all were out there for hours one day last week."

"That's right. We drove down as soon as he got home from the sorting session. He went off with some of the men to clear underbrush and I painted. There were six cabins to paint and we did three of them in one afternoon! I thought my arm would drop off I was so tired.

"But you don't want to hear about an old woman's aches and pains. Now, if you really want to help, you just call Jeannie Campbell and get on the list. We'll let you know when the next work day is scheduled."

I copied down a telephone number I'd never use and felt guilty at deceiving a sweet woman like Mary Mabry. Maybe a cash contribution to the Boy Scouts would smooth out my karmic debt. I made a note on my calendar to send a check the next week.

I was cheered by what I'd accomplished. I could now destroy Carlton's file. Only Cassie Waycaster remained. Once that was done, I'd turn over the box of files and try to make everything right with Steve Ballard.

I thought about calling Edward to confirm our date for Saturday night's Fifties-Sixties Dance, but doubted he was in the mood to think about dancing. So I turned my attention to the business of paying my only employee.

It took me nearly half an hour to figure out the intricacies of doing so. There were forms we both had to fill out and state and federal deductions to be made. Luckily, I was able to find the forms online and print them out. Otherwise, it might have been weeks before she saw a penny of her pay.

Pandora's pouting didn't last long. She left at noon, happily clutching several books and her first week's paycheck. The check was for considerably more than I'd planned because of the extra hours she'd worked, but the freedom she'd given me was worth the money. The books she took with her were a result of her taking advantage of our newly-created employee discount.

I'd brought the morning paper with me and, as I relaxed with it and a cup of coffee, I read the front-page story of Reg's murder. His body had been discovered by a groundskeeper early Thursday morning. Death was due to a gunshot wound. He hadn't been robbed and his car was untouched beside him. I couldn't tell from the brief description exactly where he'd been in Rose Hill.

There was no obituary notice yet. I realized with a little shock of surprise that I didn't have any idea who his next of kin might be. Reg had talked very little about his family, yet I was well versed in his opinions on books, food, and travel. It's odd what we choose and don't choose to share with others.

For the hundredth time since learning of Reg's death, I wondered if it was my fault. Would things have turned out differently if I'd given the files to the police in the beginning? Had I been so sure that the people in the files weren't involved, so confident of my own superior opinion, that I'd withheld something critical in the investigation? And was this just another piece of the pattern I'd created out of conceit? After all, Donald would still be alive if I hadn't been so sure of my abilities as a cop.

Shaking my head to clear it of such dark thoughts, I poured more coffee and puzzled over the deaths. There had to be a connection, but I was damned if I could see it. Nothing in those files should have led to murder, but what else was there? I never thought Reg and Glynnis had anything more in common than membership in Friends of the Library, but there must have been something. However, it wasn't up to me to discover what it was. My goal was to extricate myself from this mess, not venture in any further.

The browsers lingered longer than usual in the shop that afternoon, a fact I attributed to the chilly weather and heartily endorsed. If a person spends enough time in a store, he or she usually finds something to buy.

I tried calling Cassie once more. This time a small child who I took to be Jason answered.

"Is your mother there?"

There were some silent seconds, then he said, "No."

"Are you sure?" I knew Cassie would never leave her children alone. "Can I talk to your mommy?" More silence. Then the connection was broken. Cassie had probably talked with one of the other Friends and learned I'd been asking questions about Glynnis's files. I tried one more time, but after ten or eleven rings, I gave up. It looked like I was going to have to drive out and see her in person if I wanted to talk to her. But I didn't have time to do that today.

I closed the shop at six and drove north out of town.

Steve was already at Reg's condo when I got there. He opened the door to my knock and led the way to the office.

"It's all yours," he said with a sweeping gesture toward the books.

I got comfortable on the carpet next to the shelves, armed with a pen and a legal pad. Steve lounged in the desk chair and told me some of what they'd found in their search of the condo.

"We've gone through all of his papers. Everything about the book selling seems to be in this desk. He had a pretty good little business going here. I'd say he was netting anywhere from five hundred to a thousand a month. Not a fortune, but it was enough to provide him with some nice extras."

The amount was larger than I expected, based on my eBay research. Reg must have had several outlets for the books he sold.

"And it was tax free," Steve went on. "From what I've been able to determine, old Reg wasn't declaring any of that income to Uncle Sam. Still he kept pretty good records of the books he sold – two sets of books, in fact. One in that green ledger there and the other on the computer. But there were hardly any records of books that he bought. Makes you wonder, doesn't it?"

I put down the Mary Higgins Clark novel I was examining and sighed. It was time to share some information. "I don't think he bought many books. I . . . uh . . . I came across an account he had on eBay. I think Reg was a thief – and at least some of these books came from Friends of the Library donations." I picked up *The Anatomy of Melancholy*. "I'm pretty sure this was one of ours."

I told him about Cassie and her lost book. His expression didn't change and I could see the news didn't surprise him.

"Glynnis must have found out what he was doing."

"It looks that way," I said, "considering the note in her purse and the fact that Red October is sitting there on the desk." The guilt was stronger than ever now. It didn't just look that way. It was that way and I had the proof. As soon as I could verify that Cassie was in the clear, I'd give the remaining files, including Reg's, to Ballard.

"One thing I don't understand," Steve said. "If he was stealing from the library, how did he get the books out of the sorting center? Surely the rest of you would have noticed if he'd waltzed out of there with boxes of books he hadn't paid for."

I was relieved to have a question I could answer without first having to censor the words. "Yeah, we'd have noticed that, but he didn't have to do it that way. We're a pretty casual group, you know. Marian has the official key, I guess you'd call it, but there are probably several others floating around. He could have gotten one of those.

"And even if he didn't, getting books out of there wouldn't have been hard to do. Marian always opens the door for our sorting sessions – gets there way before anyone else – but the last one out locks up. The lock is just one of those push button things – you push it in and pull the door to behind you and it's locked. All Reg had to do was arrange to be the last one out. He could have left the door unlocked and then come back later and taken anything he wanted."

Steve nodded. "Could all these books have come from the library donations?"

"I don't think so." I considered the books stacked around me on the floor. "There're just too many. He must have been getting them from other places as well."

"Like where?"

"I don't know right offhand." I pushed a hand through my hair, trying to think. "Even though you didn't find any records, he could have bought some of them. And we already know he was a thief. Who knows where he might have stolen from? Private collections, even some stores, if he didn't mind running the risk of being caught. He could also have volunteered with other library organizations."

Steve stretched his legs straight out in front of him. "It's a hell of thing. If I'd found out about all this last week, Anderson would have been my number one suspect." He'd learned about the files somehow, I decided. I waited for him to drop the net, but he didn't. "But now – it's hard to be a suspect when you're dead." He shook his head. "Still there has to be some connection between the two. You got any ideas?" His eyes bored into mine like a priest asking questions of a penitent.

"No, not a one."

At the end of an hour, I'd examined and cataloged all 163 books. I got to my feet and stretched.

"Well, that's it."

"You're done?"

"Not finished, no, but I've got the raw information I need. I'll try to get the complete valuation to you some time tomorrow."

We walked out to our cars. The sun had disappeared beyond the horizon and it was even cooler now.

"Listen," Steve said, "since we're already here, why don't we check out the Balloon Glow? It's right up the street there and it's free."

"Mmmmmm. I don't think so." I glanced at my watch. "Besides, it's after seven. It must be over by now."

"Nah, they never do the glow thing until it's full dark. Come on. Have you been before? It's really a neat thing to see."

The fact was that I hadn't been before and I'd always wanted to go. More than that, I loved spending time with this man. So I let myself be persuaded. I locked my car and climbed into his Toyota for the three-minute ride to Wesleyan College. That Steve was driving his own vehicle and not one that belonged to the city of Macon underlined the fact that he believed this evening was more a social occasion than a professional function.

As it turned out, we'd have done better to walk over. We followed a slow-moving line of cars several blocks down Tucker Road before Steve found a place to park. Then we joined the stream of people walking back to the campus.

The Balloon Glow was one of the most popular Cherry Blossom events. On the last Friday evening of the festival, the natural bowl and rolling meadow that was the center of the Wesleyan College campus filled with hot air balloons of different sizes and every imaginable color. People began gathering by late afternoon to stake their claims to the best spots for watching the spectacle.

By the time Steve and I arrived, the place was packed. Picnics were laid out on blankets. Wine was being poured. Kids ran off their excitement, shouting and twirling the lighted plastic tubes their parents bought from the vendors scattered around the edge of the field. The same vendors sold food, soft drinks, and beer. Music, just slightly too loud, was broadcast over a public address system, adding to the air of pleasant confusion. But it was the balloons, most now fully inflated, but still anchored to the ground, that were the undisputed center of attention.

We strolled down the gentle slope, the new grass springy beneath our feet. Steve took my hand. There was nothing awkward about the action – joining hands was as natural as breathing in the fresh night air. It was a cool, one might even say cold, evening, but the carnival–like atmosphere around us seemed to raise the temperature. Or it might have been that all those bodies milling around simply blocked the chilly wind. We wandered along the edge of the field and Steve got us hot chocolate. The paper cup was a welcome warmth in my hands.

Below us the bright canopies undulated over their baskets. People who seemed to know what they were doing moved quickly among them, clipboards in hand and serious expressions on their faces. They stopped often to converse with the different balloon crews. Every few minutes, a whooshing sound could be heard above the other noises as a burst of heated air was released to keep a canopy upright.

By seven-thirty, night had overtaken the day. Above us, a few stars competed with the streetlights along Forsyth Road. The music stopped and a man's voice issued a quick welcome over the public address system. He thanked those people and corporations that evidently needed thanking and then asked the crowd to watch the field.

Dramatic music swelled in the air and then was almost drowned out by a low roar that built in volume as all the burners fired at one time. A collective exclamation of awe rose from the crowd. Each balloon on the field glowed from the fire within, shining like huge, multicolored fireflies in the dark.

"What do you think?" Steve asked, his lips close to my ear to be heard over the crowd.

"It's magical," I told him truthfully. "I've never seen anything like it."

"You should come back tomorrow morning and watch them all take off. That's a sight to see."

I just grinned. The sight of all those balloons ascending together would be magnificent, but I never planned anything for six-thirty in the morning.

CHAPTER FOURTEEN

As he drove me back to my car, Steve lobbied hard for continuing the evening.

"Let's go get something to eat. Or maybe listen to some music. You like jazz? Alphonso Thomas is at 550 Blues."

There was nothing I'd like better than to spend more time with him, but I knew exactly where a couple of drinks and sitting close together in a dimly lit club would lead. And that couldn't happen as long as I was holding back information from him. By this time tomorrow he'd know everything. It would have been better to get it over with tonight, but I wanted to try one last time to talk to Cassie. I only hoped that I'd be able to explain my reasons for the delay well enough that he'd forgive me.

"I'm really exhausted," was my excuse, "and the house is a wreck with the construction. You are still coming to dinner Sunday, aren't you?"

"I wouldn't miss it for anything."

It was nearly nine o'clock and I was starving. I pulled into a drive-through and ordered a burger and fries. During the five minutes it took to reach my house I'd eaten half the potatoes. That took the frantic edge off my hunger, but I was eager to finish the rest.

No key was necessary at my side door. It swung open at my touch. I was furious. Not only had Edelman not fixed the latch, his men hadn't even secured the door when they left. I was going to call him tonight and let him know just what I thought about it.

There was no feline wailing. Maybe Hot Shot was getting used to his daily confinement. I found a place on the crowded dining room table to set my paper bag and climbed the stairs to release him.

The bedroom door was ajar. How, I wondered, had Hot Shot managed to turn a doorknob, then realized the absurdity of that. He might have been able to pull open drawers and unlatched doors, but unless the cat had suddenly grown thumbs, he hadn't manipulated a doorknob. But if Hot Shot hadn't done it, who had?

I'd warned the contractors to stay on the ground floor. The note announcing that a cat was inside was still taped to the bedroom door. Oh, Edelman had a lot to answer for. If Hot Shot had gotten out of the house because of the workmen's carelessness, I'd fire the whole bunch of them.

One step into the bedroom and I stopped dead still. In an

unpleasant echo of Delia McCullough's burglary, the contents of my bureau and dresser had been tossed into the floor. The bathroom had suffered the same fate. Hot Shot couldn't be blamed for this. It was definitely the product of human hands.

The house had an empty feel and I was sure the intruder had gone, but I was still cautious as I looked through the remaining upstairs rooms. They'd been searched as well. But security wasn't my major concern right then. Although I called his name, as well as repeating 'here kitty, kitty, kitty' over and over, there was no sign of the kitten.

Heart pounding, I hurried downstairs, still calling the cat. In my past life, I'd encountered instances of burglars injuring or even killing pets. An icy fear settled in my stomach. Room by room, I covered the first floor, calling Hot Shot's name and noting the debris of a thorough search. Nothing appeared to be missing, but I wasn't looking that closely. My whole focus was on finding the cat.

In the kitchen, I examined the lock on the door. It didn't seem to be in any worse repair than when I left home that morning. The burglar may have gotten lucky here and not even had to force a lock to get in. If the back door hadn't been secured when the workmen left, then the house had been wide open for anyone.

I forced myself to take a deep breath, then methodically checked that all the other doors and ground-floor windows were shut and locked. Unless the cat had gotten out through the kitchen door, he was probably still in the house. Maybe he'd hidden as soon as the intruder entered, but I doubted it. He was such a friendly little animal that he probably ran to greet whoever it was. He always appeared when I came in the door. Would he have been any less welcoming to a stranger?

I got a Harp from the fridge in the hall and opened it, all the while calling for the cat. I made my voice as warm and unthreatening as I could, but still got no response. After a long swallow, I went out onto the screened porch. I didn't bother with a light, just stood there staring out into the night, trying to calm my fears and damp down the anger at having my home violated.

It was the files, of course—both here and at Delia's house, the files that were now locked in the Blazer. But why? There was nothing that incriminating in any of them. The only evidence of criminal activity concerned Reg Anderson. The worst thing that might come if the other files were made public was embarrassment. There was nothing there important enough to provoke murder.

Tears of self-pity were rising in the back of my throat. It was all my fault. My intentions no longer mattered. Sure, I'd been trying to protect people I thought were innocent, but what gave me the authority to make those decisions? My friend Reg was dead and my poor cat was gone.

The flood of misery was interrupted by a faint "maow?"

"Hot Shot!"

The little tabby poked his head through the doorway and stretched one tentative paw onto the stone floor of the porch. Very slowly I dropped to my knees. I didn't want to spook him, but I had to make sure he wasn't hurt.

"Hey, there, buddy," I said, pitching my voice low so as not to startle him and slowly extending a hand. "Come on, come see me."

I stayed perfectly still as he first sniffed, then rubbed against my outstretched fingers. "That's it. Just get comfortable again." I scratched a spot between his ears and heard the purring crank up. Still moving in slow motion, I picked him up and took him to the love seat. As I rhythmically stroked his soft fur, he – and I – gradually relaxed. From somewhere out in the darkness a bird song reached my ears. Camouflaged by the petting motions, I examined his tiny body to make sure he wasn't injured. When I was assured he was okay and ended my examination, he curled up in my lap and slept. I didn't know where he'd been, but I was grateful he'd found safe refuge.

My next move should have been calling the police. Lord knows I'd insisted that Delia do exactly that after her burglary, but I just couldn't stand anymore tonight. Handing over the files was going to trigger some serious unpleasantness, I knew, especially since I could no longer claim that they weren't somehow relevant. There would be questions, accusations, and recriminations, and I'd have no defense whatsoever. Tomorrow was soon enough to start that ball rolling.

I got little sleep Friday night. When I wasn't fuming with anger over the break in, I was tossing with guilt over withholding the files. Hot Shot slept peacefully through all my thrashing around. As daylight brightened the windows, I gave in and got up. The cat stayed behind, curled peacefully in the tangle of covers. I had work to do.

It was several hours before I returned the house to something close to order. I was more fortunate than Delia had been. Although my place was thoroughly searched, there'd been no intentional destruction and nothing was missing. Most of the work consisted of retrieving the contents of closets and chests and putting them back in the appropriate places. I stopped only twice during the clean up – once to make coffee and once, when he'd managed to drag his lazy self from the bed, to give Hot Shot his breakfast. It was very physical work and the exertion helped to dispel some of my anger. And I already knew that I'd be taking a giant step toward getting rid of the guilt when I turned the files over to Steve that morning.

I called Delia McCullough around eight-thirty.

"How are you?"

"I'm doing all right." She sounded tired.

"Did you get the house cleaned up?"

She sighed. "We tried to do it ourselves, but it was such a disaster that my brother hired a crew to come in. I stayed with him and his family. It's almost back to normal, I suppose, although I have a lot of broken things to replace. I'm going to work on the insurance claim today."

"Was anything taken?"

"The only thing I can find missing is poor Glynnis's camera."

"Your daughter was quite a photographer, wasn't she?" I remembered all the pictures in her files.

"Yes, she was." Pride drove the weariness from her voice. "She could have been a professional – she was that good. Sometime you'll have to come over and I'll show you her work. Glynnis always said you just never knew when you'd see something to photograph. She got to where she took that camera with her all the time."

"Did she use a digital camera?"

"No, although she ..." There was an audible gulp and I knew she was fighting to overcome tears. "She was going to get one, she just never got around to it. And now she never will."

She gave in to a brief bout of sobbing. I wished there were something I could do or say to ease her suffering, but I knew that the only way to get past the grief was to live through it. As I waited for her tears to subside, I had the stirrings of an idea.

"I'm sorry, Dixie," she finally said. "Was there anything else you wanted?"

"Just one thing. Did she develop and print her own pictures?"

"No. She said she could do that if she wanted, but that was the easy part and she didn't have time to waste on it. Most of the time she took her film to a little camera shop on Riverside Drive."

It was a long shot, but worth a try. "You didn't find any receipt stubs for photos in her purse, did you?"

"No...why? Do you think she might have taken pictures of something important?"

I didn't want to get her hopes up. "I don't know, Delia. But why don't you go by the camera store and see if they're holding any pictures for Glynnis?"

"I'll do it!" Her voice lifted a bit, buoyed up by the prospect of constructive activity. "I'll do it this afternoon."

I decided to wait until I got to the shop to call Steve. After a quick shower, I was ready to go. Since Edelman and company took weekends off, Hot Shot was allowed to roam free that day. I double-checked the lock, then started down the driveway. Furious squawks filled the air. A squirrel streaked down the sidewalk with a mockingbird flying after him in hot pursuit. The squirrel, who must have looked too much like a cat for the bird's comfort, finally dove into the safety of a dense hedge. The bird flew off, pleased with a job well done. Just one more reason to keep Hot Shot inside.

As I drove through the waking streets, I couldn't help picturing Glynnis gloating at her own cleverness and relishing her victims' pain. I could imagine her smile when she showed Marian Saxby the record of her father's first marriage and her enjoyment in presenting Deannie with the evidence of her past crime. She really was an awful woman, and I now believed that was what got her killed.

Saturday wasn't as busy as the early part of the week had been. The Arts and Crafts Festival would bring a lot of people downtown during the next two days, but most of them would stay a block south on Mulberry Street where hundreds of booths were set up to sell paintings, crafts, woodworking, and pottery.

I kept busy for a while with the valuation of Reg's inventory. Using some of my own reference books and a few online resources, I was able to produce a fairly accurate list of values for the books. My final calculation was $15,500.

I sighed, knowing I couldn't put this off any longer. I called the police department first, but was told Lt. Ballard was off and wouldn't return until Monday. Next I called his house, but only got his machine.

"Give me a call, please, Steve. I have the information ready on the books and I need to talk to you about something else. Something important."

I dreaded the confrontation. Once the truth was out, I feared Steve would be as angry as Kaminsky had been the day before. No, angrier. The prospect of his forgiving me had become pretty much a thing of the past as soon as I discovered my house had been searched.

Edward called just before noon. "Here I am, risen from the dead, or at least from feeling like death."

"You sound so much better. How do you feel?"

He chuckled. "About how you'd expect a human punching bag to feel a week after the main event. But, all things considered, I'm doing okay. George's check cleared the bank, so that's a load off my mind. And tonight I'm planning to try out some really devastating moves on the dance floor – that is, if you don't mind being seen in public with someone whose face bears a striking resemblance to an eggplant."

"Of course I want to go! I've even got a new dress."

"I hope it's suitably retro, sweetie."

A lot of people who attended the annual oldies dance dressed in what they believed to be the style of the Fifties, heavy on the poodle skirts, bobby socks, and saddle shoes. But I wasn't going to follow that crowd. "Not really retro, I'm afraid, but I think you'll be pleased. The skirt should twirl nicely."

"Then I'll pick you up at five till eight. And don't worry about food or drink. Uncle Eddie is providing everything!"

Hearing him sound so positive lifted a weight that I didn't even know had been pressing me down. I still thought George should be reported to the police and I'd probably revive that subject later on, but for today and tonight, I wasn't going to do anything to spoil his good mood. Edward deserved some fun and, I decided, so did I.

Steve still hadn't called by the time I closed. Since I had a short reprieve, I thought I'd try and see Cassie that afternoon. Maybe I could eliminate her and destroy her folder as well. She lived in Shirley Hills. It was only a short drive across the river from my shop.

The Waycaster house was a brick ranch about forty years old. It was attractive, but the yard needed some work. Weeds competed for space in the flowerbeds and bicycles had ridden away the grass in parts of the front yard. A rolled-up newspaper lay in the drive where it'd been delivered. Only one car sat in the carport and no one answered my knock. I'd struck out again. It seemed extreme, but it looked like Cassie had taken her family out of town just to avoid me.

I tried four more times to get hold of Steve Saturday afternoon. When I still hadn't been able to reach him by six o'clock, I decided to forget it until the morning. I couldn't bring myself to try and find Kaminsky. Steve was going to be bad enough, but telling Kaminsky what I'd done would have been so awful I didn't even want to consider it.

I had no first-hand knowledge of how women dressed for dances in the fifties, although I suspected it was much like it is today – a little of this and a little of that, with few absolutes constituting the most current style. But, no matter what the year, I couldn't imagine anyone not liking the dress I'd bought for Saturday night. Pale lavender cotton blend with a scoop neck, short sleeves and a full skirt flaring out from the fitted waist, it made me feel sixteen again – at least until I looked in the mirror. Then my thirty-four-year-old face quickly dispelled that notion.

I showered, dried and fluffed my hair into a pixie style that I thought fit the period, applied more make up than I usually did, and was ready when Edward arrived at the front door. He was the epitome of Fifties chic. He'd slicked back his thick blond hair like a modern-day James Dean. The look was complemented by a white tee shirt, tight jeans and, of course, the requisite leather jacket. The only jarring note was his bruised face, but he seemed determined not to let it bother him.

"Let's get going, baby doll. We're going to rock the night away!"

Then he whipped a white florist's box out from behind his back. Inside was an enormous purple orchid with a matching satin ribbon.

"My goodness," was all I could manage.

He gave a delighted laugh. "Isn't it ghastly? But it's just the thing for tonight. Here, put it on. See, it goes on your wrist with this little elastic band."

When we walked into the City Auditorium fifteen minutes later, I felt like I was sporting a funeral spray on my left arm, but needn't have worried about being conspicuous. I wasn't the only orchid transporter. As we threaded our way through the tables to find the one we were assigned, we were surrounded by a sea of bouffant hairdos, poodle skirts, and an extraordinary number of white sport coats adorned with pink carnations. There were also quite a few James Deans milling around, but none could hold a candle to my date.

Edward had packed a picnic basket. With a flourish, he arranged wine, crystal glasses, linen napkins, and elaborate cold cuts, fruit and miniature dessert platters on the table before us.

"I know, I know," he said, leaning close to my ear to be heard above the band performing an enthusiastic version of "At the Hop," "you don't like wine, but darling, the occasion simply cries out for it."

I didn't mind a bit. For once in my life, I enjoyed the wine. In fact I enjoyed everything. The whole evening was infused with whimsy, good spirits, and celebration – a welcome change from the two weeks just past. We became immediate friends with the other eight people at our table. During the band breaks, we swapped stories and wine. We danced nearly every dance and laughed at everything.

When Edward dropped me off at home, it was after one. I was happy, exhausted, and a bit tipsy. He reached for his door handle, but I hopped out as soon as the car came to a stop.

"Wait a second. I'll walk you to the door."

"Thanks, but there's no need."

He got out anyway, came around to the sidewalk and gave me a kiss on the cheek.

"It was a great evening, Edward. Thank you so much."

"It was spectacular, as were you. Just what I needed."

I waved as he drove down the hill.

Hot Shot came running as soon as I let myself in the side door. I picked him up in mid-stride and he purred like a well-tuned engine, butting his head against my chin.

"Well, I'm glad to see you, too. Did you miss me?"

I put him down and made sure the food and water bowls were full. The light on my answering machine was blinking. The first message was from Delia McCullough.

"Glynnis did leave a roll of film for developing. I got the pictures this afternoon, but I don't see what good they are. Just some pictures of men having dinner—I think one might be the mayor. And some kids in a park with their father, or maybe their grandfather. It's not a good picture of the man but something about him is familiar. I'll try to remember where I've seen him. Call me tomorrow."

The second message, the one that made my pulse race a bit, was from Steve Ballard.

"Hey, sorry I missed you, especially since you said it was important. If it can wait, I'll see you tomorrow about six. If not, give me a call in the morning. Sleep tight."

He sounded so cheerful, so affectionate that I cringed. I knew that good mood wasn't likely to last much longer, not once he learned what I'd kept from him. I just hoped I could make him understand why I did it.

Cat at my feet, I climbed the stairs. The last thing I remembered was Hot Shot turning in circles as he settled beside me.

CHAPTER FIFTEEN

Later I could never say for sure what woke me. Was it a dream? Maybe it was thirst or the first faint stirrings of a hangover headache behind my forehead? I remembered now why I didn't drink wine. The mockingbird was back outside my window, filling the night with liquid song. Moonlight streamed in the windows, throwing silver squares across the floor. I turned over and closed my eyes again, but the quick return to sleep wouldn't come. Once awake, my mind refused to release its grip on consciousness.

It was the whole mess of the murders, Glynnis's files, and my part in it that wouldn't let me sleep. Why, why, why hadn't I had the good sense to tell Delia McCullough 'no'? Sure, some of my friends might have been embarrassed, but Reg Anderson might still be alive. I'd honestly believed that I was acting for the best, but good intentions don't mean much in the harsh reality you encounter at three in the morning. Seeking comfort, I reached out to stroke the cat, but the bed beside me was empty. It wasn't surprising, I supposed. I didn't want to be with me either—I just couldn't get away from myself.

I flipped over again, punched my pillow a couple of times and tried to get comfortable. At that moment, the mockingbird stopped his serenade in mid-note. The sudden silence seemed to press against my ears.

After a couple of minutes, I sat up, sure I'd never go back to sleep. The house felt different somehow. Had the burglar come back? I strained to hear, but there was nothing. I threw back the covers and, even as I told myself I was just overreacting, I slipped silently to the floor.

But then there was a noise and it wasn't the cat. It was muffled, but substantial, maybe a body bumping against a large piece of furniture, but loud enough that I couldn't ignore it or explain it away. I drew my hand back from the bedside lamp I'd been about to switch on, choosing darkness over light.

I grabbed a pair of jeans from the bedpost and added them to the oversized tee shirt I wore. A person is somehow less defenseless wearing pants. Then I slid open the drawer of my nightstand for the gun I kept there. The little .22 revolver wasn't the more substantial pistol I'd been carrying since Glynnis's death – that one was in my purse where I'd left it in the dining room – but it was better than nothing. I slipped it into my pocket and, as an afterthought, picked up the cell phone I'd left on the dresser.

There had been no more unusual sounds and I was starting to feel a bit foolish, equipped as I was for a natural disaster or an armed invasion. But I wasn't quite ready to relax. I moved as quietly as I could from the bedroom into the hall. Across the way moonlight brightened the guest room window, but to my left toward the steps there was nothing but darkness. That triggered an alarm. I routinely left on a small light in the living room so that its faint glow illuminated the top of the stairs. Had the bulb simply burned out or had an unknown hand turned it off? And where was Hot Shot? By now he should have been right under my feet, his usual position any time I was up and moving. Had he rushed back into hiding in the face of another invasion?

My hand, sliding along the wall, encountered open space. I was at the top of the stairs. I edged along in the darkness until I made contact with the banister, then eased down onto the first step. The darkness was too deep to see anything, but I suddenly sensed a subtle change in the feel of the air around me. It was warmer and somehow closer.

Before I could react, someone grabbed me. Big, hard hands fastened like clamps on my shoulders. My attacker didn't speak, he only grunted with exertion. He smelled of sweat, garlic, and dogs. I fought hard, but not hard enough. He outweighed me and, when he pushed me backwards, we landed with a crash on the wood floor. I was pinned beneath him. The air whooshed out of my lungs and my left ankle twisted painfully under my right thigh.

Like a drowning swimmer, I struggled against the weight of him as his hands groped their way up my body to my throat. They found my neck and began squeezing. I tried prying them off, but it was like trying to bend steel. My head felt suffused with blood and about to explode. I couldn't breathe. For a brief weird moment, an eerie calm settled on me and I was resigned to having my life end right here. It would soon be over and it wasn't so bad after all.

Then I came back to myself. Squirming enough to get my right leg underneath my attacker, I slowly began raising it. It took a desperate strength I didn't know I had, but I managed to lever him up high enough that he had to loosen his grip. I gulped in air, then pushed my leg up and away as hard as I could. He fell away from me with a clatter of bumps and crashes.

Getting to both my feet wasn't an option. My left ankle refused to hold any weight, so I scooted across the floor until I found the banister and pulled myself up on one foot. Then I found the light switch.

It's only in the movies that people routinely die from falls down flights of stairs. Carlton Mabry was very much alive and his face was dark with fury. He was in the process of getting to his feet when I pulled the gun from my pocket.

"Stay right there," I told him. "Don't come any closer."

He took a step up the stairs. His down-home grin looked incongruous beside the bruise that was beginning to color his forehead.

"Aw, Dixie, we can work all this out." He climbed another step. "You're not going to shoot me with that little toy, are you?" Another step.

I pulled the trigger and his leg, just below the right knee, bloomed with blood. He howled in pain and collapsed in a heap, both hands wrapped around the wound.

"Goddamn it, you shot me!"

"And I'll do it again, Carlton, if you don't stay right where you are."

I'd like to be able say that I deliberately aimed for his leg, but I just pointed the gun and pulled the trigger. He could just as easily have been hit in the chest. I was damned lucky I hadn't missed him completely.

He moaned. "Help me, Dixie. I'm gonna bleed to death!"

"You might." I put a hand to my bruised throat. "You just might."

The cell phone had tumbled two steps down. I half-fell into a sitting position on the top step and stretched forward, using my fingertips until I finally had it in my hand.

"If you stay absolutely still, I'll call an ambulance. But you need to understand that your health isn't something that's real important to me right now. You move an inch toward me and I'll shoot you again. And I will let you bleed to death."

"Bitch," he muttered through clenched teeth.

I snapped open the phone, praying the fall hadn't knocked it out of commission. The press of a button produced a lighted screen and, seconds later, the happy little musical notes that signaled I was now in contact with the rest of the world. I released the breath I hadn't known I was holding and punched 9-1-1. It took only a minute to explain the situation. The emergency operator assured me that help was on the way and instructed me to stay on the line. I said I would and set the phone on the floor beside me. I'd leave the connection open, but I wasn't going to distract myself by holding the phone to my ear.

Carlton was crumpled at the bottom of the stairs, blood puddling on the floor under his leg. He might have been hurt, but I wasn't fooled for a minute into thinking he was no longer a danger. And while he had strangled Glynnis and tried to do the same to me, I hadn't forgotten that Reg had been shot.

"Where's your gun, Carlton? Do you have it with you?"

"No." His voice was thick with pain.

I didn't believe him. "Yeah, well, just in case, don't move your hands in any way that might make me think you're reaching for one. If you do, you'll be dead before that ambulance ever gets here."

He looked up at me and, for the first time that night, I saw a trace of the man I'd known and cared about for two years. It was beyond comprehension that we were here now facing each other this way, ready to kill if the need or opportunity presented itself.

"Carlton, how did this happen? What the hell were you thinking?"

I thought he was going to call me some more names and he did, too. He sneered and opened his mouth. Then it was as if someone had suddenly let the air out of his body. A look of sheer misery replaced the sneer. He didn't release the grip on his leg, but the rest of him sagged.

"Oh, God, I can't believe this is happening to me." He swallowed hard. "I never meant to hurt Glynnis. You've gotta believe me. She just made me so goddamned mad. She had this newspaper clipping. It was forty years old, for God's sake. It had nothing to do with now or with the man I am now."

"What clipping?"

I thought he might be talking to take his mind off the pain, but I didn't care. I wanted to hear the story. Besides, it was taking my mind off of my own pain. My ankle throbbed and I was fairly sure it was broken.

He shifted his leg a millimeter and inhaled sharply. "Huh? Oh, the clipping, yeah. See, back when I was a kid, there was this guy who taught our Sunday School class. We all liked him at first, but then . . . well, he got me and some other kids involved in some stuff. . ." He shook his head as if to banish an ugly memory. "He even made me do some things with the others, but . . . I mean, I was the victim of a child molester, not a criminal. I was only fourteen years old, for Christ's sake. But they arrested me just the same. And this was back when newspapers published kids' names in cases like that."

He moved to sit a bit straighter against the banister. My hand tightened on the gun until his body relaxed again.

"But Glynnis found out," he continued. "Do you remember how she talked that morning about child molesters?"

I did and mistakenly thought she was referring to Edward.

"She was a disgusting woman!" he went on. "And then later, I met her downtown and she showed me the clipping. She leered at me like we shared some horrible secret. It was just more than I could stand. I grabbed her and – Dixie, I honestly don't remember anything else until I saw . . . what had happened."

He swallowed again. I knew extreme pain could trigger nausea and I hoped he wasn't going to throw up on Grandma Evelyn's Oriental rug.

"Where the hell's that ambulance?"

I glanced at my watch. Only two minutes had passed. "They'll be here soon. You know, I almost understand about Glynnis. But why Reg?"

He made an exasperated noise with his lips. "He overheard me and Glynnis talking that day – after the work session when she asked me to meet her near your shop. When Glynnis . . .died, he called me and he let me know what he'd heard, said he wouldn't tell anyone . . . but then he said, then he wanted money to keep quiet." He shook his head again. "I never would have expected that from Reg.

"So I agreed to meet him, told him I'd give it to him. Of course, I didn't, give him any money, I mean. Once that started I knew it would never stop. He'd have bled me dry. I . . . uh . . . I shot him. There just didn't seem to be anything else to do."

"But what made you come after me?"

His lips tightened. "You as good as told me you'd seen me with Reg at Rose Hill. And then you called Mary, checking up on me."

"But I didn't! I only saw Reg that day. I never had any idea you were there. As for Mary, she confirmed your alibi. Guess she never knew you slipped away from the camp that afternoon, huh?" I sighed. I felt tired and old. "God, Carlton, you did this for nothing. You had no reason to come here."

He laughed without humor. "Ain't that a kick in the ass?"

I listened for the sound of a siren, but there was only silence. If

177

I could hold my ankle with one of my hands, it might lessen the pain, but I didn't dare drop my guard even a little. Carlton's story sounded plausible, but killing someone over a forty-year-old incident, even one as potentially humiliating as this one was, was extreme. Something just didn't ring true. And why did he search my house? Then I got it.

Clear as a bell, I could almost hear Glynnis talking at that last sorting session. 'People like that can't be cured, can they? I understand that even if they get caught when they're very young, they don't stop. They'll still be at it years and years later. You just never know who might be abusing children, do you?'

I'd thought it was just another dig at Edward, but now I understood Carlton had been her target. "Glynnis was right, wasn't she?"

He frowned.

"She knew, didn't she?" I kept pushing. "You didn't stop when you were a kid. There have been more victims and she found out. How did she do it? Did she follow you? Did she have pictures of you with the Boy Scouts? I bet that's it. That's what she showed you that made you so mad, not a newspaper clipping from forty years ago. Were you afraid she had more evidence? Is that why you broke into Delia's house? Glynnis knew something that would send you to prison today, didn't – "

Fury propelled him up the stairs toward me. His hands held no weapons, so I didn't have to shoot him again. I just lifted my good leg and kicked him back down the steps. He must have hurt something in his neck or back that time, because he didn't move after he came to rest. He was lying in the same position when Steve Ballard came running into the downstairs hall a minute later. He beat the ambulance there by a full minute.

After a quick check to see if Carlton had a weapon, Steve ran up the stairs and gathered me in his arms.

"Thank God, you're all right."

I was feeling pretty thankful myself. It was wonderful to be safe and held by someone who really cared about me. But, of course, it didn't last.

CHAPTER SIXTEEN

An ambulance delivered me to the Medical Center where an emergency room doctor pronounced my ankle badly sprained, but not broken. Still they admitted me, put me in a room and kept me there 'for observation' until Sunday afternoon. Kaminsky arrived about the time they wheeled me into the room and I laid it all out for him and Steve.

There was nothing I could do to keep the whole story of Glynnis and her files and her blackmailing under wraps. Too many people, including Carlton Mabry, knew about it. If I hadn't told the police everything, someone else would have. The only bright spot in my giving them the remaining folders was that they already had their murderer, so there was no reason to investigate anyone else.

"You could have saved us all a lot of trouble if you'd turned over those files as soon as you got them," Steve told me, standing by my hospital bed. The easy smile had been replaced by a stiff expression completely devoid of humor. Kaminsky stood nearby, enjoying every minute of my disgrace.

"I know you don't think much of our ability to solve crimes," he went on. "You've made that damned clear. But we just might have found out about Carlton Mabry in time to keep him from killing Reg Anderson. That is if you hadn't decided you were better qualified than we were to investigate."

His eyes met mine in a merciless stare. "You might want to do some serious thinking about that, Dixie. You seem to have a habit of getting people killed because of your inflated opinion of yourself. Maybe it's time for some self-examination."

They didn't charge me with obstruction, although they could have. And I'm sure it was discussed. Probably my nearly being killed and shooting Carlton saved me from arrest.

I hoped that I wasn't responsible for Reg's death. Since the information and photos that incriminated Mabry were never found, I didn't really think the files I had would have led the police to him. But I'd never know that for sure. I added that possibility to the rest of the guilt I carried around with me. It was one more thing to be taken out and examined on those nights when sleep refused to come.

Edward got me home later that day and took care of everything. I just sat back on the sofa, my ankle in a walking cast and elevated on three pillows, with reality softened by pain pills, while he fed the cat and made me a grilled cheese sandwich. In between bites, I told him what had taken place between Steve and me. Like the good friend he was, Edward tried to cheer me up.

"He'll be back, Dixie. He's just upset right now. But he'll come back. You'll see."

But I knew the truth. "No, he won't."

Pandora was a godsend in the days after my injury. Although I hobbled into the shop most every day, I was nearly useless for any sort of physical activity. She put in more hours than I could count, stocking shelves, unloading and sending orders, and running the place when pain and exhaustion sent me home to bed. I paid her what I could, but it was nowhere near what she deserved.

As the end of the semester approached, I began to dread seeing her leave for home. One morning over a cup of tea, she surprised me by announcing that she'd be staying in Macon over the summer and would continue working for me.

"That's if you want me to."

"Of course I do. I'm not sure I could run this place without you now."

She sighed. "Good, because I sure don't want to go back to home for three months. There's nothing to do there. I'd be bored to death!" Then her lips curved into a smile. "I knew you'd want me stay. The cards said you would."

Pandora wasn't the only one with a surprise. Two weeks after I'd shot Carlton, Delia McCullough sent me a check for $5,000 and a note thanking me for 'solving the murder of my baby'. I couldn't face the argument I knew would follow if I tried to return it to her. I called to thank her the next day and then I endorsed the check over to a local ministry that provided interim housing and job training for the homeless. I never heard from Delia again.

As it turned out, the second fall down the steps didn't do Carlton any lasting damage. He just knocked himself out on one of the risers when he landed. The gunshot wound, however, was more serious. He lost a fair amount of blood and, because the bone was shattered, he'd never walk again without a limp.

When the police searched his house the next day, they found a cache of photographs of him and a number of young boys in sexually explicit poses. And Delia turned over the last photos Glynnis had taken. It turned out they were pictures of Carlton and some of the Boy Scouts he'd worked with. The pictures weren't incriminating in themselves, but by identifying and interviewing the boys in them, the police discovered two more of his victims. So in addition to the two murder charges, he was indicted for numerous counts of child molestation and exploitation. There were rumors that he'd even victimized his own grandchildren, but I never learned if that was true. Considering he'd probably spend the rest of his life in jail, I guessed walking with a limp was the least of his problems.

In the end, Carlton's attorneys negotiated a plea for him. It was about the best he could hope for. In return for the state not seeking the death penalty, he pled to life in prison without parole. The sentencing took place in the big courthouse on Mulberry Street one blisteringly hot July morning. I heard it on the noon news and told Deannie about it when we met for lunch.

"You know, I kind of feel bad for him," she said. We were at her table inside Chimera. With the temperature topping ninety by 11:00 a.m. every day, no one was interested in sidewalk dining. "I mean, he was Glynnis's victim just like I was."

"No, he wasn't just like you. You didn't kill anyone and you're not a child molester. As far as I'm concerned, he got what he deserved."

She shrugged. "I guess you're right." She gave my sandwich a critical look. "What do you think of the new chicken salad?"

And as quickly as that, Carlton was dismissed from the conversation, if not from my thoughts.

For months afterwards, I still didn't feel entirely safe in my house. I had dead bolts installed on all the doors and locks put on the downstairs windows. The gun, which I'd thought of as temporary, now became a regular accessory for me. The summer dragged by slowly and the heat was relentless. I spent most of the hot months inside – either at work or at home – and socialized even less than usual.

It would be nice to report a happy ending, but life doesn't often cooperate by tying up all the loose ends in a big pink bow. Although we'd known each other only a couple of weeks, I believed Steve Ballard and I had been on the way to a good relationship. The chemistry had certainly been right. But that was before he learned about the information I'd kept from him. And, although it hurt, I understood exactly why he felt the way he did and that it was entirely my fault.

I only saw Steve once after that day in the hospital. On a muggy August afternoon, I was entering the Kroger over on Pio Nono Avenue at the same time he came out. His arms were loaded down with bags and a pretty, dark-haired woman was at his side. I know he saw me because our eyes met for a quick moment, but he didn't speak. I went on inside and bought the frozen pizza I would have for dinner and a can of tuna for the cat.